SiSTER MiSCHiEF

SISTER MISCHIEF

LAURA GOODE

CANDLEWICK PRESS

4 Meer Rae & Vix

12% Ladies

Thuggette Sisters 4 Life

Why does everyone have to put you in a box and nail the lid on it? I don't know what I am—polymorphous and perverse. Shit. I don't even know if I'm white. I'm me. That's all I am and all I want to be. Do I have to be something?

—Rita Mae Brown, *Rubyfruit Jungle*

Contents

Part III

I.

Yesterday I told my girls, I told them, if somebody interesting talks to you, you say a few things too. You might as well breathe at the same time and let the words out in the air. Don't ask questions, I told them. Give things away. Give yourself away.

—Anonymous

PROLOGUE

Holy Hell, Evening

I guess I'm here because I wanted to be sure.

Breaking news: it's Friday night. The Holyhill Fighting Loons won the first game of the fall against Rosemount a few hours ago, not that I could see much of it from the meadow behind the concession stand, where a few of us straggled together after halftime to pass around a few beers, not really enough to get everyone drunk.

"Do you feel anything?" I lean over to Marcy.

"Shut up," she says, then finishes her Leinenkugel, crushes the can in her hand, and goes back to making out with this wrestler who looks kind of like a hammerhead shark.

"She's not driving, right?" Tess grimaces at Marcy, who's peeled the polyester jacket off her marching band uniform and is wearing just the green trousers and her ubiquitous men's undershirt. Marcy's rank lieutenant of the Holyhill High School drumline. She makes all the freshmen call her Captain.

"Eh." I reach for another swig from someone. "She's not actually drunk. And also probably not going anywhere for a while."

"I can hear you," Marcy growls, coming up for air.

I hear another beer crack open behind me. Charlie Knutsen is shyly offering me a can. Speaking frankly, Charlie's wanted to punk my junk since sixth grade, when he caught a glimpse of me in my training bra as the girls' locker room door was closing. Now we're juniors. He's patient—I'll give him that.

I take it. "Thanks."

"No sweat. There was more in Anders's car."

"Does he know you took it?" Charlie shakes his head, smirking.

Over in the parking lot, most of the football team has arrived and is pumping one of the predictable Biggie songs—"Juicy" or "Big Poppa"—and dancing like morons.

"Jesus," I mutter to Charlie. "Check out the white man's overbite parade over there." He cringes.

"Uh-oh," he says. "Mary Ashley's trying to booty-dance again. This can't end well."

Sure enough, I look back at the crowd around someone's bass-thumping Chevy pickup, and Mary Ashley Baumgarten, super-Lutheran teen queen of Holy Hell and Tess's ex-BFF, is jerking her skinny flat ass around to the beat.

"Tessie." I jerk my head toward MashBaum and take another sip as I watch the scene unfold. The guys are clearly drunker than Mary Ashley realizes, and her feeble dancing attempts slow as they get bolder in grinding on her. Mary Ashley is obviously starting to freak out. Suddenly, Ryan Hoffstadt, who's pretty much your standard-issue ass-hat, crashes face-forward into Mary Ashley's B-cups and kind of deliberately dumps Captain Morgan and Coke all over her white sweater. Mary Ashley lets out a feral scream, shoving Ryan into the Chevy.

"Aw, jeepers." Tess takes off after Mary Ashley, followed by Anders.

"Let's bounce," Marcy says, getting up, pitching her beer can into the Dumpster fifteen feet away, and summoning Shark-Neck. "MashBaum'll totally call the cops on them, and next thing we know, her dad'll be campaigning for the state senate on an anti-tailgating platform. You drive." With a wave, she disappears into the Shark's car. I'm stranded; Marcy drives me everywhere.

"No, that's okay—don't worry about me," I call after her. "Dick."

In a matter of seconds, it's just me and Charlie Knutsen.

"Fuck," I say.

"What?" he asks.

3

"They were my ride," I tell him.

"Oh. Well. I mean." Charlie clears his throat like a douche. "I could give you a ride. If you wanted."

Maybe Charlie Knutsen's all right, I think, taking a sip, and a few more sips. Maybe then I'd know for sure. God knows this night isn't going anywhere else.

"Sure," I say. "Thanks."

This parking lot, another one, is a vigil of streetlights, too bright, making us conspicuous. My head is shoved against the window of Charlie's Camry's backseat, the manual window handle jutting into the back of my neck, and I can see two dogs copulating in the shadows on the other side of the empty lot. The thing about Holyhill (I'm partial to Holy Hell) is that the night I'm having, if I play it right, could be big shit on Monday morning. Some people grow up places where things happen, where you get discovered in diners or whisked off to far-flung cities with glamorous frienemies, but here I guess we don't have the weather for it or something.

Despite the fact that I'm regarding the whole situation as an experiment, I can say that, regardless of the chain of events leading up to it, Chuckles is pretty psyched to be crammed in the back of this Camry with me. He's worked his hands under my shirt, groping my stomach, and is steadily moving north as he sucks on my neck.

"Give me a hickey and I'll end you," I growl, wrenching his leechy mouth off my neck with a pop.

"Sorry." He actually looks sorry. "Sorry, Esme. Did it hurt?"

"I mean, it didn't *hurt*, but it wasn't exactly awesome. I don't know. Try something else," I order him. He obediently begins a tentative nibble along the ridge of my earlobe. Slightly better—I guess.

I wonder if Dad's already eaten the leftover bacon from this morning. I begin to get sick of Kings of Leon on the iPod plugged into the car's cigarette lighter. I look out the window.[1] Out of nowhere, a woman in a lilac terrycloth tracksuit runs screaming toward the still-coupling dogs. She's got the crazy in her eyes as she pulls the unwilling retriever off with some difficulty. I guffaw. Terrycloth's head snaps up. Shit, the front windows are open. The painfully camel-toed figure in question is Darlene Grinnell, Tess's mom, and one half of the doggie couple is Stinker, Tess's puggle. Catching full view of what's going on, she turns to us with an accusatory

1. Scribbled in notebook (SiN) later that night: *I've spent my whole life trying to be more than one / Like I could up and make the earth revolve the sun / Don't get how that wanting make a girl feel invisible / Divisible: is it, though? / I wanna get physical / With an unfuckwittable / Visible mistress who / Got girl guts and sinew / Dark eyes or blue, I don't care who / Let's screw through curfews / Tell me who soon / Wanna get with you, boo.*

finger, but no sound comes out of her mouth; it just opens and closes like a guppy's.

Almost hysterically, she makes a thrusting, splay-fingered phone gesture at her ear, mouthing, *I'm calling your father, young lady.* I shrug, wishing I could see Pops's face during that call, and she snatches Stinker's leash and flounces indignantly off. Chuckles, like a wiener, lets out a sigh of relief.

"Whew. That was close," he says, miming a wipe of his brow.

"What was she going to do? Sic her postcoital dog on us?"

Chuck lets out a nervous snicker. "You don't have to be, like, mean. Or whatever," he says, losing his nerve.

"This is so pointless. Can you take me home?" I say, folding my arms across my chest.[2]

"Come on, Ez. It's real early. Stay a little longer. We just got here." He massages my scalp. It feels okay. I guess.

"Fine," I say. "Take off your pants."

"What?"

"Take off your pants and let's get on with it."

"Seriously?"

"I'm counting to three and then I'm changing my mind. One."

2. Tess: *Why did my mom just txt me demanding your dad's phone #? Where r u?*

6

"Okay, okay, okay." He fumbles first with his belt, then his zipper. His hands are shaking. He succeeds in removing his jeans, which are far too tight and make him look like some sort of Hot Topic refugee. His boxers are speckled with cacti. I try to remember which underpants I have on under my homemade wrap skirt; I think it's the Superman briefs I've been getting in the little-boys section at Target for most of my life. I hoist up my skirt but don't take off my hoodie or my boots.

"Knutsen! You've got a boner!" I exclaim.

He blushes. "Uh. I know."

I poke it curiously through his boxers with one finger. It swerves like a sailboat boom, disturbing the cacti-patterned sail, then swings back at me. I am not at all sure about this thing. I take a deep breath and wriggle out of my Supermanderpants. I nod toward the cacti.

"Off."

He obeys. I don't get a good look at it, but I also don't try too hard. He fishes a condom out of his wallet as I look out the window, half hoping to catch more canine entertainment. I hear a snap.

"*Ow.*"

"Shit, Knutsen, did you break it?"

"What, the condom?"

"No, your dick."

I hear an unsticking sound, then he puts both hands in my hair. "Think I got it."

"*Think* isn't fucking good enough, Knutsen. Did you get it?"

"I got it." He looks terrified.

"Okay." This is what girls dream about?[3]

"Okay."

"So." Again, I'm getting impatient. "Just do it already."

He looks down, then at me. I feel a pushing. The pushing gets harder. It doesn't hurt, exactly. It's bigger than a tampon. Not a lot bigger. He retreats, then pushes again, harder. Then it starts to hurt. I wait for it to stop hurting, closing my eyes. This is stupid, I think. Nothing about it feels right. Not because I don't love Charlie Knutsen and his bony hipster bod, which I totally don't, and not because I mildly boozed myself into it, even though I sort of did. Charlie Knutsen is meat and I want fruit. I'd known it all along. He keeps grunting and jerking. I close my eyes. My mind drifts further.

My girlfriend Rowie—it's funny how girls talk about their girlfriends without batting an eyelash, but you'd never hear a straight boy mention a boyfriend; anyway, I mean Rowie's my friend and she's a girl, but she's not

3. SiN later: *He was a cramped Camry backseat and an indie rock blare / It was hard to believe I was supposed to be scared.*

8

my *girlfriend,* not like *that*—and I share a passion for Value Village, this kind of janky Goodwill-type thrift store on the way to the airport. We're there at least twice a month, and earlier this summer we were panning for gold in the old ladies' castoffs.

"Ugly-cute, or just ugly?" Rowie asked, holding up a kind of outrageous orange minidress.

I squinted, considering. "Cute. If they had that dress in purple, red, and yellow, we could be the Fanta girls for Halloween."

"Marcy'd throw a conniption," Rowie said, dismissing me.

I held up a pair of acid-washed jeans. "They're too short, but good cutoff candidates, maybe?"

"Mmmm," she said as she examined them. "Could be. I'm gonna try this bad girl on." She trotted off to the dressing room. I was pawing through the bathing suits, debating whether buying secondhand swimwear is gross or not, when my eye caught Rowie's bare feet bopping under the dressing-room curtain. The curtain had a handwritten sign safety-pinned to it: WOMEN. I heard Rowie rapping the lyrics to Roxanne Shanté's "Roxanne's Revenge" as she changed, her shorts dropping over her feet. I was transfixed for a moment, knowing she didn't know anyone was paying attention.

"Whew-eee, this article is tight!" she called out to me.

"I think I gotta go commando to make this one work." I heard her wiggling and rapping for a moment more, then I saw her step out of her underpants. I felt suddenly pervy for looking and turned my back to her, returning to the bathing suits, which were all gross. A woman in a green dress was perusing the sweater vests across the aisle from me. When she turned, she looked so much like my mother that I took a step forward, but it passed quickly, the interrupted recognition, the way it always does.

My thoughts return to the present—Chuckles, the Camry. Charlie's still moving on top of me and his moans have grown stronger. It's stopped hurting, mostly, but more than anything it just feels like some kind of intrusion. I watch the way his face contorts in the fluorescent yellow of the streetlight above his car, the way his pale ass moves below his ironic 1999 Saint Stephen's Church Johnny Appleseed Festival T-shirt, which he hasn't gotten around to taking off. I start to sweat under my skirt and my hoodie. I wonder why it's taking him longer than sixty seconds to come—wait, could it be possible that I'm the only virgin in this Camry? No *way.*

Before I can ponder the question further, the flash of headlights glints off the rearview mirror.

"Crap. Chuckles. Car." We turn to see who it is. The headlights blind me for a second, and then I see the dreaded lettering on the side of the sedan as it pulls toward us: HOLYHILL POLICE. Jesus, this night. Why don't they have anything better to do? Not even, say, a postgame tailgating party to break up? Misery, thy name is Holy Hell.

"Shit. Shit. Shit. Shit." Charlie falls on the floor in the struggle to get his pants back on. I can't find my underpants. I pull my skirt down and hope the cops don't see them before I do. It's cosmically clear that this night was not meant to be.

"I bet that dog-walking trollop called the cops on us."

"What if they smell the beer?" He sounds kind of panicky.

"Oh, calm down. They're not going to." I lunge for my purse and dig for those little minty breath strips that burn the roof of your mouth.

"Jesus, Esme. What if they call my parents?"

"Lighten up, Knutsen. Just play it cool." One of the cops — it looks like there are two — is getting out of the car. He walks slowly, like he's trying to show us his nonchalant, absolute authority. Sergeant Jackass taps on the window, shining the flashlight in our eyes. I roll the window down.

"Officer. Haahhrya, sir?" In Minnesota, "How are you" is one drawled word: *Haaahhhrryaa.*

"Everything okay in there tonight, miss?" He searches my face.

"Oh, real good, thanks a lot. And how's your night going?" I flash him a smile. I hear my phone get another text.[4]

"You kids been drinking tonight?"

"No, sir." Knutsen and I shake our heads back and forth in unison.

"So I'm sure there's no beer cans stashed under those seats."

"No, sir." Thank God we unloaded them in the concession Dumpster.

"So what are you kids doing in there?"

Before I can come up with something, Chuckles, the genius, replies, "Talking, sir." His voice cracks on the "sir." I stifle another giggle. Knutsen flushes crimson.

The cop keeps looking at me. I look back.

"I'm going to need your license and registration."

I waggle a thumb at Chuck. "His car."

"Ah," he says, smirking. "Hard to tell when everyone's in the backseat. License and registration, son."

Charlie pulls his license out of his wallet. "I, um, don't know where the registration is."

The cop shakes his head, more in a pitying than an angry way. "Just stay where you are."

He returns to the squad car. Knutsen and I sit in

<hr />

4. Marcy: *Did u walk home, or did u get a ride from/on Chuckles? Story?? PS Sorry I ditched.*

hangdog silence for a minute. He looks as though he's trying to say something.

"Chuckles, what is it?"

"I don't know. I mean, I just wanted to say—"

"What?"

"I think you're beautiful. You don't look like the other girls. I mean, in a good way. You look real."

I'm dumbstruck. What do I say to that?

"Um. Thanks."

"That was nice," he continues. "I mean, before the cops—it was sort of—nice."

"God, Knutsen, you are so *emo*." I can't let him like me. Fortunately, the cop's on his way back. He leans into the window.

"All right, boys and girls. Well, Mr. Knutsen, since you don't seem to have any offenses on your driving record, I'm going to let you off this time with a warning. I'm not gonna give you a ticket, which I could, or call your parents, which I think I might enjoy. Do you know why?"

Chuck, aware that he's hanging on the edge of reprieve, shakes his head violently.

"Because I like you, Mr. Knutsen. I like that you're an organ donor. And goddamn it, I like you for managing to get this good-looking girl into the back of your car. But son, I want you to drop this honey off and then go straight home. Curfew's in fifteen—" Officer Friendly's walkie-talkie explodes in a crackle of voices and numbers. He turns away from us.

"Eleven-sixty-five, copy. You bet. We're right near there." He turns back. "Look, I got a noise complaint on a Friday night fish fry. Don't let me catch you"—he coughs—"talking around here again."

Charlie looks like he's about to piss himself in relief. "Thank you, Officer. Thank you so much." The cop swaggers, a little bowlegged, back to his squad car, still shaking his head.

Knutsen and I scramble up to the front seat, and he starts the car.

"Close call," he says, looking at me. I shrug.

"So . . . do you think we could find somewhere else?" he asks hopefully.

"Christ on a bike, Knutsen," I sigh. "Give up. This isn't meant to be."

"What do you mean?"

"Never mind."

Our headlights hit the cop car, and I see two blue uniforms shaking in laughter. Charlie shifts oddly in his seat as he drives.

"Hey, you got ants in your pants?"

Charlie cracks a grin. "I never got a chance to pull the rubber off."

For the first time tonight, I let out a good, long laugh. When he stops at the next intersection, I reach into his pants, yank off the spent Trojan, and throw it back at the cops, eliciting a yelp from Chuck. "Take that, mofos!" I crow, but not too loud.

We drive the rest of the way home in silence. When he stops in my driveway, I get out without saying anything, not seeing the need for conclusive small talk.

"Wait," he whispers out his window.

I turn around. "What the fuck, Chuckles?"

"Can I call you?"

"Look, Chuckie, this was a one-time thing, you feel me? Just—it's really not your fault. You're a really nice guy. Thanks for the ride. Home." I put my key in the front door without looking back.

When I walk into the kitchen, Pops is sitting at the table, painting the shutters of a birdhouse that looks like Versailles. He raises his eyebrows, and it occurs to me for the first time what I must look like: hair mussed and frizzy, curls springing out around my hoodie, skirt rumpled, face flushed. I shrug. He nods toward a BLT on the table. We both love bacon. It's our private little Jew screw-you to Mom, who took off when I was five. I think it's kind of weird that I'm Jewish just because the womb of which I am fruit was. We haven't really, like, practiced anything since she left. My pops is crazy, but I'll give him this much: he stuck around for me, he doesn't shock too easy, and he knows when to feed a girl.

"Haaahhrya?" he asks, still painting. "Kinda looks like a rough night."

I open my mouth, wondering if this is the right time. He probably already knows.

"So it turns out I'm gay, Pops."

He looks hard at me, not upset, probably just checking if I'm serious. When he doesn't say anything, I keep talking.

"Definitely a homo. Like, Same-Sex City, population Esme. Just a big gay, gay lesbian."

He nods.

"Cool with me, kiddo. Eat a sandwich."

CHAPTER ONE
Spoonbridge and Cherry

Saturday night with my girls. We—Marcy, Tess, Rowie, and me—are seriously the four fiercest, baddest rhyming lionesses these few miles west of the Mississippi. In our hip-hop lives, we make rhymes, we make beats, we go big or go home. Marcy once said that hip-hop is what happens when a bunch of disparate parts explode into a big swaggering corners-sticking-out Technicolor whole. I think the four of us are kind of that way, too. We are MC Ferocious (me), MC Rohini (Rowie), DJ SheStorm (Marcy), featuring vocalist The ConTessa (obvi). We write sex-positive reflections on our location in the present; we are a sisterhood of lyrical explosion, and we first throw down mad props to the following: all hail the most righteous Queen Latifah, all hail our fierce sister from the East M.I.A., all hail the powerful partnerships of Salt-n-Pepa, M1 and stic.man, Mos Def and Talib Kweli. All hail Slug and Dre and B.I.G. and Pac, and Lauryn and Kim and Missy and Lyte. We claim comradeship with Jay-Z, with Mary J., with Nas, Pras, the GZA, the RZA, Raekwon, Rahzel, Rakim, and Roxanne, Ghostface Killah and Killah Priest, K-OS, K'naan and KRS-One, Black Star and Gang Starr, and we are also a fusion of our lonesome hometowners: with Prince of many purple names, or with Robert Zimmerman, the Jew from Minnesota who later became one Bob Dylan, and with David Bowie, James Brown, Patti Smith, Tina Turner, Freddie Mercury, and Lady Gaga, just to up the glamour factor.

The four of us have another life together, though, a quieter, costumes-off kind of understanding. For example, last summer, we all got curious about liquor and stole some bottles of wine from Tess's parents' wine cellar. We sat in the gazebo Pops built for the Grinnells and got drunk for the first time, so drunk that Marcy pissed on my leg in her sleep. I told them I thought I didn't like guys like that. I hadn't told anyone else. But I did tell them, and Tess looked mildly rattled, but it could have been the spins. Marcy'd gone back to sleep before I finished the sentence. Rowie just nodded, not a nod exactly, more a gentle rock of her head side to side, an acceptance.

Tonight we're piled into Marcy's '97 GMC Jimmy on our way to the light rail. Minnesota has crap for public transport, save the twelve-mile Hiawatha Line, a modern reincarnation of the Twin City Rapid Transit streetcar system, which stopped operating in 1954. I think there's something about the in-betweenness of transit that appeals to me, the fact of being changeable in motion.

"I'll tell you what you love about me." Tess pushes me, laughing. "You love that I thought up this whole adventure. None of us would be making our first public performance on the light rail if it weren't for me."

"We worship you, golden-headed queen," I mock her, bowing with my hands in a steeple. "We revere you." Tess is so blond her dome glows in the dark.

"'How thou art fallen from heaven, O Lucifer, son of the morning! How art thou cut down to the ground, which didst weaken the nations!'" she quotes back.

"Where have I heard that?" Rowie asks.

"Isaiah," Marcy says, showing a little of the Catholic in her.

"Naw, dude," Tess says. "I mean, yeah, but it's also straight out of the book of Jay-Z." We all place the reference as Tess busts the hook: *Lucifer, Lucifer, son of the morning.*

"It kind of freaks me out how you can quote Jay-Z and the Old Testament in the same breath," I say.[5]

"I didn't do it. He did," Tess says with a shrug, a dreamy look coming over her face, her I'm-fantasizing-about-Jay-Z look. "What can I say? The man is as obsessed with moral authority as I am."[6]

"And world domination," Marcy says.

Tess's sitting in the backseat with Rowie in our standard Jimmy seating configuration. We're driving east on 394, heading for the Warehouse District/Hennepin Avenue mouth of the light rail. I'm sitting shotgun next to Marcy, who's flirting with the Ford pickup driver in the lane next to us. It's probably the Golden Gophers bumper sticker that caught her attention; Marcy's a sucker for sports fans.

"Take the wheel!" she yells over the blare of Atmosphere's *Lucy Ford*. I reach over and hold the wheel

---

5. Me on Tess's Facebook wall a few months ago: *I first noticed Tess when she sang the pants off all of Plainview Middle School at the sixth-grade talent show. I was biting my nails in a magenta wool poncho I knit myself, too chicken to perform anything, when in walks this radiant girl in some sort of preteen power gown, poised like a pageant queen. Tessie brought the damn house down with her rendition of "How Can I Keep from Singing?" and after the talent show, she told me my homemade poncho was fresh. Tess is bomb.*

6. SiN: *Just like Jay-Z's preaching on moral authority / We're just four girls teaching an aural majority.*

steady as Marcy makes a litany of obscene gestures at the truck. Golden Gophers honks in delight.

"Marce, that's disgusting. Does that really feel empowering to you?" I scowl in her direction as she waggles her tongue at the truck.

"Whatever, dude. You're the one sitting around listening to rhymes about bitches and hos all day. If that isn't demeaning to you, I don't see how this is."

It's a typical Marcy-and-me exchange. Marcy of the men's beaters and slouchy low-riders, of the thick biceps and cropped shock of black man-bangs, anti-pretty but tall, blue-eyed and luminous, the butchest straight girl I know,[7] is my oldest and best friend, having entered my life at age five, the year both of our dads joined a playgroup for single fathers. Marcy and me were raised by men; we have the same mother part missing. We missed the same lessons on how girls are *supposed* to be,[8] the lessons pretty girls with pretty moms like Tess

---

7. Text from Rowie, during lunch on Friday: *Is it just me or is Marcy's outfit today a page straight out of the A.C. Slater guide to style?*

8. Me on Marcy's Facebook wall: *When we were about eight, Marcy made me play Dog Fight with her, and she bit me on the leg so hard that I had to go to the ER for stiches and I still have a scar. She let me borrow her Game Boy while we were in the waiting room. That wasn't the only time Marcy and I've injured each other in fun gone wrong, but it was the only time she's let me borrow her Game Boy.*

got in spades: no one ever taught us how to put on eyeliner or what to do when you just up and start bleeding
all over your Supermanderpants one day. The last time
I saw Marcy in a dress, she was six years old and looking like she was about to pitch a shit fit on the way to
Mass for her First Communion. Later, we cut up the
dress and used it to turn a bunch of plastic flamingos
in her front yard into flaminghosts for Halloween.
Her dad thought it was too funny to punish us; he'd
just bought the dress at K-Mart because he thought he
should, or something.

I guess the difference between us is siblings. I don't
have any, but Marcy was an oops baby, born six years
after her closest brother, Rooster, and two years before
their mom died of breast cancer. Her two oldest brothers,
Paul and Allan, were in high school by the time she could
talk. Between the three boys and her dad, Bob, who's the
wrestling coach at Holyhill, most of Marcy's early life
was spent learning how to evade ringworm and surprise
half nelsons. Paul and Allan have both been in Afghani-
stan for a little over a year now; Marce doesn't bring it
up a lot, but she worries. Rooster, whose real name is
Thomas, just finished college at the university in Duluth
and works now as a cameraman for KIND-11 News. And,
probably because of all those dudes, Marcy, while by no
means someone anyone would compare to a swan, or
really any kind of water bird, has a confidence with guys

like nothing I've ever seen. Her dad has no idea about her adventures with athletes, and God knows no one's dying to spill the beans to Coach Bob, who, by the way, benches a cool 250. Marcy defies the term *brazen*. Marcy's solid bronze.

"I have a question," Tess says.

"Imagine that," Marcy replies, wiggling her tongue in between two fingers at the pickup truck.

"I mean, I have lots of them," Tess says.

"Ask!" Rowie says.

"I guess I want to know if we really have any right to be doing this," Tess says.

"What do you mean?" I say, intrigued.

"I mean, don't you ever wonder if hip-hop really belongs to us?" Tess asks. "It had to travel from black urban areas to the radio and MTV to the suburbs. It's, like, it goes from being this spontaneous kind of performance at block parties and clubs to being this huge moneymaker, and all of a sudden what used to be a black-owned industry moves to bigger labels owned by old white men, and this is how a movement born out of poverty and oppression arrives in our tender suburban hands." She reaches the end of her lung capacity and takes a long breath. "You don't ever feel conflicted about that?"

We take a collective pause.

"Your white guilt is overpowering," Marcy mutters.

"I know," Tess snaps. "Why isn't yours?"

"But the progression isn't really that simple," Rowie says. "All that commercialization also sent hip-hop out into the rest of the world, where it became a whole new global uprising. I mean, if you frame this only in black and white, where do I fit in?"

"Dude," says Marcy, "what we should really be asking is how your people win so many spelling bees."

"It can't be genetics. Spelling bee kids all die virgins," Rowie sighs.

"Naw, spelling bee kids all become horny debate kids," I say. "I heard debate camp is basically a big nerd sex party."

"What about band camp, Marcy?" Rowie says, shoving her. Marcy raises one eyebrow and keeps driving. "Everyone knows the trombones were sweating you hard this summer."

"What happens at nerd camp stays at nerd camp," Marcy says, shutting down the topic. "But as for the rest, with hip-hop and everything, the question isn't whether or not it's, like, kind morally and racially messed up. Of course it is. The problem is that if you stop listening to music that makes you uncomfortable because it was stolen from black people, you're basically starting with Elvis and working your way backward. There's really no way to listen to just white music or just black music anymore."

"Seriously," I say. "And look, I love a good white guilt pity party as much as the next mope, but isn't the whole tradition of hip-hop based on artists taking samples from each other out of respect and composing new musical collages? Rhythm and poetry. So if you think about it, by taking in hip-hop and spitting out our own rearrangement of what we've heard, we're really just doing what everybody else in hip-hop has been doing for thirty years. I mean, that's gotta be more respectful than just stealing samples for our ringtones, right?"

"Even my church friends listen to it," Tess says. "I mean, only what's on the radio, but still."

"Your church friends listen to the Jonas Brothers," Marcy says. "And dry-hump."

"You don't have to crap all over them for being different from you," Tess shoots back defensively. "They're mostly good people."

"Mostly posers," I mutter.

Tess goes to this big Lutheran church that sort of unofficially, like, *governs* Holyhill, and her parents are sort of Those Holyhill Parents. There's Darlene, Holyhill's 1976 homecoming queen, a lawyer elected to the school board last year, and Dr. Gary, of *Minneapolis/ St. Paul* magazine's "Best Physicians in the Twin Cities." Tess's older sister, Ada, was wilder than Tess, notably causing a minor scandal when she turned down

Princeton to study musical theater at NYU. Anthony, the youngest, was adopted from Guatemala when he was five and is so charming and easy to love that you almost don't notice his right arm is gone. He was just born without it, some kind of congenital thing. Anyway, until last year—that is, until she really started chilling full-time with us—Tess spent a lot of her time with her Old Best Friend, the wicked stepsister, Mary Ashley Baumgarten. I think Tess found other believers easier to relate to for a while.

"*They're* the posers?" Tess asks incredulously. "We're the suburban white girls trying to be rappers."

"Speak for yourself," Rowie says pointedly.

"Well, yeah," Tess says. "Sorry."

"The possibility of our being posers, or people thinking we are, doesn't make MashBaum a better person than she is," I say. "That girl's a straight-up gay-hater."

"Which is why we should stop talking about her. Spot me," Marcy orders me as she reaches into her purse for a Parliament. She and MashBaum are old nemeses, and it still causes some friction. The car swerves.

Tess screams. "Are you effing crazy? Keep your mother-loving eyes on the road! You're going to get us pulled over!" Tess always tries not to swear. After a while, you start to find it endearing.

"Dude, can you chill out?" Marcy says. "We're fine."

"Marcy, that's gross," Tess whines as Marcy lights

up, coughing for effect. "You're bringing me back to Ada chain-smoking while she drove me to grade school. I have to sing."

"If you don't look at the road sooner or later, *I'm* calling the cops," Rowie says.

"Dude, I've got the five-oh karmically taken care of this week. Lightning ain't gonna strike twice," I say with confidence.

"Did you get busted for something?" Rowie asks.

"Like, something to do with the fact that my mother is swearing she saw you in Charlie Knutsen's car last night?" Tess asks.

"*Shut up*. Is that true? Is *that* why you never texted me?" Marcy says.

"Jesus, this is all getting so teen rom-com. So maybe I got busted by Darlene and then by the cops during my first tour of a boy's backseat. Do I have to, like, get my period and cry next?" I say.

"I heard the cops broke up the parking lot party later, too," Marcy says. "Holyhill sucks so hard."

"Can I just come out and ask the obvious question here?" Tess asks more insistently. "What were you and your Superman panties doing in the back of a car with a male *Homo sapien*?"

"Key word there being *homo*," Marcy adds, snickering. I blush, exactly one second before I start hating myself for blushing.

"Charlie Knutsen? Surprising." Rowie regards me with curiosity, then bursts into laughter.

"Did you—?" Tess asks, knowing that sentence finishes itself. I feel myself go from pink to maroon.

"You so did! Look at her! You went to the bone zone with Chuckles!" Marcy crows.

"Oh, my God, I barely did," I say. "It was so gross."

"You dirty little hooligan, you're going straight on us," Marcy hoots, dissolving into yuks.

Rowie reaches up and ruffles my hair. "So why'd you decide to make Chuckles's day, anyway?"

"I don't know, man. I just wanted to be sure, or something." I pause. "I mean, my pops's been through enough raising me on his own already. The least I could do was check for sure before I told him once and for all that he completely failed at raising me normal."

"Queer little word, *normal*," Rowie says, smiling at me.

Tess starts to make a sound, then stops. I turn around.

"What?"

"You know what I'm going to say."

"Tess."

"I'm just saying that *maybe* it's *possible* that you're sixteen and you just weren't ready."

"Okay, let's take a ride on the real-talk express. Is this a Christian thing?"

"Of course, but not in the way you—"

"Tess, I want to know. Do you think it's a sin to be gay?"

She shakes her head emphatically. "Absolutely not. Don't make me into something I'm not. I think you're perfect the way God made you."

"Then what's your problem?" Marcy and Rowie have grown uncomfortably silent.

"Homeslice, I don't *have* a problem. I love who you are and *I* can't tell you who to love with your body, mind, or otherwise, and any Christian who does isn't hearing or practicing Christ's message of unconditional love. It's not that I don't think you should have gay sex. I just don't think anyone is really ready to have sex before they're married."

"What's sex?" I ask. "Is it sex if you use your mouth, or your hands, or are we just talking ugly-bumping here? And how am I supposed to get married?"

"You know what sex is better than I do." Tess sounds exasperated. "You had it."

"Because what you do with Anders Ostergaard every weekend isn't sex," I say. Tess looks stung.

"Ez, lay off," Marcy intervenes.

Rowie says something too quiet to hear.

"What did you say?" I ask.

"I said, Did you like it?" Rowie repeats. "When you did it, did you like it?"

I pause, not because I have to think about it, but

because sometimes Rowie has this way of cutting through the bullshit. I shake my head.

"That dick was nasty, dude."

Tess throws up her hands. "They're ucking fugly! It's a totally normal first-time reaction to seeing one." She pauses. "Or so I hear."

From under her breath, I hear Rowie quietly ask, "What the fuck is normal, anyway?"

Rowie always hangs back a little from the rest of us somehow. The Rudras—Drs. Raj and Priya, Rohini, and Lakshmi—moved to Holyhill from St. Paul around the time Marcy and I were cackling over beheaded Barbies buried in my backyard, but we didn't really get to be friends with Rowie until last year, when her family moved again into a house down the street from Tess. Tess's dad and Rowie's mom are doctors at the same hospital. I guess Rowie wanted something to make her sound or feel less foreign[9]—I can't blame her, Holyhill is a shit place to be a non-Anglo[10]—and so she shed *Rohini* and

---

9. On Rowie's wall: *Rowie sometimes has better words for things than what they're actually called. One time we were in Marcy's car and it started raining, and she told us to turn on the windshield vipers.*

10. SiN later that night: *There's something about people of color in an all-white place. I don't know—it's like once you start noticing how complicated it is, you can't stop noticing. Maybe some people can. It's a white thing to say, I guess.*

became *Rowie* to most, including us. The nickname suits her in a quirky, buoyant way, so I keep the fact that I think *Rohini* is a beautiful name to myself, but it puzzled me when she picked it as her MC tag, a stage name. We're a good fit as MCs-in-arms, partners in lyrical crime: she writes choruses and hooks; I write verses.

Rowie's one of those people who doesn't speak much unless she really has something to say. She's beautiful; I like looking at her. There's a strangeness about her that feels familiar. And most of the time she dresses in living colors: eggplant plum, Florida orange, chlorophyll green. Today she's wearing a red felt dress with white polka dots and a green-feathered headband capping her hair. Somehow she makes her strawberry look hip and not like she's an extra in the third-grade play.

"Yeah, man," I agree, studying her. "Eff normal."

Marcy pulls off the highway and we snake through downtown Minneapolis. I'm in love with its small-city seediness, its throngs of hipsters outside First Ave., its skyways suspended like arteries, the light emanating from the Basilica and the highway's swoop past *Spoonbridge and Cherry*. This is my real home, I think, and not the sterile minivan parade of Holyhill. We pull into the parking lot, where the light rail sits jacketed like a hornet in yellow and black. It's Saturday night and we came to drop bombs. We buy four tickets and get on the train.

"Guys, seriously, I don't know if I can do this," says Rowie, looking a little pale. I plunge a hand into my bag and pull out my trusty Nalgene. I believe in hydration.

"Drink some water and sit down while we warm up," I say, handing her the bottle and stroking her hair.

Rowie has the shiniest hair ever, thick and lustrous in her vampy bob. Marcy is pulling our portable beatbox out of her backpack, a hot-pink heart-shaped set of iPod speakers, and cueing up our newest track. Tess sits a few feet away, practicing her breathing exercises. She looks like she's practicing Lamaze, but homegirl can *sing*, so I don't say anything. Rowie, still swigging my water, looks slightly better, but she's clearly fighting to duck the monkey on her back.

It's about seven thirty and there are only a handful of people in our car: a couple of worn-out-looking construction workers, a Hmong woman toting three children, one of whom can't keep her eyes off Marcy's magic pink sound machine, a black girl who looks a year or two younger than us, two camera-loaded Japanese tourists clearly on their way to the Mall of America.

"Ladies. It's time," I declare.

We are four points strong and near to bursting. Each one of us glances around the circle, waiting to see who'll light the fuse. I like to think I'm reliable for tasks like this.

"LADIES AND GENTLEMEN!" I howl like a WWF

announcer. "Twin Cities commuters! We do NOT apologize for the interruption. You are in for the best light rail ride of your life. Me and my sisters are four mud-slinging, bomb-dropping, clam-jamming bringers of mischief, about to spit some rhymes like you've never heard."

I trip on a purse strap loose on the floor and tumble forward, eliciting a few snickers.

"So, uh, ladies and gentlemen," the Ferocious in me continues, rising and brushing myself off, "hold on to your hosiery, because we're about to load you up with a fat dose of wickedness, whimsy, thievery, sensation, charm, and general ruckus-making. Without further ado, here now, making our Twin Cities public transportation debut, is Sister Mischief with our soon-to-be hit single 'Gynocracy.' "

I lope back to the ladies, who are still exchanging bewildered looks. Marcy raises her eyebrows at us. Swallowing the anxious mass of bile rising in my throat, I nod.

"Let's do it," I say. "Count it off, SheStorm." Marcy does. She fumbles with the speakers, but they won't turn on. Frustrated, she smacks them with the butt of her hand. The loop loaded on the magic pinks coughs and begins, a sample we lifted from 9th Wonder's "No Comparison," and Marcy begins to beatbox over it a measure later, picking up the slack. Tess leans into her

opening vocals, belting in that rangy voice that makes
the church ladies twitch in their seats:

"I got sisters on one side and mischief on the other
Saying that we better recognize our foremothers
We got a positive psychology of peace and camaraderie
So get with positivity or you best not be botherin' me."

I grab Rowie's hand for a moment, squeezing it for
courage. She gives me a tight deer-in-headlights smile.
The first verse is mine.

"We're done with sex hypocrisy
up in this here gynocracy
So what's with dudes up in my grill
I'm all get over it, get real
I see you there, you think you fly,
You think you're stealthy, smooth and sly
Frontin' like girls who say they're bi
Just to entertain some guys
So step up, bro, and recognize
That I'm rolling deep to ride
On with my girls, and tell you why
We're over it with paradigms
The gaze we play ain't for your eyes
My conscious sisters realize

I got to roll with Tess and Ro
And DJ SheStorm got my vote
We're out to throw some pro-ho flow
Sex-positivize your language, yo."

Rowie leaps into the transition with both hips and both shoulders, rushing it half a beat, but recovering after a little stutter.

"So listen close, we'll spell it slow
I take attitude and add tempo
My girls is high and you too low
So Lawdy, Joe
Already tole you so
Y'all best find some solo hos and go . . ."

My vision is cloudy with exhilaration, but I can make out the Hmong woman clapping politely and her little girl jumping up and down in delight as Rowie continues. Small victories: no one throws anything, and no one boos. One of the workers is alternately fiddling with his iPod volume and scowling at us, but the other one bobbles his head and smiles. One of the MegaMall-bound Japanese tourists raises his camera to his eye and snaps a souvenir photo of us, and I imagine what he will see when he flips through his vacation back home in his bedroom, or telling stories to his buddies at work, saying something like *And we were going through the city on our way to the biggest mall, and there they were, three whitegirls and a desi-girl rapping on the train. No, I don't know why. They were Americans; it could be anything.*

CHAPTER TWO

3 Non-SWASPs

It's lunchtime, and we're parked in the commons. I don't know why they call it *the commons* when it's nothing but a big hallway. There's nothing common about it; it is, at best, reluctantly shared. Little pockets of people are scattered throughout: the weird, formerly homeschooled Christians near the horny debate kids, all eating baby carrots; the theater and lit magazine kids spreading barbecue sauce on someone's math homework, glaring at the popular Christians; Anders Ostergaard, Tess's douchey sometimes-boyfriend, and his hockey harem, all pretending to ignore her, and finally us, the alienated smartgirls who couldn't find a group to belong to.

They say that only ten percent of the population is naturally blond and blue-eyed, but in Minnesota, it's more like sixty percent. You can find members of the diaspora in Holyhill, I guess, if you squint. Making an unscientific count around the commons, I spot a handful of Asian kids—Jisoo Kim, Iris Hong, Rowie, Prakash Banerjee, a few others—a couple of them adopted, a couple more with engineer or doctor parents who had enough degrees to get visas and came here to work for Honeywell or 3M, the U of M or the Mayo Clinic. There's even fewer black kids, most of whom seem kind of marooned in Holyhill's ABS program, which, like, recruits smart kids from the inner city or whatever and ships them out to the sub-urbs, where the property taxes are higher and the public high schools are better. They all sit together at lunch. I think they live together in a chaperoned program house on the outskirts of town, and ABS actually stands for A Better Shot. There are these de facto boundaries that no one talks about, and I feel weird about them, and I think other people must too.

"Well, as I live and breathe, it's Dykes with Mikes!" Mary Ashley Baumgarten taunts as she saunters by in her SWASP sweatshirt, earning a round of cheap laughs from the hockey dudes and her cake-makeuped lunch gaggle. Every year the senior girls make sweatshirts with some kind of taboo acronym beginning with "SW" for "Senior Women." This year, its SWASP, and apparently it stands for "Senior Women Always Say Please" or some stupid shit. But we know it stands for the model Holy

Hell student: Straight White Anglo-Saxon Protestant. "I heard about your little girl group, bless your hearts."

"Hey, Marcy, your boxers are showing!" Anders calls.[11]

"Yeah, Marcy," Mary Ashley croons viciously. "Didn't you see the new policy?" She throws a packet of paper at us. "It says the administration doesn't want to see your lesbo man undies either."

"Mary Ashley, I can see two-thirds of your butt and three-quarters of your thong," Tess slings back. "You better hitch up your skinnies or we dykes might get the wrong idea."

Mary Ashley glowers as she hikes up her jeans. "Tess, can you please just ditch the freak flock and come sit with us? We're talking about the Save Unborn Lives event and you haven't been around in forever. You even missed choir practice last week. We had the auditions for next month's Sunday solo."

"I don't need another episode like last month. Just lay off, Mary Ashley." Tess throws up her hands. Tess always used to get the Sunday solos at their church because she has this kind of voice that can't just sink into the curtain of a chorus: this bold, rangy, obscene voice, a voice that stirs something in you, the kind of voice you might say might make you believe. Except last month, Tess

11. Text from Rowie: *Why does Tess suck face with that ass-clown every weekend?*

was apparently so stirring in her rendition of "Amazing Grace" that it made the church moms kind of uncomfortable, and they complained to the pastor that it was too *edgy*, by which they really meant too *sexy*. Tessie was heartbroken. She just sang it how she felt it. It's not her fault she knows how to let music have its way with her.

"Hey, I've got a great idea. Maybe you guys can perform at our Save Unborn Lives fund-raiser. Oh, I forgot—they're all just a bunch of feminist lesbian vegetarian baby killers," Mary Ashley hurls back.[12]

Tess jumps to her feet, seriously pissed now.

I grab her arm. "Don't waste your breath."

"Where'd she get vegetarian?" Marcy laughs, taking a bite of her cafeteria cheeseburger.

I turn to face Mary Ashley and the band of boneheads. "Look, your ignorance is ruining my lunch. Tess doesn't want to hang out with you anymore. Deal."

"You also ain't much at parking-lot dance partying," Marcy says.

"You can't mess around with me," Mary Ashley sputters, the right side of her face puckering slightly. "Don't you know who my family is here? My dad's going to be a state senator. I don't need to sit here and take this just because you're, like, angry athlete girls."

"I don't play any sports," I say. "I guess I'm just angry."

12. Text from Rowie: *i hate her. i hate her so much.*

"Yeah?" Mary Ashley says levelly. "I heard you got a workout in the back of Charlie Knutsen's car. And Marcy—well, everyone knows Marcy's in great shape too."[13]

"Mary Ashley, if you're going to insult my friends, at least don't be a dumbass while you're doing it." Whoa. Tess said *ass*. "Is she a lesbian or a slut?"

"I call trash trash. You can call it what you want," MashBaum spits.

Marcy rises to her feet, glowering, and lets out a faint growl. "You hungry for mud, dollface?" According to varying accounts, during a marching band practice last year, Mary Ashley, who's one of the flag girls, called Marcy either Captain Tranny or Fat and Manny. Marcy retaliated by stopping drumline practice to give her a mud swirly on the football field. A mud swirly is just like a regular swirly, except Marcy actually ran in a circle with Mary Ashley's feet in her hands, wheelbarrow-style, to swirl her face in the mud. Some people say the drumline started marking time with Marcy's revolutions.

Mary Ashley stands up in Marcy's face like she's actually about to step to her. Marcy, my beautiful six-footer, has probably seven inches and forty pounds on Mary Ashley. "I should have gotten you expelled when I had the chance," Mary Ashley says to her. "And Tess,

13. Text from Rowie: *I'm going to poison her diet coke.*

41

honestly, what's with these freaks you hang out with now? Like, you were suddenly just *dying* to spend all your time with a psycho dyke from hell and her freaky loser friends?"

Rage rises in my throat like mercury in a thermometer. It's not fair that they pick on Marcy for a secret she isn't keeping. It makes me feel guilty, makes me wonder what Mary Ashley would do if I just told her the truth right now.[14]

"Bitch, you better—" I begin to gutter up a loogie to spit in Mary Ashley's eye, but Tess steps in front of me just in time.

"Back off, Mary Ashley." Tess's voice is low, boiling. "I'm sorry you're mad at me, but you are so not allowed to talk to my friends like that."

The bell cracks the mounting tension, signaling the five-minute warning before the dreaded return to afternoon classes. Mary Ashley's big green eyes are smoldering with rage. "Catch you later, traitor," she says to Tess. Flanked by her IQ vacuum, she huffs off.

I'm struggling to get my temperature back down. "Tess, how could you have hung out with those assholes?"

---

14. SiN before bed that night: *I'm learning the urge to blurt my hurt / Emerging to burn the cold hard out / Just wanna be the free me, get on the she on she in me / Gotta be real easy, curly-haired Esmeezy / Learning never to say please, just being real out loud.*

She looks at a loss. "I'm so sorry. She's not always that bad. It's just—she's been like this since I told her I couldn't go to her house in Door County this summer, when the four of us went camping in the Boundary Waters. I'm going to tell our pastor what she said. She'll get in trouble. Don't worry."

Marcy shakes her head. "Great. Backup from the church." She takes out her drumsticks and tattoos restlessly, looking down at the concrete floor.

Rowie, who's been silent and seething in the fetal position through this whole exchange, finally rises. She hates confrontation. *"Bitch!"*

We look at her in surprise.

"MashBaum is the one going to hell," Rowie heaves. "If there even *is* a hell. Who the hell does she think she is?"

"Whatever, she's so not worth getting worked up about," Marcy says. "Shake it off. She's just a mean girl with a Christ complex. No offense, Tessie."

"Yo, have you guys seen this?" Tess asks, picking up the packet Mary Ashley tossed at us.

"No, what is it?" I ask, popping a cold French fry into my mouth. I have a weakness for French fries, especially in times of crisis.

"It's apparently a copy of Holyhill's new code of conduct. 'Holyhill High School cannot condone violence in any form, nor can it condone any material known to incite violence. In this interest, loud, violent, heavily rhythmic music such as 'rap' will be prohibited on campus or at school events. Additionally, any apparel or other materials associated with this violence-inducing culture, such as pants sagging below the underwear line, gang apparel, or promotional artist material, will also be prohibited and punishable by suspension.'" Tessie expectorates the words as she reads aloud. "And get this. They're making everyone *sign* it."

"WTF?" Rowie asks in disbelief. "That shit is unconstitional."

"They think there are gangs in Holyhill? West Side!" Marcy laughs, throwing an upside-down finger W.

"Let me see that," I demand, grabbing the handbook from Marcy. "Where is this coming from? Like, what suddenly inspired them to outlaw the hip-hop nation?"

"Isn't it obvious?" Marcy says, slapping her forehead in jest. "There's been a large and dangerous — *influx* — into the community." She jerks her head toward Jane Njaka, a Somalian girl in a few of our classes, who's working on calculus and poking at something in Tupperware across the commons. Jane's sitting alone.

Rowie nods, aping concern. "Them coloreds, they're taking over the neighborhood."

"And the White House!" I holler, proudly exposing my Obama button.

"Yo, I meant to tell you, I have this hook that's like *We wanna cause some drama like Barack Obama*," Rowie tells me.

"Sick!" I say. "I love it. Let's work on it this weekend."

"OMG, do you think this policy is because of Friday night?" Tess asks. "When Mary Ashley got clowned on by those drunk guys? It would be just effing like her to get her dad to make the administration write some wack policy because she was pissed her shirt got ruined. Plus Herb Baumgarten's superconservative: I heard his education platform would actually make it illegal to teach evolution in Minnesota."

"No way," Rowie says. "Do the Baumgartens seriously have that much clout here?"

"I forgot his name was Herb," I say. "Ha. Ha, ha."

"Oh, mos def," Marcy says. "They almost got me expelled. But why hip-hop?"

"Why not?" Tess says. "Her dad's running for the state senate; he probably needs an issue. And people like that just like to feel powerful. This isn't the first sagging-pants policy I've read about. I saw an article about some kid in California who actually got arrested and held overnight because his pants were hanging off his butt."

"Held overnight? For real?" Marcy says. "I guess I can kiss ever fitting in here good-bye."

"Were you holding your breath?" Rowie asks drily.

I throw a fry at Marcy. "Fuck here."

"I'm sick of Holyhill's shit," Marcy says. "I mean, how can they confiscate, like, the most important musical movement of the last fifty years?"

"I'm not signing anything," I say. "And I don't see how they can make me."

"For real," says Rowie. "I mean, what if we wanted to learn from hip-hop? Like—what if we wanted to discuss it, or study it in an academic setting?"

"Isn't that sort of against what hip-hop's about?" Tess suggests. "I mean, do you really think Tupac would've wanted to be hauled into the classroom by a bunch of kids in the suburbs?"

"Isn't that something to discuss in and of itself?" I say.

The girls nod.

"So let's fucking discuss it." Marcy licks her lips, gunning for a fight. "Let's start a student group for hip-hop, a group to listen to it and talk about it. I wonder what they'll do if we all refuse to sign the policy."

"But a group like that'd never get approved by the administration. You saw the rules." Rowie sounds skeptical.

"That's totally the point," I say. "We refuse to sign the policy and challenge it by applying to put a hip-hop group on the official roster of school-sanctioned student groups."

"I'm not signing anything without a lawyer," Tess says, sounding like her mom. "And if they deny the application, we'll appeal and draw all kinds of attention to how unfair the policy is in the first place. How can they keep us from *talking* about why hip-hop is so complicated and offensive to some people and so effing bomb to all the awesome people?"

"They let the prayer group meet on campus. That's offensive to some people," Marcy says.

"Jesus is bomb," Tess mumbles through a bite of her sandwich.

"You know what else this shithole doesn't have?" I say. "A safe space. Of any kind. We don't have a gay-straight alliance, or any group that deals with issues like that. All the shit Holyhill tries to sweep under the rug just stays there."

"You're totally right." Marcy punches me for emphasis. "Even more to talk about. We should start, like, a queer hip-hop alliance." The four of us bust out laughing, then trail off, thinking.

"Wouldn't we need a gay to have a gay-straight alliance?" Rowie asks gently.

"Not necessarily," I say quickly. "I mean, maybe we could have a gay—after we have an alliance." Rowie nods understandingly, popping a dried apricot in her mouth.

Tess looks at us dubiously. "Let me get this straight. You guys are going to apply for school approval for a queer-friendly hip-hop student group?" A grin spreads like dawn over her face. "Damn. That's bold."

"Fucking right." Marcy is grinning. "We can call it Hip-Hop for Heteros and Homos. Code name: 4H."

"Are you sure that name isn't taken?" Rowie says.

I bust up. "This is fucking inspired."

Tess steals one of my fries and chuckles. "I'm so down. You dames may be crazy, but that policy is a violation of justice in ten different ways."

"So it's on," Marcy says. "None of us signs the policy. The dissenters shall be named 4H: Hip-Hop for Heteros and Homos. Oh, *hell* yes."

The bell rings again, urging us into afternoon classes. Slouching, groaning, resisting, we get up to go. Marcy balls up her paper bag and shoots it into a trash barrel fifteen feet away without so much as a kiss of the rim. "Three points!" She pumps a fist in the air.

"Marcy, how long am I gonna have to hound you before you get a reusable lunchbox?" Paper lunch bags drive me crazy; it's a hang-up of mine.

"I should get a lunchbox so I can have a gay little accessory like that?" Her face darkens. "Uh, I didn't mean—like, not *gay* gay—you know."

"Chill out, dude," I say. "Gotta do a lot better than that to offend old Ezmeezy."

I've never known an openly gay person in Holyhill, so I don't have a lot of precedent to go on in terms of, like, coming out to the world. I don't think I'd get beat up, but I can't say for sure—I'm pretty sure if I were a gay dude, I'd get the shit kicked out of me. How does a person go about coming out, anyway? I already told my best friends and my dad. Am I supposed to go around doling out high fives, all "Hey, what up, I'm Esme the Wonder Gay?"

Besides, Holyhill is a giant public high school, the best in Minnesota, 99.9 percent SWASP, or at least it feels that way. There are about twenty-five people in our five-hundred-person class with 4.0 averages: Tess and Rowie are two, and Marcy has a 3.95 because last semester she got her band grade docked for the MashBaum mud swirly incident. My friends are kind of over the whole social scene—the Holyettes danceline and their revolting highlights, the hysteria over hockey, the shiny cars in the senior lot. I think we all try to get really good grades because we know that college will get us out of this sand trap of a suburb, which I sometimes call the Orange County (gross) of Minnesota. Everyone graduates from Holyhill, everyone goes to college, and everyone seems to be Christian.

The Christian thing is a tricky stick to dip, because the girls like MashBaum who wear the little gold and silver Tiffany's crosses every day are the same girls we see wasted on Friday nights at Perkins, the only twenty-four-hour joint in town, eyeliner melted into dark half-moons under their eyes, hair backseat-ratted, tormenting poor Pearl, the weekend waitress. It gets to me sometimes, the way the moms complain when teachers assign too much homework on Wednesdays, when all the church youth groups meet, or get their knickers all in a twist about sex ed in health class and evolution in biology and gay teachers anywhere, or the way a lot of Holyhill moms don't seem to have anything to do but Botox their overcooked faces, cling white-knuckled to their lame middle-management husbands, and make their kids go to church. Living in Holy Hell is like being under twenty-four-hour Jesus surveillance.

Rowie's inquiring face startles me.

"Chemistry?" Rowie often speaks in single words.

"What?" I shake my head. "Sorry, totally spaced for a sec there."

"Come on, you know I'll do most of the lab work anyway."

Rowie's so good at chemistry it makes me want to vom. She's a super Hindu model minority at math and science. I'm good enough to be in the advanced class, but I'm still pretty destined for the humanities. I don't really like subjects where there's only one right answer. Ambivalence is practically my middle name.

I slump at the phrase "lab work," dragging my backpack behind me like a recalcitrant kindergartner.

"Is it more lab today? If we're not blowing anything up, I'm so out," I whine. I skip Chem a lot. Mr. Halverson is either too bored or too resentful of his job to protest my excuses—the nurse's office, an emergency newspaper meeting. One time a forged note claiming a phony meeting with the superintendent. Another time, as soon as Halves the Calves (more cankles, really—terrible, terrible man cankles—mankles?) started talking scientific method, I just got up, pointed to my crotch, declared, "Rag. Major rag," and walked out. That shit makes male teachers so uncomfortable that they let you go every time, especially if you've got the cojones to try it in a non-gym class. Totally catches them off guard, and you just slip out amid the stuttering and confusion.

"Unclear. Come on. Whenever you leave, I have to stay so you can copy my notes later," Rowie says.

I consider her point, which is fair. Casting an arm around her shoulders, I walk toward the domain of Mankles. "Fine. But you owe me five bucks if he's wearing mint-green again today." Halverson has a seemingly infinite collection of orthopedic sneakers. White and black, obviously, but also—we have a running record in my notebook — mint-green, ecru, gray, red, brown, and navy.

"Deal," she says. We fist-pound.

As we walk to class, I see Jane Njaka packing up her bag. What I know about Jane is that she's from Somalia, she commutes from Minneapolis, and she's wicked smart — she always knows the answers in AP Chem, sometimes even before Rowie.

"Hey, Jane," I call, waving at her. She turns around and looks a little surprised. "Do you know if it's more lab today in Chem?"

"Oh, God, I hope not. Prakash Banerjee is my partner, and he makes me do everything while he plays with his funny little Magic cards." Jane's voice is lilted in a tone I find reassuring; its articulation sounds a little islandy, but with some desert too.

Rowie and I bust out laughing.

"Prakash is a Magic *fiend*," Rowie says, giggling. "That kid is dork on a stick."

"I know!" Jane says. "I thought I was the only one who noticed what a freak he is! Do you know he always keeps four GI Joes in his pocket?"

"No," I say in disbelief.

"Not five, not three." She nods. "He takes them out and looks at them sometimes."

"Wow. Always good to know there's people out

there who are even shittier at fitting in than you are," Rowie says.

"No shit," says Jane Njaka, nodding with conviction.

The third bell rings, and Rowie and I hustle to our lab-table-for-two. I elbow her in the ribs.

"Powder-blue today."

She nods at my notebook. "Note it in the report." My phone buzzes.[15]

Mr. Halverson briskly claps his hands three times, which is his way of beginning class. He's not a bad guy, I guess, but he's one of those teachers who seem constantly disappointed. Maybe what Halves the Calves really wanted was to open his own cake shop or play pro cricket or, I don't know, tickle the baby grand for shoppers in the Galleria. Maybe a lot of grown-ups are disappointed.

In his dejected drone, Halverson begins. "Sit down. We're going to—well, we're going to try to—go over the principles of valence electrons and atomic bonding. Valence electrons tell us how well or poorly atoms play with others. Write this down, please, you'll need it for Thursday's quiz. Or don't. Fail the quiz. I don't care. Valence electrons orbit the nucleus on the outermost

---

15. Stealth-text from Marcy: *Dude, sorry about the gay lunchbox comment. Didn't mean it.*
Me to Marcy: *Dude, stop hitting on me.*
Marcy to me: *I wish I knew how to quit you.*

electron shell of the atom. They determine how stable or reactive the atom is. A high number of valence electrons makes a stable atom, and a low number makes the atom likely to react, or bond, with other atoms.[16]

"While there are five primary types of atomic bonding," Mankles continues blandly, "the two we'll cover today are covalent and ionic bonding. In the covalent bond, a reactive atom, one with a small number of valence electrons, shares valence electrons with a nearby atom. In an ionic bond, a reactive atom steals valence electrons from another atom. This is caused by electrostatic attraction."

I reach over and scribble in Rowie's notebook.[17] She muffles a giggle like a wind chime, and I feel distracted. Trying to get her laugh unstuck from my ringing ears, I decide it's safe now to take out my book and read under the table. Rowie can teach me chemistry later, and better than Mankles will now. I'm rereading Anne Frank; I love her. When I was eight, I started a journal just so I could call her Kitty, and began it by cataloging the entire contents of our kitchen cupboards in an attempt to imitate Anne's record of the annex's food supply, but I had to stop when I found a dusty box of matzoh and burst

16. *I have very few valence electrons,* I scribble in my notebook. *I think my nucleus is showing.*

17. *Let's get ionic.*

into tears. It's Mom's copy of the diary I have. I don't have much of hers, but there are still a ton of books she left behind in our house. I read the notes in the margins, or underlined passages, and I scrutinize them for evidence of her intent to abandon me, for a flight plan.

Her last letter, from almost a year ago, drops out of the back cover as I turn the page. She sends me a letter every birthday from a kibbutz she lives on in Israel. It's virtually the only contact we have, a yearly reminder that we're both still alive, even if we don't really know each other. Pops didn't understand, and I certainly didn't understand, *why* she left—I guess she had some kind of breakdown. The letters I get from her are more like lists.

1. *Esme Ruth.*

2. *Today you are sixteen, or maybe you are already sixteen and the mail is late.*

3. *Today I woke up at five and did my chores, and it felt as though you were there next to me, folding the other end of the sheet, picking fruit.*

4. *You were born in a blizzard.*

5. *I'd imagine you are angry with me. I'm so sorry. Not because you're angry, but for my giving you a reason to be angry.*

6. *When you were three, you stuck a Raisinette so far up your nose, we had to take you to the emergency room.*
7. *Someday we'll have a long conversation over a bottle of wine and you might begin to understand.*

I tuck the letter away and return to the book. I'm at January 6, 1944. A Thursday. Anne's been in hiding for about a year and a half. She's writing about her mother, about her exasperation with her mother and her sister. She loves her father, like I do. She has a mother and a sister, but I don't. She's thinking about her body, like I am, and she's embarrassed about it, which I guess I am, sometimes. Isn't everyone? I'm just coming to the passage that made everyone snicker when we read it in eighth-grade Language Arts, the passage I remember best of Anne's definitive edition, the restored version with all the sex and nasty observations her father once extracted, the passage that still rings like a bell inside my hollow places:

> *Unconsciously, I had these feelings even before I came here. Once when I was spending the night at Jacque's, I could no longer restrain my curiosity about her body, which she'd always hidden from me and which I'd never seen. I asked her whether, as proof of our friendship, we could*

touch each other's breasts. Jacque refused. I also
had a terrible desire to kiss her, which I did. Every
time I see a female nude, such as the Venus in my
history book, I go into ecstasy. Sometimes I find
them so exquisite I have to struggle to hold back
my tears. If only I had a girlfriend!

I close the diary and look at Anne's picture on the
front, at her grainy black bob, and in profile, I see the
black wall of Rowie's bob, its smooth surface disturbed
by the rapid action of her pencil, her head bowed,
unaware of me just on the other side, watching.

CHAPTER THREE

Let's Get Free

Fall is a heady apple-tree season in Minnesota; the sinking feeling of winter hasn't quite sunk, and the wind is aromatic with embering pumpkins and unpacked quilts and dirty, wet red leaves and a distinct, immodest scent of anticipation veiled over it all. Football season bleeds into hockey. The bottle blondes begin to lowlight a little. College scouts sniff around, and it rains until it snows. I'm in my last-period art elective on Friday, which would be the easiest class in the world to skip if I didn't actually like it, when Ms. Mayakovsky, the severe-looking but appealingly crazy art teacher, hands me a note summoning me to the principal's office directly after class. It doesn't say why, though I have an idea. My suspicions are confirmed: all three of my comrades-in-arms are gathered outside the office, waiting to be called in.

"Guys, this is going to sound pathetic," Tess confesses, "but this is the first time in eleven years of public school that I've ever been called to the principal's office."

"Me too," Rowie says. "There goes my perfect record."

"I punched Ryan Hoffstadt for tripping me in kickball in first grade," Marcy says. "He lost four baby teeth, they made me sit at the bad kids lunch table for three days, and people called me the Tooth Fairy until middle school."

"Savage from day one," Rowie says, chuckling.

"Well, ladies, you must be happy to be sharing your first time with us public-school menaces." I headlock Marcy and noogie her hard.

"Oh, eff off, poser," Marcy says, calling me out and wriggling free in a matter of seconds. "Name one time you've ever gotten sent to the principal's office."

I blush. "I got sent to the guidance counselor once for telling everyone in my second-grade class that Santa Claus was invented by advertisers." I hadn't even known what that meant, really, I'd just heard Pops say it.

"Doesn't count!" Tess gleefully points at me. "You're just as big a square as we are."

Principal Ross Nordling opens his door, quelling our clowning. "Ladies? Would you like to join me?"

We straighten up and hustle in. Principal Ross Nordling is a tawny man, the same golden pink from his hair (mustache, eyebrows, eyelashes) to his skin to his dress shirt. He's youngish—I'd say late thirties—and not particularly intimidating, though you can tell he thinks he is; he gives off that red-meat scent of hanging on by a thread all the time.

"Please, sit down." He gestures us toward four chairs. His demeanor suggests a host's, as if he's just invited us to sit for tea. We sit.

"The office is collecting and sorting this year's signed Holyhill school policies," he begins, glancing through the new copy of the *Holyhill West Wind,* the school paper, on his desk. "And I was surprised to learn that four of Holyhill's most outstanding students hadn't yet responded to a second reminder to sign the policy."

None of us says anything for a moment.

"You don't say," Marcy replies, earning a raise of two strawberry-blond eyebrows.

"In fact, Miss Crowther, I do," he challenges her.

"*Ms.* Crowther," she corrects him. He takes a moment and gives us all a long elevator-eyes scan.

"Ms. Crowther"—he offers a shyster smile—"would you like to tell me why you did not sign the policy?"

"I'd be happy to," she says. "We didn't sign the policy because it's narrow-minded and counterproductive. First of all, outlawing hip-hop is ridiculous, considering it's everywhere, and second, a policy like this prevents anyone from *learning* from hip-hop."

He sizes up the rest of us. "And this is how all of you feel?" We nod.

I pull out a folder with a copy of our application to be a recognized student group.

"The four of us are definitely in agreement on that," Tess says, "and that's why we've applied to create a discussion group about hip-hop music and culture." She smiles at him. "We thought that if we showed how hip-hop can be a positive force for debate and learning, the administration might reconsider its ban on it. In case you haven't gotten a chance to look it over, here's a copy of the application we submitted about a week ago."

Nordling takes the paper and gazes vacantly at it for a moment.

NAME AND PURPOSE OF GROUP:

Sister Mischief: Hip-Hop for Heteros and Homos is proposed as a discussion group for queer inquiry— inqueery—into the language, music, and culture of hip-hop. As a safe space for GLBT students, the group will also serve as Holyhill's first gay-straight alliance. By directing our questions about gender, race, class, and art toward both the discipline of hip-hop and the terrain of Holyhill High School in a spirit of tolerance, we hope to break down bound-aries of what a hip-hop language, or a Holyhill stu-dent identity, may include.

NUMBER OF MEMBERS (ESTIMATED):

There are currently four members, though several hundred are expected to join when they realize that our group is way more fun than other groups.

ARE YOU REQUESTING FUNDING?

Not at this time.

MULTIMEDIA/TECHNOLOGY
REQUIREMENTS (PLEASE LIST ALL):

Audio/video equipment for listening to music and viewing films; Internet-equipped meeting space.

FACULTY ADVISER:

We're working on it.

Nordling clears his throat. "Yes, Ms. Grinnell, I'm familiar with this application, and I'm sorry to have to inform you that it's been denied."

"Why is that?" I ask. "Because it violates your hip-hop policy or because you don't want to deal with the fallout from creating a gay-straight alliance at Holyhill?"

"Is that what this group is?" he asks dubiously, holding up our application. "Because to me, it looks like a group without a faculty adviser dedicated to the study of a music and culture of violence, drugs, and licentious sex. I must say, I'm surprised that four bright girls such as yourselves would be so devoted to music that objectifies and degrades women."

"I think if you studied it more, Mr. Nordling," I retort, "you'd find that hip-hop isn't nearly that simple, and that discussing and exploring its questions of culture and gender and identity are fascinating, legitimate courses of inquiry. Inqueery."

Our conversation is interrupted by a knock at the door. Marilyn DiCostanza, our AP English teacher and head of the department, pokes her head in.

"Ross," she says, "sorry to interrupt, but what are these signed school policy sheets my homeroom is handing in? I don't remember any new school policies being discussed at the last faculty meeting."

"This isn't the ideal time to discuss it, Marilyn." Principal Nordling maintains a forced smile.

"Now's the time to discuss why a Christian prayer group is allowed to meet on school grounds but our hip-hop GSA isn't," I say.

"We could use a faculty adviser, Mrs. D.," Tess pipes up.

Mrs. DiCostanza smiles. "It looks as though you have your hands full right now, Ross. I'll catch up with you later."

"Thank you, Marilyn," he manages through pinched lips.

"Mr. Nordling, not all Holyhill parents are Christian, and neither are its students. And I think you should consider the idea that maybe students who don't fit your Holyhill SWASP ideal might need a space where they feel safe too," I say.

"SWASP?" he asks.

"Straight White Anglo-Saxon Protestant," Rowie rattles off.

Nordling takes a deep breath and massages his temples. "Listen, girls. Whether we all like it or not, we live in a Christian community in a Christian nation. Don't you think it'd be much easier for everybody if you just accepted the administration's denial of your student group application and pondered all these things on your own time?"

"Mr. Nordling," Tess says in a voice full of honeybees, "we are not interested in what is *easy*. We live in a melting-pot nation in which our freedom of expression is protected by the First Amendment. Our Christian community wouldn't want the ACLU breathing down your neck. A First Amendment, or gosh, a church-and-state lawsuit—that would be so *pesky*, wouldn't it? Hmm?" She sits back, crossing her legs.

"Ms. Grinnell, I must say I'm a little surprised at you. I wouldn't have expected a stunt like this from a young woman such as yourself," Nordling says.

"Actually," Tess replies, "I believe this stunt, as you call it, is perfectly in line with my Christian values of love and tolerance. Nothing offends those values more than when people use Jesus's words as a lame justification for their own small-mindedness."

"Well, I'd hardly say—" he starts.

"We have some contacts in the local media," Marcy says. I wonder who she's referring to until I remember Rooster's KIND-11 gig.

"There must be some way we can reach a compromise here," Tess says, sweetly pounding Ross Nordling into the ground. "I'm sure my parents, Darlene and Dr. Gary Grinnell, would be so pleased to hear that you listened to us and made a fair decision. Hmm?"

Tess's laid her whole hand on the table now: everyone, and I mean *everyone*, in Holyhill knows the Grinnells. Darlene is not a woman one wants as an enemy, and Principal Ross Nordling knows this exceptionally well, having overseen the education of both her daughters. However, he also knows that she's not a woman one would think likely to support a queer hip-hop collective.

Principal Ross Nordling drops his head and furiously kneads his forehead with his thumbs, weighing his options.

"How about this: you keep your group quiet, sign the policy, and"—he glances back at our application—"Hip-Hop for Heteros and Homos can meet in the old warming house out by the track."

"Wait one hot minute," Marcy says. "That warming house isn't even technically on school grounds if it's past the track."

"It's the best offer I'm making, Ms. Crowther. And how do you know so much about school boundaries? Does *your* father know about this group of yours?"

Marcy starts a little, but holds her bluff. "Of course he does."

"Good. Do we have a deal, ladies?" He holds up the unsigned policies.

We exchange looks.

"Ladies?" he says.

"Well—all right," I say.

"Really?" He brims over with glee.

"Naw, I'm just playing with you," I say. "I'm not signing anything. And if that warming house isn't on school grounds, it seems like we can pretty much meet there whether you say so or not."

"I'll have to check with my mother about signing."

Tess folds her hands delicately on her lap and smiles. "And possibly our family lawyer."

"No, thank you." Rowie smiles.

He looks unoptimistically at Marcy. "Seriously?" she scoffs. "No way."

"All right, ladies. I'll meet you halfway. You meet in the warming house for the rest of the semester. If, in that time, you can demonstrate to me that this group is truly positive and purposeful and that other students are interested in having it, we'll find a space on campus for it next semester."

"That"—Tess stands up, sticking out her hand—"is a better offer." He shakes it.

"So you'll sign?" Nordling asks, hoping this meeting is over.

"We'll think about it," Marcy says. Nordling shakes the rest of our hands and we retreat, holding in our laughter until we make it to the parking lot.

Later that night, waiting for Marcy to pick me up for our celebratory jam session with the ladies,[18] I'm painting my nails black and white and watching *Hedwig and*

18. Text from Rowie: *I just got an original-release LP of CunninLynguists' Will Rap for Food. When are you coming over?*
Me to Rowie: *Omfg, that's like seeing a unicorn. On our way in 10.*

the Angry Inch for the five hundredth time when I hear Marcy and Coach Bob walk into the kitchen, shooting the shit with my dad. They're all old buddies, and I think I hear Marcy and Pops practicing their secret handshake. Sometimes I think my dad knows more about Marcy's life than her dad does. No doubt he's easier to talk to than tank-like Coach Bob, who's shaped like a refrigerator and learned how to communicate in the Marines. I know my dad isn't like other dads; I mean, he carves wood furniture for a living and miniature houses as a passion, for one. We're pretty broke by Holyhill standards—it's a good thing Marcy inherited Rooster's old car, because Pops and I could never afford a second one—but I guess that's just the price I pay for having a dad who's pretty chill and empathetic and liberal by Holyhill standards, too.

Blowing on my piano-key fingernails, I attempt to shove on my emerald-green boots without using my hands, no easy feat considering the boots are eighteen inches tall. I hook my bag over my elbow crook, turn off the TV, and clump out to the kitchen.

Per usual, Dad is pushing food on Marcy.

"Seriously, Luke, I *just* ate," she protests weakly.

"Little girl, you haven't tasted egg salad like this in your life. Did you know curry powder makes everything better?" Dad's going through a curry phase. Coconut curry, various veggies in curry sauce, now curried egg salad.

"I gotta admit, the egg salad is pretty tricked out," I chime in. "But I contest the allegation that curry powder makes *everything* better."

"Cite your evidence!" Dad cries, actually shocked.

"Uh, last Sunday's maca-curry-and-cheese? Not meant to be, Pops."

Bob guffaws. "Luke cooks like a girl." This sends Marcy and me into peals of laughter.

He laughs. "Okay, okay, I'll chalk that one up to my overzealous palate. But for real, just try one bite of this." He spoons a lump of today's special into Marcy's mouth, and her eyebrows shoot up.

"*Damn*, that's tasty." Marcy coughs. "Nice work, Rockett man."

"Ez, you want some? Skinny girl, you're wasting away."

"Dad, we had dinner like half an hour ago. Marcy and I really gotta bolt. Bob, didja bring *Forrest Gump*?"

He bashfully produces the DVD from under his coat, along with a six-pack, a bag of corn chips, and a can of Frito-Lay nacho cheese dip. Bob Crowther wears John Deere hats unironically. "Now, how'd you know it'd be that and not *Platoon* this time?"

I grin. "Lucky guess."

Pops throws his hands up in mock exasperation. "What do you expect the man to say? We old men are creatures of habit. Bob likes war movies. I love by feeding. Go. Get out of here. Consider your welcome overstayed."

I remember my hobo feet. "Wait, Pops, can you lace me up? My nails are wet."

Dad shakes his head a little, chuckling, and kneels down to work on my magnificent shitkickers.

"Luke, I gotta bail on Sunday night," Bob says as Pops laces.

"Why?" Pops looks crestfallen. "We haven't, um, been bowling in months."

"You know you guys sound a lot gayer when you come up with euphemisms for playing blackjack at Mystic Lake, right?" I say.

"Seriously," Marcy says. "The jig is up. No one can come home from bowling smelling that much like Kool cigarettes and despair."

"Well," Bob says, "I suppose you were bound to figure it out."

"Why can't you go?" Marcy asks. "You don't have practice on Sunday nights."

"Maybe I should ask you," Bob says. "You got any idea why Ross Nordling wants a meet with me first thing Monday morning?"

"Nope." Marcy suddenly appears engrossed in cracking open the dip can.

"Mary Marcella, are you sure?" Bob asks sternly. Marcy *hates* her full name.

"You bet," Marcy says. Pops and I exchange a look in which I try to convey *I'll tell you later.*

"Did I buy you these?" Pops interjects. "They're kinda nutty."

"You mean they're kinda *beautiful*? No, you didn't buy them. I got them for ten bucks at Value Village with Rowie. Can you believe someone left these homeless?"

Marcy, Bob, and Dad exchange a look, then nod in unison.

"I'm breaking up with all of you. Later, Pops. Love you no shit. Later, Bob."

"Love you no shit. Where are you going? Do you have your phone?"

"Just over to Rowie's, and yes. *Bye.*"

I toss Dad a quick peck on the cheek, followed by an identical peck from Marcy. Marcy kisses my dad, but not her own. Just as we're about to walk out the front door, the doorbell rings. Surprised, I turn back to the kitchen.

"Hey, Pops, you expecting someone?" Is Dad dating behind my back? That hasn't happened in a while, not since Marcy and I scared away his last girlfriend, Felicia, by stealing a sign from the Holyhill Veterinary Clinic that read BUFFALO MEAT FOR SALE and putting it on her front lawn. Sign stealing is one of Marcy's and my favorite pastimes. Truth be told, I still feel kind of bad about Felicia. There wasn't anything overtly wrong with her except that she smelled like cottage cheese.

"Nope," he calls back. "See who it is."

I open the door to find none other than the despicable Mary Ashley Baumgarten, along with another girl who looks like her freshman doppelgänger. Why can't I ever get away from this girl?

"What in God's name are you doing at my house?" I ask MashBaum.

She pretends to gawk. "This is your house?"

I roll my eyes. "Yes. And this is my door." I begin to close it, but Mary Ashley thrusts a foot in and comes back with a syrupy smile.

"Go ahead." She nudges her mini-MashBaum.

"I'm canvassing today because the Holyhill Teens for Christ are selling poinsettias to support our Preserve Unborn Lives initiative," the girl starts.

"Who's the clone?" I ask.

"This is Kristina, my freshman buddy. She's learning how to canvass for Christ." MashBaum wraps an arm around her minion. "Right, Stina?"

"Perhaps you'd like to know that the first poinsettia is seventeen ninety-five, and each additional plant is just fifteen ninety-five," Kristina rattles off, looking eagerly back at Mary Ashley for approval. "We guarantee delivery by December first, and for today only, we have a special offer of five plants for eighty-nine ninety-nine."

"Oh, spare me," I groan.

"That's a total rip-off," Marcy mutters. "If you buy

one plant at seventeen ninety-five and then four at fifteen ninety-five, the total is only eighty-one seventy-five."

Mary Ashley's face twists, and she says, more for Kristina's benefit than ours, "Look, it's never too late for you girls to come to Bible study sometime, and just own up to your sins and learn about Jesus, and hear about everything we're doing to save the unborn. Everyone is welcome. Teenage pregnancy is a big problem in Holyhill—"

Marcy cackles. "You should know, right, Mary Ashley?"

"We meet Wednesday afternoons, third lunch . . ." I can hear Kristina's waning voice as I slam the door in her face.

"Unbelievable," I say.

"Now we have to wait for her to leave before we can," whines Marcy, watching through the window as Mary Ashley and Kristina cross the street.

"Like hell we do. Let's run her over," I say, opening the door and walking out.

Marcy follows. "Not worth the mess they'd make on the driveway. We should seriously call the ACLU on that Bible group. Bob's always said pinko lawyers love that church-and-state shit."

"Maybe," I say, hopping into the passenger side of the Jimmy. "But don't you think legal's more flexible when you're rich?"

"Shit is fucked."

"For real."

Marcy starts the car and I stick my tongue out between two fingers at Mary Ashley as we pull out. Dead prez's *lets get free* blasts from the CD hookup. Marcy's been heavy into hip-hop for as long as I can remember, and it was her endless lyrical parroting and beatboxing that got the rest of us rhyming in the first place.

"You're good with words," Marcy said to me about a year ago. She'd figured out how to break songs down for their parts on her computer. "You say things right. Can you make them rhyme?"

I wrote and I wrote, and it rhymed, but I couldn't make it sit in a song shape. I just wrote lyrics like a highway without any exit ramps.

"I was thinking about Rapunzel," Rowie said out of the blue one day. "I think I wrote a hook about Rapunzel."

"Yeah?" I said, intrigued. "Lay it on us." Rowie was so nervous as she read from her notebook that her voice shook.

"Bumping up against the edges of a blond-yawn town
She's stuck up in a tower and she can't get down
But she's got beats in her feet and she's drowning in sound
Break out, babe, obey it, get down."

"That's it," Marcy marveled. "Thank God you came along. Miss Poet Laureate over here can't write a chorus to save her own ass." Then when Tess started hanging around, Sister Mischief was born.

People think it's weird, I know—four suburban teenage girls, three white, one brown, making this kind of music. Maybe some people think a white girl from Minnesota doesn't have any right to rhyme. But how am I supposed to keep from rhyming? To me, hip-hop is a reflection of your surroundings, and an instrument of change. And if that's true, it can't belong only to black people, or to white people, or to brown or green or blue people. Within a medium of subversion, I like to think that all subversive people are, or should be, welcome, because busting rhythm and poetry loose is the only way anyone with hip-hop pumping in their veins can feel free. We're getting free. So fuck anyone who thinks we shouldn't rap. If we're being really honest with ourselves here, we rap exactly because a lot of people think we shouldn't.

"Hey," Marcy says.[19] "Where you at, Ferocious?"

I smile. "Just thinking."

"Wanna find a new sign to bring Rowie?"

---

19. Text from Tess: *On my way to R's now, but I gotta hit choir practice for a while tonight or MA's gonna call a Lutheran jihad on my a**.*

"No doubt, ladyfriend."

Marcy pulls off the highway and we hunt for targets. I point out a generic handwritten GARAGE SALE THURSDAY sign and shrug; she shakes her head.

"We need something more ironic. Something with a little more smack to it."

"What does that sign say?" Marcy asks, pointing at a sign on Mary Ashley's mammoth yard.

"Oh, my God, we would have to be seriously stealthy to make off with that." The lawn sign reads *Herb for Holyhill: Herb Baumgarten for State Senator.*

Marcy cackles. "Herb for Holyhill! That shit is ours."

"Can you believe he's actually running?" I say. "We're basically doing Holyhill a nicey by sabotaging him."

"I still can't believe he's running as a Republican with 'Herb for Holyhill' as his campaign slogan. Let me pull through the side street—it'll get us closer." She hangs a left and kills the lights. "I'm going to roll slowly by the edge of the lawn, and you dash out and grab it from your side, drive-by–style."

"Someone should confiscate your DVDs of *The Wire,* but I'm on it." We roll by the yard and I bolt across the lawn, twisting my ankle a little as I pivot back, sign in hand. The sprint leaves me panting when I jump back in the Jimmy and toss the booty in the back as Marcy peels out, cackling wildly. Marcy and me, we take care of business.

Rowie and Tess live at the end of a long cul-de-sac near the fire station, in houses facing each other from about a block's distance. The Baumgartens live on the next street over, which lends a literal quality to Mary Ashley's acting like we invaded her territory. Anyway, what I love most about Rowie's house, apart from the old treehouse in the backyard, is the smell. It's sweet and spicy and totally unlike the smell of any other house I know; I love that it's full of scents unfamiliar to me. Before I knew Rowie's family, I'd never really eaten Indian food, except for a samosa here and there, but Dr. Priya Rudra is a force to be reckoned with, in the kitchen as well as the ER. It took me a few tries to brave the Rudra chutney gauntlet without weeping from the heat, but that shit is legit. Marcy parks on the street, and we walk up to the embossed-copper door.

Dr. Rudra—well, one of them—Rowie's dad—answers. "Ah! Friends! Rohini is expecting you. Do you want some chicken?" As the only non-veg member of the Rudra family, Raj Rudra is always trying to recruit companions in carnivoraciousness.

"You have no idea how full we are," Marcy answers. "Esme's dad just pushed me over my limit."

"Maybe later," I add. "Thanks a bunch, though. Is Rowi—Rohini down in her room?"

"Yes. Please go ahead." He steps aside softly down

the hall. "You girls have a nice time writing your rap rhymes." He sends us off with a glance at the Herb sign ill-concealed behind Marcy's back.

Just then, the other Dr. Rudra, Rowie's mom, appears. Her face lights up when she sees Marcy and me.

"Girls! I'm so glad I caught you. Oh, I loathe that man." She points to HERB FOR HOLYHILL. "He wants to destroy science education in Minnesota." She laughs at the shocked looks on our faces. "My mother always says that American medical school turned me into a crazy radical. I say, what's radical about dispersing information? Please, don't get me started. How is your writing going?"

"Fine, thanks, Dr. Rudra."

"I'm so glad." She smiles. Rowie's mom is really beautiful—not young, and not pretending to be, but she has a kind of glow that's lit from within. "I was thinking about your verses. I studied poetry at university, you know."

"I didn't know," I say, wondering when she had time to read poetry as she was learning how to save children's lives.

"I have to get to hospital, but—" She looks conflicted for a moment, then relaxes. "Oh, it's all right. I'm always early anyway. I want to show you this lovely poem I found. It made me think of you girls."

"Yeah?" I say, surprised. Marcy looks awkward but intrigued. "Okay. I'd love to see it."

She motions for us to follow her down the hall into the office she shares with the other Dr. Rudra. Marcy and I hover in the threshold, surveying the piles of paper and pictures of Rowie and Lakshmi, her little sister. Rowie's mom plucks a sheet off her pile and scans it, smiling.

"Here it is," she whispers. "It's by a Minnesota poet, and it makes me think about those early friends, the girls you love first, before all others. This is the stanza that made me think of Rohini and you American girls." She begins to read in a musical voice:

"How we could talk!
Translating back and forth. We knew hundreds
of lines by heart, the endless
rhythms, counterpoint to the ocean waves. We wanted
to take in all the wonder in the world, all
the ecstasy, all the tenderness. Ömhet,
you loved to say this soft word for tenderness, ömhet.
I loved to listen to you.
So strange to have loved something so much
and not to have known it was a calling."

She finishes reading and looks up, gently searching our faces for a reaction.

"That's—that's beautiful," I croak, clearing my throat.

"Isn't it? I think it captures a kind of magic feeling, something mystical about the way life feels when you are young, and the love between women. It's truthful that way. Do you know?" Dr. Rudra's eyes return to the page for a moment.

Out of the corner of my eye, I see Marcy slumped, staring at the floor.

"I know we all need a little poetry sometimes," I say, to break the silence, and because it's true.

Dr. Rudra nods firmly. "Yes. You are a very wise girl, to know that already."

I clear my throat again. Marcy shifts her weight.

She looks at us again, searching. "Well, any time you feel like you need some poetry, you come to our house."

"Thanks, Dr. R. Have a good night at work." She places a hand on both of our shoulders and slides past us, smelling like Rowie—gardenia and almond and something else. Marcy is still all hunched over and quiet. This mom shit, she's never looked it in the face. I nudge her.

"You cool, fool?" I ask.

She raises her head, taking in a rush of breath. "Yeah"—it hangs for a second—"yeah. Let's do this." Without providing further opportunity for discussion, she walks out of the study.

We scamper downstairs to find Rowie nestled in her

bed underneath her enormous headphones and Tess humming "Poker Face" on the floor. Before I can nudge Rowie's shoulder, Marcy leaps in front of her bed and flashes the Herb sign.

"Herb for Holyhill!" Marcy cries.

Rowie jumps like she's been electrocuted and falls off the bed, on top of Tess.

"Jesus Christ, Marce, you almost killed me," Rowie gasps, yanking her headphones off her ears, rolling over, and catching her breath. Marcy doubles over, yukking.

"Me too." Tess coughs. "Where'd you get that?"

"Some asshole's lawn," Marcy says.

"What's got you so lost in thought, girl?" I ask Rowie, patting her hair.

"I'm trying to figure out how to isolate this beat and bassline from 'Testify,'" she tells us. "I think we could use a sort of similar structure, like, give Tess a vocal hook that repeats throughout the whole track and lay the rhymes on top of it. Here, listen." She unplugs the cord from her MacBook and Common fills the room.

"I can pull that beat for sure," Marcy says. "This track is totally post Common's selling out, but still good shit."

"Have you started working on lyrics yet?" I ask, knowing she has.

"Affirmative," Rowie replies. "I'm thinking 'Lemme

81

Get a Hit of It' as the title. But in the actual track, I want to put a pause between the two clauses so they sort of rhyme, like 'Lemme get / a hit of it.' So it's like a call-and-response thing, like you'll say something, and we all say 'Lemme get / a hit of it,' and then I'll say something and everyone responds. . . . You get what I'm talking about?"

"I think so. If you can work that into a chorus, I can write some verses around it. What you got so far for the call and response?"

"Okay, so I think it just starts with you and me doing some MC improv as the beat starts and Tess's vocals come in, you know, just talking like 'Turn that up in the headphones' style."

"Got it. Tessie, you got a melody?"

"You know it." She grins, splashing an arpeggio into a circular hook.

"And then you come in with 'Sisterhood!' " Rowie instructs me. "Then we all say 'Lemme get / a hit of it,' and then maybe I say 'Equality!' and everyone responds, then maybe the TC, rollin' with my homegirls, Roe v. Wade, you know, some other sweet shit."

Rowie's door flies open and thirteen-year-old Lakshmi appears.

"What the hell? Get out of my room!" Rowie hurls her pen like a javelin at Lakshmi, which strikes me as somewhat vicious, but what do I know about siblings?

"Can you cover for me?" Lakshmi asks.

"While you do what, exactly?" Rowie snorts.

"There's a party, *obvs*," Lakshmi says, rolling her eyes.

"Will there be boys at the party?" asks Tess, bemused.

Lakshmi looks at us like we're all shit-for-brains. "Why would I be going if there weren't going to be boys there?"

"Excuse *me*," Rowie says. "I will not cover for you so you can go do whatever you do with those skanky little Holy Hellions. Go to bed."

"Come *on*," Lakshmi whines. "It's only three streets over. You know how Dad gets as soon as he hears *party*. I'll be back by eleven. It's not even a *bad* party."

"No." Rowie holds firm.

"Damn, Ro." Marcy whistles through her teeth. "You're kind of a tightass." Rowie looks at her wide-eyed, then relents.

"Fine. Eleven. Don't get hit by a car or anything. Bye."

Lakshmi leaps with delight, blows us all a kiss, and dashes out. We exchange looks.

"That one's gonna be *trouble*," Tess says.

"Don't remind me." Rowie shakes her head. "She's on the Holyette Express. Let's just talk about the song."

"I was digging what you had going on," Marcy says as she pulls her computer out of her backpack and starts isolating more samples. "Carry on as I work on technical support."

"What if," I start, thinking out loud, "at the last call and response before we get into the first verse, I say something funny like 'Yo, Ro, you got some deodorant in that purse?' and you say, 'Yeah, Ferocious,' and I just say, 'Lemme get a hit of it' by myself?"

Tess giggles and her dimples indent her cheeks. "Your face is crazy, crazy-face."

"That should be a lyric in the chorus." Rowie lights up, trying it. *"Your face is crazy, crazy-face."*

We die laughing. "Lemme get a hit of it," I choke.

"Got it!" Marcy proclaims seconds later. "Listen to this." She plays another sick polyrhythm for us.

"Sick," Rowie says.

"Word." Marcy is pleased with herself.

I agree. "That shit is heavy."

Tess checks her watch. "Buttfudge, I gotta run." She begins to get her purse together.

"Sometimes I think your non-swears are nastier than actual swears," I comment.

"Where you going?" Marcy asks.

"I gotta go to choir to make sure Mary Ashley hasn't put out a hit on me-slash-us after our little showdown in the commons," she says.

"She did show up at my house pushing poinsettias," I say. "With a mini-MashBaum."

"That girl is a Percocet dependency waiting to happen," Marcy says.

84

"Yeah, uh," I stutter. "I meant to say earlier, sorry she, like, thinks you're gay. I sort of feel like it's my fault."

"Eff that," Marcy says. "What comes out of that girl's mouth is not what thinking sounds like."

"Why are you afraid of Mary Ashley?" I say to Tess. "I mean, why do you care what she thinks of you or your friends?"

Tess sighs. "It's all politics, girlfriend."

"Plus you feel guilty for breaking up with her," Marcy says.

"I always felt like she blamed *me* for that. Once I moved into the neighborhood, it's like she got demoted or something," Rowie says.

"She did," Marcy says simply, shrugging.

"Look, you're not wrong," Tess says. "But strategically, it's better for us and for 4H if Holyhill still thinks I'm in with the A-list Christian contingent."

"I guess then they can't say we're all degenerates and aliens," I say.

"Just some of us," Rowie mutters.

"Oh, quit it with the Indiangst," Tess teases her gently. "That betch is perverting my church and effing with my friends, and her unconstitutional Bible group is the best leverage we have with Nordling. As long as I can help keep our plan moving forward intact, we have something he doesn't want to leak to the local media and their lawyers."

"I feel you," I say. "You're like our secret ambassador. That's some devious shit."

"Yeah, get a hit of *that*." She beams. "Plus, you know, I like to sing."

"We'll fill you in on *this* scheming later." Marcy raises her hand in a good-bye salute.

"Tell the girls we said namaste," Rowie adds drily.

"Mazel tov," I contribute.

"Body of Christ." Marcy makes the sign of the cross over Tess.

"Good night, God bless you, and God bless America." Tess flashes us a peace sign and disappears out the basement door.

CHAPTER FOUR

Fruit

"Speaking of scheming," Marcy continues slyly, producing an Altoids box from her bag. "Anyone wanna get a hit of this?" She opens the box to reveal a joint that looks like it's been through a dishwasher.

"Oooohh, shit," I crow, a smile spreading across my face. "I'm wicked down. Where'd you get that?"

"Rooster's glove compartment," Marcy informs us without a hint of remorse. "I think it's pretty old, so I doubt he'll notice it's gone." Things we've stolen from Rooster over the years include the first porn I ever saw, $7.86 in change for a late-night Perkins run, a whole truckful of Legos, and one shoddy little doobie before this one. Marcy's been a lifelong beneficiary of the fact that she's smarter than her brothers.

We look at Rowie, who looks a little nervous.

"Down. I think," she says hesitantly. "Lemme just run up and assess the Raj situation." She darts upstairs.

Even though we like to act like hardened criminals, truth is, our experience with the sticky icky is pretty limited. Marcy's smoked a few times with her brother, but I've only tried it the once before. I didn't think it really worked, but we did polish off six personal pan pizzas between the two of us, the kind Pops always buys from Anthony Grinnell's Boy Scout troop. Marcy says no one gets high the first time they do it. Kind of like sex, I guess.

Rowie bounds back into her bedroom. "The news just finished and he's snoring so loud I'm surprised we couldn't hear it from here. We're golden."

"You wanna call Bob and tell him you're spending the night?" I ask Marce.

She whips her toothbrush and retainer out of her backpack and grins. "Check, check, dirtbag. No one's expecting me home tonight."

"Okay, lemme just give Pops a heads-up." I dial home.

"Hey, parakeet," he says.

"I've never understood how that became a term of endearment. I hate birds."

"You should be counting your blessings that I didn't pick *budgie*."

"And I am. Is it cool if I sleep at Rowie's?"

"I s'pose. Do you have all your stuff?"

"More or less. Marcy can give me a ride home tomorrow."

"Are you going anywhere but Rowie's? I'm not saying you can't. I just want to know where you'll be."

"Don't think so."

"Then have a nice time and I'll smell you in the morning."

"Love you no shit."

"Love you no shit."

Honestly, I could probably tell Dad I'm about to go get stoned in Rowie's treehouse without incurring so much as a brief lecture, but the thing about permissive progressive parents is eventually you've talked about your feelings so much that you want to keep secrets just to have a feeling that belongs to you.

"All good?" Marcy says.

"Holler," I say.

"I call the trundle bed!" Marcy gives a sleepover fist-pump.

If Marcy's in the trundle, that means I've got the other half of Rowie's bed.

"Looks like you're stuck with me." I turn to Rowie. She smiles, doesn't say anything. I feel warm.

"Let's smoke that in the treehouse."

"Treehouse-ho, yo."

Rowie grabs two blankets and her old camp flashlight and unlocks the basement door. Rowie has the easiest house to sneak out of in the entire world. There's a door leading out to her backyard ten feet away from her bedroom, her parents sleep upstairs on the opposite end of the house, and her mom works four nights a week anyway.

The three of us tramp across the wet grass to Rowie's big oak tree. The treehouse is the gift of the previous owners, and it's ugly as shit but a good third space— something neutral, not school and not exactly home, just a place we go to have someplace to go. It's not much more than a shack that happens to be in a tree. Recently, we waterproofed it by throwing a tarp over the roof so we could bring electronics up, namely, my ancient battery-operated CD player.

"Why do you even bother calling a bed when we all know you're just going to sneak out to meet some wrestler later?" I tease Marcy, climbing up behind her.

"Oops, so sorry." She kicks off a shoe, which smacks me in the forehead, just like she planned.

"Asshole," I say with a laugh.

Rowie hands up the blankets and flashlight and emerges through the hole in the floor like some kind of backward birth, up instead of down. I spread out a blanket, and the three of us arrange ourselves in a triangle upon it as Marcy loads her M.I.A. disc in the boom box. I feel nervous. *Why?*

Marcy ignites the joint with a yellow Vikings lighter. She pulls hard to get it lit, resulting in a barrage of coughs. I can tell that she's embarrassed to cough, that she wanted to be the experienced one.

"Herb for Holyhill," she chokes, cracking up. I dig the Nalgene out of my Mary Poppins bag and hand it to her; she gratefully takes a swig and recovers.

Marcy passes the joint to Rowie. "Be careful. It's super dry 'cause it's so old."

"Question. Can you, um, talk me through it a little?" Rowie asks bashfully.

"Yeah, I wouldn't kick any instructions out of bed," I say, both to make Rowie feel less bashful and to help me do this without looking like a moron.

"No sweat," responds Marcy, reclaiming her position of superior badassery and puffing up a little. "So basically, first you're going to suck on the joint, and then you're going to breathe in a little bit of air to push the smoke down into your lungs. Then you hold it for as long as you can stand it and try to blow it all out before you start coughing."

"Okay, here goes." Rowie takes a teensy hit, then sucks in a huge gulp of air. Her brown eyes widen as she holds her breath, making her look astonished at what she's doing. After a second, she exhales a small cloud of smoke.

"Take one more. It goes puff, puff, pass," Marcy says, officiating.

Rowie pulls a bigger, braver hit, which doesn't leave as much room for clean air, and she loses it, coughing herself into a momentary veil of smoke. She thrusts out the arm holding the joint as she hacks, and I take it. Like Rowie, I make my first hit conservative, not wanting to push my luck. I breathe in and hold it. Exhale. Repeat. As I hold my breath, I begin to feel a little dizzy, maybe even a different kind of dizzy than what dizzy usually is. I feel a little surprised to see the thin jet of smoke pluming from my lips. It smells like skunk and incense. This is exciting. I take another little drag and hold it again, and this time the dizziness is palpably stronger.

"So how exactly is this going to make me feel?" Rowie asks.

"First your mouth will start to feel really dry," Marcy says matter-of-factly, taking the joint from me. "Then you'll start to feel it all over your body. It's hard to describe and I'm pretty sure it's different for everyone, but it just makes all your senses stronger. Music sounds different; light looks different; food tastes different. Not bad different. Good different. Don't be scared." She inhales.

"It's from the earth," I say. "I'm not scared."

"What if it doesn't work?" Rowie asks, but no one responds.[20]

The three of us fall silent through the next few rounds of the magic stick. "Paper Planes" comes onto the sound track, an overplayed song I've heard a million times before, but a song that right now feels more perfect than ever, like I'm hearing it in Technicolor for the first time. I reach up and look at my own hand as if I've never seen it before, watch the way it wavers around the edges. Using this new instrument, I pull the tarp over a bit to witness the moon, a half-melon in the dark clear sky.

"I like the way it smells," Rowie notes as she takes a two-puff turn. "I like it." She trails off a little.

I look over at Rohini and ponder the vague, dreamy expression on her face, her eyes half-closed and her mouth arched in a sphinx-like smile. I remember how the night I came out in the gazebo last summer, she told me that in Vedic astronomy, there are twenty-seven *nakshratas*, which are the divisions of the sky—like the Indian version of Virgo and Sagittarius and stuff. Rohini is the fourth, the favorite wife of the Moon.

"Rohini, married to the moon," I murmur, not

20. Text from Tess: *MashBaum says her mom got the license # of a car registered to Robert Crowther when its passenger stole their Herb for Holyhill sign. Know anything about that?* Me to Tess: *I saw the sign, and it opened up my eyes. Hehehehehehee*

93

totally sure if I'm thinking or speaking aloud. No one seems to hear. I think she must be wearing the music, must be buried so deep in it that I can't reach her. Just then, the song changes.

Rowie's eyes open more. She parts her lips as if to speak. I lean forward. Time slows down.

"Hey, do you guys ever think about animals just, like, *making out?*"

Silence hangs like a dead man for a split second before I start laughing literally harder than I've ever laughed before. Marcy begins to howl, slapping her palm on the treehouse floor. Rowie looks startled for a moment, then cracks up too.

"What?" She giggles.

"I — I think it worked," I sputter.

"Was that really stupid? I can't tell." She giggles some more. "This is so funny."

"What?" Marcy asks as she struggles to catch her breath. "Do you have, like, pervy farm friends?"

"Seriously guys, I have no idea where that came from," Rowie answers amid a new peal of laughter. "This is *so funny.*"

"I know," I say. "Good coaching, Marce. Bob would be proud."

"Bob!" This sends Rowie into a fresh conniption of laughter. She rolls around on the treehouse floor, convulsing. Seeing Rowie this stoned is hilarious and

wonderful and more intoxicating than anything we could ever swipe from Rooster. I can't stop laughing, either. Marcy is clearly more together than either of us; I think she's more laughing at Rowie than from the ganja.

Without warning, Marcy rises to go. "Okay, I'm out," she says.

"What? Why? We were having such a good time!" Rowie looks stricken.

"I know, toots, but I got . . . somewhere to be."

"Bullshit!" I scream, pointing an accusatory finger at her, dissolving into laughter yet again. "You're going to meet a *boy*. You have a *date*."

"You want another shoe in the face, Ezbian? By the way, can I call you *Ezbian* if I promise not to do it at school?"

I can't help but laugh. "Sure. Ass."

"Sweet. I'll be back later on. Just leave the basement door unlocked."

"Who are you meeting?" Rowie makes the mistake of asking. Marcy just shrugs.

"Hey," I say, remembering, "you're not driving, right?"

"Naw, I got my bike in the back of the James. No worries. If you fools start to get paranoid, just drink a bunch of water and then crunch on some munchies. Don't call unless there's an emergency. Peace." Marcy disappears through the hole in the floor.

I look at Rowie, wondering what comes next. She looks back and grins.

"Hi, honey." She tinkles with laughter.

"Hi, honey."

"I'm pretty sure we're stoned, honey." She giggles.

"Yeah, honey, I'm pretty sure we are, too." She's so cute like this.

"I'm just glad we know, you know?"

"Know what, funny honey?"

"That we're stoned."

I laugh. "God bless Rooster."

"So how did you, like, know?" Rowie blurts out.

"How did I know I was stoned?"

"No, not that. The other thing."

"What other thing? You're being kind of cryptic."

"How did you know you were—gay? Or whatever."

"I don't know. Because Chuckles didn't exactly get my rocks off?"

"I'm serious."

"I think I always knew. Why are you asking?"

"I don't know. I mean—I guess . . ." Rowie stumbles a bit. "I mean, you haven't ever kissed a girl, right?"

I wonder if I should act more experienced than I am. I decide not to. "Um, I mean—no." A breeze begins to drift through the night air as we sit spider-legged and confessional in the trees.

"I've never really kissed anybody. Boy or girl. Is that

normal?" She picks at a hole in her green tights, pulls a thread from the hem of her peach dress.

"What the fuck is normal?"

"I don't know. But really, if you've never been with a girl, how did you know?"

I think for a minute. "I feel like being with Charlie just confirmed something I already knew. I think I've always known. Like, for example, when all the girls used to argue about which guy on *Gossip Girl* was the hottest, I always thought Serena was the hottest."

"That's because Serena's a total fox!" Rowie cries. "I've always thought she was really hot, too."

"Really?" I feel like my jaw must be on the tree-house floor. "I never thought—I just never knew anything like that about you."

"I mean, I don't think I am. But I don't feel like I can really decide until later on, when I have, like, more information. That makes sense, right?"

"Maybe you're both."

"I don't know. Maybe."

For a minute, neither of us says anything. Rowie's never been this candid about anything sex-related before. I suddenly feel like I'm hanging on the precipice of something enormous.

I cock my head to one side.

"Honey," I say slowly, "can I ask you something?"

"Yeah." The wind begins to pick up, blowing with

more urgency. The treehouse is better insulated from it than I expected.

"You can totally say no."

"Okay."

"Um." I nod, acknowledging that there's no going back now. "Do you think that maybe, um, I could, like, kiss you? Just, like, to see?" I feel like I'm sitting on a downed power tower, like I'm buzzing.

She looks at me with the same wide-eyed astonishment as when she was holding in her first hit. "I guess — I guess so."

"Really?" I ask incredulously.

She takes another big gulp of air.

"Sure, what the hell. It's about time I get going in this department, right?"

I giggle. "Glad to be of service?"

We pause awkwardly for a second.

"So, are you going to —?"

I don't have the patience to wait for her to finish the sentence before I grab her face with both hands and kiss her. I grasp handfuls of her hair as I kiss her hard. I pull away for a moment, resting my forehead on hers, searching her lips, their improbable color. She kisses back and it frightens me how much I want to keep kissing her. This is an unbearable kiss, unbearable, unreal, unimaginable. Tentatively, I part her lips with my tongue, meeting hers. She doesn't resist; her tongue tastes sweet. I can feel her beginning to respond. She arches her back a little, and I can feel her small breasts press against mine. I imagine for a moment what they must look like under her dress: brown, round, perfect, her nipples like twin figs.

I feel her hand rest on my midsection, cautious as a moth's landing. I pull her closer. It doesn't seem like she wants to let go, either. *This is what it feels like to be completely human,* I think breathlessly as I grasp her. Rowie's face is so soft, so much softer than Charlie's or any other boy's. Her skin is like warm caramel in my hands. No Camry, no Leinkugels, no cops, just this girl and her impossible handfuls of black hair and her delicate hand on my waist. I tingle inside out; I pull away to catch my breath. I look her dead in the dark velvet morass of her eyes. She is so luminous I can't speak. Rowie is alive in a way I've never seen a person be alive; she emanates something sweet and warm and the color of tea, something that smolders, something I lack. Something I've always been missing.

"Does that help?" she asks. She smiles. Her white teeth are chattering a little, terrified and exuberant.

I nod. "What about you?" I manage.

"No," Rowie says, just before she leans in and kisses me again.

II.

Come to me now: loose me from hard
care and all my heart longs
to accomplish, accomplish. You
be my ally.

> —Sappho, translated by
> Anne Carson, *If Not, Winter*

CHAPTER FIVE
The Undies Club

The wind rushes into the moment after I pull away and look at her. My ears are attuned to every detail of sound as acutely as a wolf's; I hear a rustle of leaves in the bracing darkness, the thump of my heart in my chest like a midnight visitor insistent at the door. I hear Rowie take a shuddering breath.

"Oh, my God," I say. "I'm sorry. I mean. I didn't mean to—"

"No," she says. "You didn't. I mean, it wasn't like—" She falls short and I feel her breath on my mouth, her face an inch from mine.

"What are we doing?" I ask.

"Something we're—not supposed to do," she says.

"Why not?" I ask.

"I don't know. I wish I could be like you," she whispers. "I want some of—whatever it is you have."

"You can. I mean, you are. I mean, take it." I kiss her again, feeling drunk.

Sometimes I think that *you* is the most beautiful word in the English language. The proximity of it, one to another. *Do you? You are. I want you. What are you?*

"You know," Rowie says shyly, later that night, "you could come over sometime after my parents go to bed. You could just wait in the treehouse if I left it unlocked."

The conditionality of her language pulls at me: *If* I left it unlocked. *If* I let you in.

"You're sure the doctors upstairs wouldn't hear you come out?" I say, my hand jerking as I go to pass it through her hair.

She shakes her head and her cheek lands in my hand; I feel her jaw tense and release. We've been kissing for hours.

"I don't think so," she says with a note of uncertainty. "They sleep pretty sound."

I look down, smiling, then up at her through my hair.

"Well . . . what would we do then?"

She giggles, shifting nervously. "Um. We could, like, listen to music, or something. We could play Scrabble. We could—"

"Not what I had in mind." I tackle her, whole in our laughter, pulling her down to the treehouse floor.

▼ ▼ ▼

The first night I go to her alone, I bury my bike in a leaf pile and wait in the distant reaches of her yard, afraid to enter the treehouse until every window in the house has blackened. Rowie's mom works the night shift four nights a week, Monday, Tuesday, Thursday, and Friday, and her dad goes to bed every night between 9:45 and 10:10 p.m. The autumning air is getting cool enough to frost, but I'm sweating so hard I begin to wonder what I'll smell like later. At 10:27, I see Rowie's bathroom light flicker off—a signal! My heart is racing as I MacGyver silently across the wet lawn and up the ladder. That door in Rowie's treehouse floor is a bastard. I try to open it to sneak in, but it shuffles too loud and gets stuck. I push it slowly and it won't give. I push it harder and it makes a protest noise. My gut clenches.[21]

I wait under my headphones in the treehouse. She texts me.[22] She doesn't know I'm already there, doesn't imagine me sitting vigilant in the elevated place, not seeing her but sensing her just on the other side of the wall. And suddenly there she is, a dark shape at the source of the tree, slouchy and shy and muffling her bangles.

"You," she whispers, her teeth glinting in the moon-light.

21. Scribbled in Notebook: *I have to get in again / Give me my sin again.*

22. Text from Rowie: *All in.*

She's brought out a sleeping bag, a few pillows, a blanket or two to soften the wood floor. Neither of us really knows what comes next.[23] We lie down and at first she giggles so much I have to smother her with a pillow for fear her voice will carry.

"All right, all right, don't go all psycho on me," she says, laughing and clutching a stitch in her side. She calms, watching me, and begins to work the axis of buttons down her orange shirt. My hands, my skin, on hers are a negative relief of her color.

"God, Rowie," I say, startled by her radiance. "You're beautiful."

"Shut up." She twists against me. "Beautiful doesn't do shit."

"You're right. But you're also beautiful." I gaze at her from across the pillow, wishing I could never look at anyone else. A beat goes by. I take a deep breath and pull off my hoodie. My hair lies beside me, a pet on the pillow, merging with hers.

"Um," she whispers, one jack-of-hearts eye obscured by the black stream of her hair. "Do you know what to do?" I shake my head, sealing her mouth with one finger.

"Um." I inch closer. She still has her PJ pants on,

---

23. SiN later, furiously: *How do you keep your hair out of your face while you're kissing? Why is it hard to unfasten a bra when it's on someone else? Has Rowie ever come?*

a worn pair of blue scrubs I'm assuming she inherited from her mother. I ask her *Can I?* with my eyes and she nods. I pull the drawstring loose and slide them down her thighs. I notice for the first time that Rowie shaves her legs above her knees—I never have. A thrill radiates from my core when I see her black underwear. My hand hovers above it like a helicopter for a moment, unsure how to land. She lifts her chin and I sink my face into the brown arc of her jaw.

"I think I know where to start."

"Rowie," I say, pulling away for a necessary breath, "you don't kiss like you've never kissed anybody else before."

"Well, shucks," she mumbles. "Actually—I did something once, but I don't think it really counts."

"What do you mean, it doesn't really count?"

"I mean, it's such a cliché."

I crack a smile. "What *kind* of cliché?" I grab her yellow bra strap and kiss her mouth.

Her chin tilts down as she grimaces. "It may have been . . . a summer camp cliché."

"Oohhh!" I say. "I'm intrigued. Who was she?"

"Um." She clears her throat. "Samir Mirza."

"Oh." I feel like a dumbass. "The plot thickens. Continue."

"It happened so fast—that's why I figured it didn't count. I was asleep."

"You were *asleep?*"

"It was on a dare, I guess. He was supposed to sneak into my cabin and kiss me on the lips without waking me up." She looks away.

I make a face. "That's skeezy."

"Yeah." She shrugs. "I woke up."

"What'd you do?"

"Punched him," she says simply. "He got kicked out of camp." She grins a little.

"You!" I grab her around the middle. "*You*, girl."

It gets easier once we've done it a few times, once it starts getting dark earlier. I can't even tell you how much it isn't like with Charlie Knutsen. I've never felt *big* before. When I'm with Rowie, I feel *enormous*—God, I don't know how to explain it. It's not like feeling fat or anything. I'm just, I don't know, aware of my *magnitude* in a way I wasn't before Rowie happened, or aware of hers. I bend over to kiss her and she feels so small beneath me, fine-boned, pebble-smooth, a feline thing, a fuse. I lack the ability to deny her anything; the way I feel when we're in the same room is like she's electricity and I'm water.

"I feel like—" I peel off an orange section and feed it to her. We've built a stockpile of snacks out here ever since Dr. Raj caught Rowie prowling the kitchen at three a.m. and she almost died of shock. She takes a bite and juice dribbles down her chin. She starts laughing and almost spits it out. I laugh and push it back into her mouth. "Anyway, I feel like there should be, like, a NO BOYS ALLOWED sign on the door of this treehouse. Like it's our clubhouse."

"Thhppp Unndweep Cwshubbb," she mumbles incoherently around the orange piece, losing herself in laughter again.

"What?" I dissolve into giggles, never wanting to be anywhere but here.

She swallows. "The Undies Club."

I lean in and kiss off the orange pulp. "I like it."

"Rhyming with you girls feels like that too. A clubhouse, I mean. Or a club," she says.

"Yeah," I say. "I know what you mean. We got an A-team."

"Our songs are sick. Being onstage with you, Ez—it makes me feel—I don't know. Alive. It's like working muscles I didn't know I had."

"Me too." I smile. "You said it just right."

"What day is today?" she asks. "I can't even remember anymore."

"Thursday," I reply. She hooks a finger in the elastic of my underpants and laughs.

"It says Lazy Tuesday on your hoo-ha." She laughs harder.

▼ ▼ ▼

The treehouse is private, but small in a way that makes me wonder if it's really big enough to contain us. We meet at school, and with Marcy and Tess, but in different skins. At first it feels delicious, our secret, though it swells, conspicuously, every day giving us more not to tell.

"Am I slutty for not making you take me out on a date before I showed you my boobs?" I ask. "Do you think I'm easy?"

She giggles. "I don't even remember the first time I saw your boobs. So yeah, you're easy. Ho."

"Maybe we should, like, go out on a date sometime," I say cautiously.

"Where the hell would we go?" She snorts.

"I don't know," I say. "Anywhere you want. Or, I guess, anywhere we could bike to."

"But I like being here."

"Why?"

"Because here I can do this," she says, kissing my ear. "And this." She slips my bra strap off my shoulder. "And this."

Sometimes we pass out for a few hours out of sheer exhaustion, wrapped in each other's arms under the pile of blankets. I wake up into another blue night and watch her sleep, studying her face. I don't know how to explain it: I *recognize* her, I see her sameness with me. Rowie and me, we rhyme.[24]

I brush my fingertips across the smooth convexity of her forehead; in her sleep she winces, swats my hand away, a refusal.

"What day is today?" she whispers, pulling awake.

"I don't know," I murmur into her hair. I roll closer to her. I extend my leg, bending it over hers. Her hand rests on my thigh. She extends her other leg across mine; our legs twin boomerangs, interhooked, splayed like two clocks' hands. I wrap my extended leg around her back, pulling her in, belly to belly, where we remain for a minute, finally seeing the whites of each other's eyes. It's like, I've always known this world was mine, but then Rowie came along and found the door, and stood there until I heard her breathing on the other side,[25] until I opened it and let her all in, let myself all spilling out on a sleepless black-haired girl. She rises to her knees and lifts herself over me, forcing me onto my back as the hand behind me acquiesces. Both of her hands are spanning my waist, holding her up as she regards me sleepily from above.

24. SiN: *When the black-eyed girl blushes / It twists me in thrushes / All flustered and hushing / The lushness of lusting / What a rush, wanna touch / Her luscious erupting / Her flush gets me gushing / we're hushing, she's blushing, I'm busting on crushing.*

25. SiN: *I hear you. / I hear you. / I hear you.*

"Do you ever get that feeling like you'll never have enough time?" I ask.

"Every day," she answers.

I nod. "That's how I feel when I'm with you."

"You too. I mean, me too," she says, leaning down to kiss me. My heart begins to thunder as I cross my ankles behind her back.

CHAPTER SIX

Girl Rappers in Minneapolis

"Tessie! Hustle!" Marcy yells with her head out the Jimmy window, leaning on the horn. We see Darlene's vexed face poke between the living-room curtains. She puts a bony finger to her lips; Marcy relents on the horn.

"Where is she? We still have to get Rowie and be at the LocoMotive by nine," I say.

"Do you think the stick up Darlene's ass is actually from a tree, or do you think she had it specially hand-carved?" Marcy says.

"You're a little harsh on Darlene," I say. "So she's a Botox queen. She's not, like, evil."

"Yo, my first memory of that woman is her refusing to take us to the grocery store before Tess had makeup on after we slept over that one time. We were, like, twelve."

"I know," I say. "That was when we found the Trim-Spa in her bathroom and tried it. We were up all night. No wonder we looked like shit in the morning."

"She's just ugly to me. I mean, you definitely freak her out, but you're still parent-friendlier than me. Try showing up to dinner at Darlene's in a men's undershirt and a Twins hat," Marcy says. "Watch the feathers fly."

"God, how'd you get to be such a little butch?" I say. "Has anyone else noticed I'm surrounded by pseudo-queers? My dad builds fairy houses. My best friend dresses like Fiddy Cent."

"Maybe we're all queer, you know?" Marcy asks.

"What does that mean?" I ask, cracking up.

"Just means that ain't none of us ever gonna fit in, so I do what the fuck I want. Sexuality spectrum!" Marcy gives a fist pump.

Just then, Tess finally bursts out of her house, tripping like a vixen in vicious heely boots. Ignoring Darlene in the doorway, we hang out the windows and catcall like heathens.

"*Daaaaammmmnnn,* girl." I reach over and slap Tess's legginged ass as she climbs in the back. "This is, like, some Debbie Harry shizz." Tess's wearing a red mini-dress with gold polka dots, shiny black leggings, and the skank heels. Tess is the kind of beautiful that makes you wonder if that much beautiful ever gets in her way.

"Naw, dude." She grins. "This is, like, some Con-Tessa shizz."

We're on our way to play at the LocoMotive, a grungy little Minneapolis club with an open-mike night. And come to think of it, we're all kinda pimped out to the teeth for our first real thing: Marcy's added chains and brass knuckles to her standard beater-and-jeans ensemble, and I could swear she's actually put a product in her hair, and I'm combining my hand-painted Timbs and leggings with a big leopard print Value Village T-shirt.

"Check out this mix I made," Tess says as Marcy pulls out of the Grinnells' cul-de-sac of a driveway. She plugs her iPod into Marcy's tape deck converter, and Lupe Fiasco's "Kick, Push" begins to blare from the speakers.

"Dude, I know you, like, *love* him, but Lupe Fiasco is pretty much just Kanye's douchebag bromance of the moment," Marcy whines.

"Yeah, well, Kanye was just Jay-Z's douchebag bromance of the moment once. At least he isn't hating on the ladies all the time," Tess says.

"Eff Lupe Fiasco. Get an earful of this and tell me he still dampens your panties." Marcy pulls a Parliament out of her man purse and switches in her iPod, putting on K'naan's "Kicked Pushed."

"I'm throwing your iPod out the window if you light that in front of me," Tess shoots back. "It's bad enough I'm still trying to get my sister to quit."

Marcy lets go an irritated sigh. "Fine. Change the song and I'll lose the stoge."

Tess switches the iPods back and bites her lip,

grinning, in the moment before the song changes. We hear the opening saxophone riff to Queen Latifah's "Ladies First" and let loose a collective holler; it's an old favorite. Marcy cranks the volume as we roll down Iroquois Lane.

"Bitch is so *fierce*," I breathe reverently.

"I've never been sure how I feel about *bitch*," Tess says. "Don't you ever feel weird using the language that hip-hop uses to describe women?"

"Oh, here we go," Marcy says. "Teenage Feminism 101. Next are you gonna tell me I shouldn't watch porn because it's sexist?"

"You watch porn?" Tess asks, visibly taken aback. "Where do you get it?"

"Please," Marcy says dismissively as she pulls into Rowie's driveway. "You can't grow up in a house with four men and a computer and not know how to find porn."

"I wish I could say I didn't know anything about porn chez Crowther," I say. "But Tessie, I think the language hip-hop uses to describe women is really messed up, but don't you think that if enough women rappers break through, it's something we can reclaim? I just think hip-hop is a medium that, like, encourages conflict over language. I mean, don't you think our whole Council of Mischief bidness of sex-positivity is about being a part of that kind of debate?"

"Yes," Tess says, nodding. "And I agree with most of what you're saying. I'm just wondering if taking part in the debate by using words that are sexually violent toward women is the right way to do it."

"Huh," I say. "I hadn't thought about words like *bitch* as being violent, but they are when you think about it. They're meant to wound."

"Well," Marcy says with a shrug, "the thing about words is you can't really question what they mean without saying them out loud."

"I mean, if you really have a problem with *bitch*, which I can totally get with, there are so many other words to use," I add. "*Girlfriends, GFs, homegirls, homeslices, ladyfriends, sisters, soul sisters, mamas, your posse, coven, fam bam, band of rabble-rousers, hooligans, troublemakers, bluestockings, alpha femmes.* No reason to stay limited to *bitches and hos.*"

"Yo, where the eff is Ro?" Marcy says, and we all realize we've been sitting in her driveway spewing nerd talk for ten minutes and she hasn't come out of her house. "Should I honk?"

"I wouldn't," Tess says. "You know how her parents are old-school. Maybe hit her cell?"

"I'm on it," I say.[26]

Just then, Rowie bursts out of her house at full clip,

26. Text to Rowie: *babygirl, we're outside. everything cool?*

rocking a purple pleather jacket and thick gold heart hoops, looking distractingly hot in skinny black jeans. She throws herself into the car and I notice her favorite green feather in her hair.[27]

"Drive," she commands Marcy, bouncing jaggedly in her seat.

"Is—is everything okay?" I ask.

She shakes her head maniacally back and forth for a moment, bouncing in her seat, then slaps the window hard, palm open.

"I'm just so *over it* with them," she explodes. "My dad is such a *fucking* FOB sometimes."

"What happened?" Tess places a tentative hand on Rowie's shoulder as Marcy rolls out.

"Nothing. It's nothing. He just thinks I'm an American hussy whenever I wear something that doesn't scream *virgin*. But he never just comes out and says it. He barely ever says anything, and when he does, it's always just lame euphemisms, always *not having my priorities straight*."

"I think you're a hot hot mess," I offer, trying for a smile.

"If it makes you feel any better," Marcy says, "I got an earful from Coach Bob after Nordling asked him if he knew about 4H. Bob was pretty pissed I didn't tell him."

27. SiN: *Is she an eggplant today? A plum?*

"Did you get in trouble?" I ask.

"Naw." Marcy grins. "He hates Nordling. Once I told him what we were about, he just sort of grunted and lumbered off to watch *Cops*."

"Look, can you guys just fight about Kanye for a minute or something?" Rowie says. "I need to get my head somewhere else." She doesn't look at me.

"Kanye's a tool," Marcy says.

"Kanye's awesome," Tess says. "But Marcy, Jay-Z is, like, the artist at which we meet in the middle."

"Doesn't get much more mainstream than Hov," Marcy says with a smirk.

"Jesus, Rowie, why do you encourage them?" I say, making the universal choking sign.

"This is the part where Tess avoids the Kanye discussion by talking about Jay-Z's relationship to moral authority," Marcy says, yawning.

"Jay-Z is the Martin Luther of latter-day hip-hop," Tess says. "Do you hear that anti-Catholic sentiment in 'Lucifer'? It's like his ninety-five theses."

"Why you gotta hate on my people?" Marcy asks. "Goddamn Protestants."

Rowie smiles weakly. "I don't know why I find this so reassuring, but I do."

A note on style: Marcy's into mostly coastal nineties hip-hop, the classics, the foundation-layers for our generation and our collaboration: Public Enemy and dead prez, Tupac, Snoop, Dr. Dre, Jay-Z, Biggie, the Wu-Tang, and Arrested Development. There are others—De La Soul, Les Nubians, A Tribe Called Quest, Digable Planets, KRS-One, and Boogie Down Productions—and all these are the early cornerstones; from them, her taste progresses outward and/or underground, into the Dilated Peoples, the Soulquarians, Gang Starr, Main Flow, Classified, the Last Emperor, Immortal Technique, the Individuals, CunninLynguists, Common Market, K'naan, more. We're also fervent upholders of the local—Slug and Atmosphere, Brother Ali, Har Mar Superstar, not to mention, you know, *Prince*—tradition of Minneapolitan reppers, which includes white rappers.[28]

Tess comes at the genre via us, church, and the radio, so she's less of an archivist than Marcy, more of a vocalist, and the only one of us who openly likes indie rock as well as hard soul: Jill Scott, Erykah Badu, Beyoncé, Jenny Lewis, Sheila E., Aretha Franklin, Patti Smith, Imogen Heap, Mahalia Jackson, Billie Holiday, Res, Feist, Janis Joplin, Karen Dalton, Laura Nyro, Lady Gaga, Dionne Warwick, Etta James, and Diana Ross. Rowie and I both fall somewhere in the middle. For me, any kind of music has always been about the lyrics—the Saul Williams and Bob Dylans and Mos Defs and Talib Kwelis and Rakims and Leonard Cohens of

28. SiN: *We had to start by understanding where we came from.*

the world—but lately I've been, like, a mixtape sleuth on the Internet. J. Period and K'naan actually did a mash-up of K'naan and Bob Dylan that almost made me crap my pants; someone else smashed Jay-Z and Radiohead into Jaydiohead, and I dug that too. Rowie brings the global beats, the less local, border-crossing and harder-to-classify: Panjabi MC, M.I.A., Nneka, Yelle, MC Solaar, DJ A.P.S., K-OS, Jamez, SA-RA. We're both also way into oldies—old country like you slow-dance to in lonesome bars, Motown soul—and, paramount of all, badass chick MCs: Queen Latifah, Invincible, Lady Sovereign, Princess Superstar, Peaches, Missy, Lauryn Hill, Lil' Kim, MC Lyte, Roxanne Shanté, Salt-n-Pepa, Bahamadia.

"I am officially changing the subject." Tess waves her hands. "In the hopes of drumming up some buzz about 4H, I invited some people to come see us at this show."

"What? Who?" Rowie panics. "Why would you do that? Who did you tell? If you invited Prakash Banerjee, you and I are over."

"Of all the people she could have told that we're playing one song at an open-mike night, why is Prakash Banerjee the one you're afraid of?" I ask.

"Because he'll tell his parents he saw Rohini Rudra at the LocoMotive when Raj and Priya think I'm just going to drink milkshakes at Home on the Range, and then his parents will tell my parents, who will then be disgraced," Rowie answers in her father's thick Indian accent, as though it were obvious. "Not so many Bengalis in Holyhill. We talk."

"We should actually go to Home on the Range later—that place is my fave. Four words: bottomless chicken noodle soup," I say, trying to distract her.

"Ro, will you relax?" Tess says. "You're totally bugging. Why would I invite Prakash? He's probably already got plans with his larper friends."

"Who *did* you invite?" Rowie asks.

Tess shrugs, playing with her iPhone.[29] "Just a few people I thought might be into it. Anders, obviously. He'll probably bring some people. Oh, and I ran into Jane Njaka today and told her to stop by if she wanted."

"Tess, did you invite Jane to our hip-hop show because she's African?" I tease her.

"I like Jane!" Tess says.

"I do too. I'm just playing with you." I go to ruffle her hair; she ducks.

"We have to plan our first 4H meeting," Marcy says.

"But where are we going to do it?" Rowie asks. "Are we seriously going to meet in the warming house? It smells like wet dog in there."

"Let me worry about that." Marcy grins. "The

29. TheConTessa @4H4life: *Come check out Holyhill's hottest hetero/homo hip-hop crew at the LocoMotive 2night. 10 pm. Free.*

ConTessa's on the right track. We drum up some underground buzz and then we can just start calling meetings. Right now all we gotta worry about is spreading our message and recruiting support."

"Wicked." I nod.

The James pulls off the big highway onto a desolated stretch of older highway cross-hatched with railroad tracks. The LocoMotive used to be a stop on the Soo Line Railroad, which ran from the upper Midwest (or, as I like to call it, the deep Midwest) to Canada. *Soo* is a synecdochic abbreviation for the Minneapolis, St. Paul, and Sault Ste. Marie Railroad; I like its whistle, a slow train shrieking in the night: *Sooooo*.

A smattering of cars sit in the parking lot. I hear a soft country voice singing Bob Dylan. I notice how cold it's getting. Little paws of anxiety begin to pad along the walls of my stomach as we unload our equipment from the back hatch of the Jimmy. I hear a harmonica through the window and think that if I liked boys, I would like boys with harmonicas.

"Hometown boy." Marcy jerks a thumb toward the music.

"Like Bob Dylan isn't country?" Tess asks incredulously.

"Not like *you're* country," Marcy snaps back.

"Bob Dylan is the prophet of the plains states and that's pretty much all there is to it," I say, silencing the argument. "Let's go get our flow on."

Rowie looks pale again. "Oh, *hell*, no." I nudge her. "Don't get freaked."

"I'm not freaked." She looks darkly at me. She forces a grin. "I'm psyched."

Tess and Marcy are walking up ahead, still bickering. I reach for Rowie's hand in the chill October night. She brushes my fingers, her depthless black eyes flickering at me for a minute, but ducks when I go to put an arm around her.

"Party looks crackin'," she says, eluding me.

I give up, ignoring the sting, and follow her into the old station, now a big, dark space with high ceilings and echoey acoustics. The Dylan boys finish as we walk in. We peel off our coats and are offered hot tea with lemon by a gentle, leather-faced, leather-pantsed woman who seems to be coordinating the bands. She has piercing blue eyes and one thick gray braid over her shoulder; she introduces herself as Vera.

"It's for your voices," she insists, refusing us as we try to offer her money for the tea. "These boys are almost done, and you're the next slot. Do you need any help setting up?"

The four of us look at one another and shrug. "I think we're good," Marcy whispers. "We're pretty portable."

Vera nods solemnly, examining us. "How old are you girls?"

"We just want to play. We're not gonna get into anything, swear," I say.

She gives a half-smile, seeming to believe me. "How do you want me to introduce you?"

Rowie grins. "We're Sister Mischief."

We take in our surroundings, preparing. The crowd is mixed: a bunch of white indie-rock-looking teenagers sneaking slurps of flasks, a lot of college-aged kids who look mostly Somalian, including the guys now onstage, a pack of Vietnamese and Hmong kids, a few older sketchy white guys trolling for God knows what. Tess goes through her breathing exercises, stretching her arms, opening her chest. Every guy in sight checks her out, inevitably. As Marcy warms up her drumsticks, I scan the crowd for familiar faces and spot Jane Njaka with a boy who looks exactly like a shorter, wider-shouldered version of her. We lock eyes and wave, and I feel relieved to see a friendly face.

As we assemble our traveling band, I stop for a minute to watch the act onstage. Guessing by the Somali audience's reaction to them, I'm guessing they're the magnet that drew the crowd; right now they're finishing up a fun, unexpected cover of Beyoncé's "Crazy in Love" with some sick Afrobeats layered underneath it. A baby's fist of intimidation tightens in my stomach. Marcy punches me.

"Ferocious. Don't forget to turn your mike on." Marcy holds out mikes to me and Rowie. We take them, and Vera raises her eyebrows questioningly at us: *You ready?* Suppressing a shudder, we nod.

"Next up, straight out of Holyhill"—a few assholes boo until hushed by Vera's ice-blue daggers of disapproval—"we have Sister Mischief. I'm going to need a round of applause for Sister Mischief, please."

Most of the audience claps halfheartedly. One African dude winks at me as I walk up to the stage, and I smile back when I see a harmonica in his back pocket. From the shadows in the back, we hear an unexpected commotion of preteen whooping. Squinting, I make out Rowie's little sister, Lakshmi, and a small company of her annoying eighth-grade cronies. Rowie herself gives me an accusatory look, but I throw up my hands, unaware of how that crew ended up here or how they got in. She glares at Lakshmi, then shakes it off.

"Check, check," she says in a low voice into the microphone. Marcy sits down at the drum kit and cues up the backbone beat, giving us a few measures to settle into it, then Tess layers in our bastardized samples on her portable Casiotone electric piano, from M.I.A. and the Wilcannia Mob's "Mango Pickle Down River."

"Hip-hopsters!" I hear someone call derisively.

"Uh," Rowie sounds tight-throated as she ignores the jeer and begins to move to the beat. "I got DJ SheStorm," she says, gesturing to Marcy, prompting a little clapping and a few uncomfortable titters from the crowd. "ConTessa in the house." Tess busts a responsive riff, prompting more serious applause.

"MC Ferocious getting down with mad flow for heteros and homos," I say, warming up to the flow, ignoring the dwindling titters. "We're Sister Mischief, Holyhill's first interracial gay-straight hip-hop-positive alliance. Let's get queer, y'all. Here it is."

We break into Rowie's newest chorus together:

"We gonna start some drama like Barack Obama
Yeah, we gonna start some drama like Barack Obama
This country needs some leaders who respect the mamas
So we gonna start some drama like Barack Obama."

"MC Ferocious," Rowie says, looking expectantly at me. I'm ready.

"I gotta give a holla for my Sister Mischief ballas
Wanna know why we only get three quarters to the dolla
MC Ro, she just wanna her tikka with masala
So why they treat her at the airport like she dirty like Osama?"

Rowie answers my call.

"We mischievous but peaceful like a naughty Dalai Lama
We got pens for guns and drums and we rhyme like
   bhangra bombas

So we gonna holla holla those three words and a comma
'Cause we wanna cause some drama like Barack Obama."

The enthusiasm from the audience builds as we repeat the chorus; some people are moving and clapping. Lakshmi and her friends begin to shake it like jailbait, which I'm sure is embarrassing the hell out of Rowie—but no, I look over, and she actually seems to be enjoying it. Jane and this guy who I think must be her brother get up and dance too—even Vera is bobbing backstage and gives a hoot. I see Anders Ostergaard and two of his douchebag white-hatted—oh, God, fucking Chuckles Knutsen is under one of the white hats—friends glowing in the dark mid-crowd.

Rowie and I are going hard at the second chorus and Marcy's throwing down some fiendish, fiendish beats when Tess lets loose with this *motherfucker* of a rangy high note. Not dropping the flow, all three of us—along with the audience, who are all wondering how such a gorgeous growl emerged from this tiny girl—look at her in astonishment. Tessie can't keep from singing.

Rowie finishes:

"She ain't no prima donna, Michelle Robinson Obama
An educated mama who's a mama role model
She's fierce on the trail speaking truth about America

How we gotta do more about the arrogance and barriers
We put up when we front about race and the state of our
Relations in our nation, how we're sick of being patient
While men legislate our bodies and they denigrate our
  matrons
She's gonna be the mama who advocates for mamas
And we gotta holla proper for Malia and Sasha
'Cause we wanna start some drama like Michelle Obama
Yeah, we wanna cause some drama like Michelle R.
  Obama."

Marcy drops the final beat, and the moment hangs thick and wordless in the air as we wipe the sweat from our brows, look at one another, and give an awkward bow, not knowing what else to do. I can feel the sweat trickling down my armpits like ants on a lemonade spill. There is staggering, awful silence for a number of seconds. It draws on. Someone sneezes. I'm looking at my knees and starting to want to die when I hear one barbaric whoop. It starts slow, and builds, and catches. The room detonates.

I raise my head slowly and people are hooting and clapping in this totally impolite way. It's the best feeling I've ever had. It doesn't last as long as I'd like it to— because ideally I'd like it to last, you know, forever— but as we hand the mikes back to Vera and she tells the audience to tip their waitresses and drive safe now, the glow just won't shake off; it hangs on to us as the people we know gather.

"Dude, you guys are going to be, like, so famous!" Lakshmi screeches, throwing her arms around Rowie, which is sort of like throwing a water balloon at a cat.

"Mimi, you little scamp, how the hell did you even know about this?" Rowie demands. "And how did you get here?"

"Anders thought he was supposed to pick Tess up, and he came over to see if she was at our house when she wasn't at hers," Lakshmi replies, smiling all Cheshirey. "We made him take us."

"They blackmailed me," Anders says. "They told me if I didn't take them, they'd tell Darlene I bought them Bacardi. I basically got hijacked."

"You little dirtbags. Sorry, man." Rowie shoves Lakshmi, but not too hard.

The girls giggle hysterically and traipse off to text someone else for a ride home. For some reason, the fact that Anders brought Lakshmi and her powder puffs here kind of makes me like him more. Then he and Tess start to make out in the corner as his entourage goes out to scam beer from the SuperAmerica across the street, and I go back to thinking he's a tool.

"That was very fucking cool," Jane says, appearing at my right elbow. "I didn't even know you rapped until

Tess told me today. This is my brother, Yusuf. He wants to be a producer. He thought you guys were really hot."

Yusuf doesn't even pause to blush. "Yo, that shit was *heavy,* girl!" he says, fist-pounding me and Marcy. "You all could be huge. We should record a demo."

"That'd be pretty tight," Marcy says. "You got a couple hundred an hour for studio space?"

"Hell, no! You gotta have money to make money," Yusuf says, shrugging. "This is America, right?"

"No doubt," Marcy says. Rowie and I nod.

"You should let us know when your next gig is," Jane says. "We could help you record it and get it distributed in the TC."

"Whoa, for real? That's really cool of you," Rowie replies. "Man, we hadn't even thought ahead that far."

"Do you have the equipment to do that?" I ask, picturing the album artwork to *Sister Mischief: Live at the LocoMotive.*

"We've got access to the parts; it's just a matter of putting them all together. With enough extension cords and duct tape, I think we could pull if off no problem," Yusuf tells me.

"What grade are you in?" Marcy asks as she dismantles the turntables she and Rowie built by miscegenating two of Luke's old EP players, part of Rooster's boom box, and some soundboard schwag from Marcy's summer stint in tech theater. She's got a good four inches on Yusuf, and she's eyeing him.

"I'm a senior." He reaches over and helps Marcy situate her bulky backpack into a carrying position. She lets him. "I go to Holyhill part-time, but I'm doing most of my classes at the U of M this semester."

"We're only eleven months apart," Jane says. "We're Irish twins."

"That's the funniest shit I've heard all day," Rowie says.

"So, you Holyhill hos gonna turn my sister into a cake-eater?" Yusuf grins wickedly at Marcy, baiting her.

"Yo, maybe I'm gonna eat your *ass*," Marcy blurts in an aborted attempt at a comeback. She blushes the color of borscht. Rowie, Jane, and I start laughing so hard that Tess takes her tongue out of Anders's inner ear and turns around to see what's so funny. Yusuf looks puzzled.

"Yo, Njakas." I grasp for an opportunity to save Marcy from dropping through a self-willed trapdoor. "So, I can explain more later, but do you think you guys would ever want to be a part of a queer hip-hop alliance at Holyhill?"

"A what?" Jane looks intrigued, but almost as confused as her Irish twin. Marcy and Rowie laugh at me as we pack up the last of our shit and begin to clear out of the LocoMotive. "Is that what you were talking about up there? Do schools have those?"

"I'm getting a ride with Anders," Tess says as she passes us, clutching his hand. "You wanna come?"

"Naw, we're going with Marce."[30]

"Remember," Tess instructs me, boring straight into each of our eyes, "that you are the finest girl rappers in Minneapolis, and that we'll all remember tonight forever."[31]

I shake my head. Tess should be a preacher. "G'night, homeslice."

I toss her a peck on the cheek. Tess, Anders, Chuckles, et cetera, and their triumphant case of MGD pile into a Suburban with a McCain/Palin '08 bumper sticker. I turn back to Jane.

"Listen, what I'm saying is — yo, do you want to just get together after school sometime, blast some beats, and piss off a whole lot of tightasses without really trying?"

Jane cracks up, clapping in delight. "Absolutely yes. Drive safe, now, y'hear?"[32] She fakes a Minnesota accent as she gets into the car, failing endearingly. Yusuf gives us a silent peace sign as he cranks the bass.

---

30. Text from Rowie: *Bike over after she drops you off?*

31. Me to Rowie: *Wouldn't it be easier to just ask her to drop me at your place?*

32. Rowie back: *Wouldn't she wonder why she wasn't invited? and my parents might not be asleep yet.*

We throw our tin-man sound system back into the Jimmy and roll out, not saying much,[33] hungover from the high. Watching the Soo Line recede, I feel warm, united with my sisters in this music we make together, in something greater than ourselves; I feel a rising again and think that if this is what gets Tess to church every Sunday, this fantastic crush of creation and communion, then maybe faith hasn't totally run out on me yet. And on the way home, from the backseat, on the door side of the car, which Marcy can't see, Rowie reaches over and holds my hand.[34]

33. Me back: *It just seems kind of overly complicated, but i guess.*

34. Rowie, last: *Everything is complicated. just come over.*

CHAPTER SEVEN
Wicked Delicious

Rowie smiles at me in Precalculus today, lifting her nose in the direction of my phone. I rummage stealthily through my backpack, defying the Holyhill classroom cell moratorium.[35] I smile, twisting my hair around a finger as I feel her eyes on me, and hold my phone under the table.[36] She clicks furiously,[37] her boatneck collar dancing with the drop-off of her shoulder, and I feel myself waffling on my promise[38] to myself to catch up on homework, to catch up on sleep, to finish the

35. Text from Rowie: *Come over tonight?*

36. Me to Rowie: *Girl, i haven't slept in days. it's only wednesday. won't your mom be home?*

37. Rowie to me: *If u come around 11 she'll be out cold*

38. Me to Rowie: *You are persuasive, aren't you?*

new song I've been toying with. She goes back to taking notes. I watch her in silhouette, her serene glance, the alluring length of her neck. I stop looking; looking wears something on the outside that we're still keeping under wraps.

I pull out the book I'm reading, Diane di Prima's *Memoirs of a Beatnik*. It's another of Mom's copies, a poet's bildungsroman, and it's chock-full of sex: sex with women; sex with men; graphic, endless sex. It's weird to think about your mother reading a book with this much sex in it. I wonder if she ever would have told me anything about sex, if that's something moms do. I see her a lot—my mom, that is. I mean, I don't *actually* see her, but I *think* I do at least once a week and I write her letters.[39] I used to wake up in night sweats from dreams that she disappeared, or that I'd found her; I'd wake up and feel bereft, in that tender place between sleep and waking, feeling like I'd just lost her again, and then find her really gone, years-ago gone, and then it would harden, the anger, and I'd try to make myself stop wanting her back. It's been too long without her to

---

39. SiN: *1. Johanna Page Rockett. Mom. 2. I will never send you these letters. You do not deserve them. 3. I had sex. With a girl named Rowie. What do you think of that? 4. Where are you? What the fuck are you doing? 5. Rowie's mom always asks me how I am. 6. Pops is a better cook than you ever were. Even though I don't remember if you ever actually cooked or not. Pops is a really good cook. 7. I don't miss you.*

keep believing her itemized fragments will ever cohere into a mother, the way you see mothers on TV, like other people's mothers.

"Ez?" Rowie pokes me with her mechanical pencil. I look up to see the rest of the class filing out; somehow I missed the sound of the bell.

"Yeah," I say, shaking my head. "Yeah."

"Gotta scoot, toots," she says with a smile. "We got trouble to make."

We scurry out and make our way toward the west exit, on our way across the track to the warming house. The October sunshine is orange, all glow and shadow, the air tonic with possibility. In a few months—weeks, really, by now—they'll flood the track for hockey, hence the warming house.

"It feels so wicked delicious to bust out of school during the day," Rowie says, rumbling down the hill, breaking into a run with arms outstretched. "'I too am not a bit tamed—I too am untranslatable; I sound my barbaric yawp over the roofs of the world'!"

"Did you just make that up?" I ask.

"No, it's Whitman," she says. "My mom loves Walt Whitman. She made Mimi and me memorize him when we first got here."

"Your mom kind of blows my mind. Hey, technically we're leaving school grounds," I say. I sprint across the track to the campus boundary, the bleachers on the far side of the track, straddling an imaginary border. "Come and kiss me. It's legal here."

"Stop," she says, loitering, shuffling her feet in the brown dirt of the track.

"Come *on*," I say. "There's no one coming. We can just duck behind that tree real quick. I thought you were not a bit tamed." I run back and grab her hand. She smiles bashfully and gives me a quick closed-mouth kiss, giggling. I grab her by the waist and plant a real one on her.

She takes a step back. It rankles me.

"You always go too far. Why do you have to shove us in everyone's face?" she says forcefully. "I said I didn't want to."

"Whoa," I say. "You didn't say that, actually. And what the hell do you mean, shove us in everyone's face? I haven't even told *Marcy* about us."

"I just mean—what was with announcing to the whole LocoMotive that we were, like, a queer hip-hop alliance or whatever? Don't you think that's going to make people ask questions?"

"Isn't that what we are? And aren't we trying to make people ask questions about the language hip-hop uses to describe women and gay people?"

"Yeah, but"—she looks exasperatedly away—"it's just getting kind of complicated to answer why we're so interested in it."

I pause. "No kidding?" I examine her, not sure what to make of that.

"Whatever. Let's go inside." She slinks into the warming house without looking at me.

I follow her inside, where Marcy is tinkering with electronics with a boy whose back I don't immediately recognize. When they turn to greet us, I see it's Yusuf Njaka, Jane's brother.

"'Sup," I say, fist-pounding them both. "What you got going here?"

"Check this shit out," Marcy says. "Yusuf brought us these old turntables. They're pretty broke-ass, but if we combine them with some new parts, we can rewire them any way we want, which is pretty dope. We were talking about how to make them portable."

"Sick," Rowie says.

Yusuf flashes a blindingly white, toothy grin. "I remembered she was the drumline girl everyone's always telling crazy stories about, and it made me wonder if we could load turntables onto one of those over-the-shoulder harnesses they use for drums in marching band."

"Word." I nod. I can't help but notice that Marcy hasn't had too many sneak-arounds with athletes lately.[40]

40. Text to Marcy: *Yo, are you gonna get with Yusuf or what?? He's like your match made in technological musical heaven.*

"I have no idea who's gonna show up to this thing. I talked to some people and passed out a few flyers." She rustles in her backpack and hands me a crumpled photocopied flyer that reads: *4H: Hip-Hop for Heteros and Homos. Think Holyhill is wack? Talk it out. Monday, first lunch, in the old warming house.* Above the handwritten text is a stick-figure couple of two dudes who appear to be some sort of homo thugs, wearing bandannas and spiked collars and holding hands.

"What the eff is this?" I hold up the flyer, cracking up. "And did you get Bob and Luke to model for it? This sort of looks like them after their Fourth of July golf game." Our dads always play golf on the Fourth of July, even if it's raining. Really they just ride around on the cart pounding beers and then come home and pretend not to be tipsy again. At this point, I wish they'd drop the charade and let us give them a ride home, but I guess it's weird to make your teenage daughter be your DD, even if it's only once a year.

"Listen, homes, you should be grateful for my initiative." She snatches the flyer back.

"I am. Seriously, homeslice, I'm super grateful for you." The confession hovers like an awkward kite between us for a minute, Marcy searching my face with a panicked look in her eyes that feelings may have entered the conversation, and then we both sputter, laughing at the thought of actually being grateful out loud for each other. Some secrets are less painful than others.[41]

"You guys are weirdos," Rowie says.

"Is this the gay-straight hip-hop meeting?" Emma Fazzio pouts her maroon lips as she enters with another theater girl whose name I forget.

"Um, yeah, I guess this is the gay-straight hip-hop meeting," I say. "Welcome."

Jane Njaka and Tess bust in behind her, pumping the magic pink iPod speakers. "What up, my sisters!" Tess hollers, breaking it down.

"Is anyone else coming?" I ask Marcy.

"Hoooooo!" Just then, a dude swaggers in and man-hugs Yusuf.

"This is my boy Angelo," Yusuf introduces his friend, a tall, good-looking kid. "I told him he should roll through here. A-nez, you know these fools?"

"I think I've seen you around." I extend a fist. "I'm Esme, and these are my girls Marcy, Rowie, and Tess."

"*Enchanté*, ladies," Angelo says, eyeing us. I know Tess is batting her eyelashes without having to look at her. He seems more interested in Rowie. I could probably take him.

"Angelo Martinez." Yusuf grins. "The only living Blaxican in Holyhill."

41. Marcy to me: *Maybe.*

"Wow," Rowie says. "Better recognize."

"Yeah. So. Welcome to Hip-Hop for Heteros and Homos." Marcy parks on a bench and clears her throat to introduce our cockamamie idea for a student group. "I guess we should start with a little background. At the beginning of this year, Holyhill's administration issued this statement and made us all sign it." She looks at me; I pull out my notebook and the copy of the policy I have in there. "Holyhill High School cannot condone violence in any form, nor can it condone any material known to incite violence. In this interest, loud, violent, heavily rhythmic music such as 'rap' will be prohibited on campus or at school events. Additionally, any apparel or other materials associated with a violence-inducing culture, such as pants sagging below the underwear line, gang apparel, or promotional artist material, will also be prohibited and punishable by suspension."

I pick up the thread. "We refused to sign the policy because we didn't like what it implied. We don't want to go to a school that doesn't recognize the importance of hip-hop music and culture. In protest, we decided to form a student discussion group to talk about hip-hop as a cultural movement. Also, because we're interested in the idea of sex-positive hip-hop, and because we thought Holyhill needed a gay-straight alliance, we combined the two beliefs into one group: Hip-Hop for Heteros and Homos. Code name: 4H." I throw down the semi-secret 4H sign Marcy and I have devised: four fingers horizontal on the left hand, crossed by one finger on the right, pressed to the breast.

"Fuck, man," Angelo says. "That asshole Nordling told all the kids in my program that we couldn't stay in it unless we signed."

"He messed around with us, too," Tess says. "That's why we're meeting out here and not in an actual classroom."

"Yo, so are we gonna listen to some hip-hop, or what?" Rowie asks. "Maybe we should play rap-and-tell. Does anyone have music they want to talk about?"

Jane and Yusuf's hands shoot up simultaneously.

"Seriously guys, don't raise your hands." Marcy shakes her head.

"K'naan!" Jane gushes. "I'm way up in K'naan's shit. I'm like getting with K'naan. With my mind." She plugs her iPod into the speakers and puts on *The Dusty Foot Philosopher.*

"Hell, yes," Marcy says.

"K'naan's a total poet," I say. "He loves Dylan. Did you guys hear his mixtapes with J. Period?"

"So you guys are, like, from Somalia?" Michelle interrupts. *That's* her name. Michelle.

Jane's tone is polite but not too warm. "We're originally from Somalia, but we were living in a camp in Kenya for a year until my father could bring us all over here."

"Why'd he pick Minnesota?" Michelle asks.

"Haven't you ever noticed there are tons of Somalis in Minneapolis? It's because of all the Lutheran missionary groups," Rowie replies. "Same with the Hmong."

"There was also a war in Somalia," Yusuf points out.

"Right," Rowie says. "And in Vietnam and Laos."

Michelle shifts in her seat. "What do you mean, a camp in Kenya? Like summer camp?" Emma thrusts an elbow into her ribs, hissing. "Ow, what?"

Jane looks disbelievingly at her. "Like a refugee camp."

"Oh. Heavy." The room goes silent as we all wonder why Michelle decided to come today.

"Sorry I'm late." The door bursts open to reveal Mary Ashley. "It took me a while to figure out where the heck this was. Hip-Hop for Heteros and Homos, is it?"

"Who told psycho?" Rowie leans over and mutters to me.

"Mary Ashley, what are you doing here?" Tess sounds annoyed.

"Well, I was just a little curious," Mary Ashley replies sweetly, "about Holyhill's first all-gay hip-hop student group."

"Being here doesn't make you gay, moron," Marcy snarls at her. "It's not, like, contagious."

"That's cute." Mary Ashley sits down. "Because I look around, and all I see is ABS losers and weird lesbos."

"Who does this girl think she is?" Angelo says.

"We're not in the ABS program," Yusuf says. "We've gone to school here since fifth grade."

"And so what if we were?" Jane pipes in.

"What's wrong with you, Mary Ashley?" Tess asks.

"Come on, Tessie, you're not like them," Mary Ashley says, staring at me. "Freak, what's in that notebook you're always scribbling in?" She makes a lunge for it before I can pull away, and when she opens it, I feel a feverish panic, like I'm about to pee and I can't stop it.

" '1. Johanna Page Rockett. Mom,' " she reads aloud. " '2. I will never send you these letters.' "

"God, what is your *problem*?" Marcy yells at her.

Without thinking, I emit an inhuman yawp and make a dive for her and the notebook, catching her around the middle. I tackle Mary Ashley Baumgarten to the ground, snatch back the notebook, and open-handed slap her *hard* across the face.

"I think you should leave," I say, getting up. "Now."

"You crazy bitch," she sputters. "I'm totally reporting you."

"And everyone here will corroborate that Esme did nothing more than politely ask you to leave," Tess says calmly. My breath heaves in the silence.

"Traitor," Mary Ashley seethes. "The baby Jesus totally hates you for this, you know."

"You are totally effing losing it, Mary Ashley. Just leave." Out of words, Mary Ashley turns on Tess and flounces out just as we hear the bell ending first lunch in the distance.

"Yo, who the fuck put pinecones in her oatmeal?" Jane asks as we all begin to pack up. Rowie's face is purpling with disproportionate passion; I want to touch her, but I know that would make it worse. It feels awful.

"Damn, girl, you bitch-slapped that bitch *right*," Angelo says, cackling and biting his fist. "I wouldn't've thought you had it in you."

"I would." Marcy raises her hand.

"I don't want to talk about her. I don't even want to think about her. What's the topic for the next meeting?" I ask.

"Female MCs," Marcy says. "Everyone bring in songs by their favorite chicks on the stick."

"Done," Yusuf says. Everyone else agrees, and I prepare to go back indoors, feeling sharply the lack of safety in space. If she'd had time to read one more line of my notebook—I don't want to think about that, either.

Rowie is feral when I climb up to the treehouse later that night, hungry. She's on me without speaking before I pull the floor door closed, clawing at my back.

"Whoa, whoa, hey." I laugh a little, covering her arms around my stomach with my own.

"Let's not talk," she muffles into my back.

I oblige, letting her pull me under the blankets, as

if under a tide. She kisses me hard, like she's been waiting for it. We make out in this way like I never have any idea how much time is passing. It could be minutes, could be hours, could be days—hardly matters. I bury my hands in her hair and kiss the curvature of her ears.

"You're so beautiful," I whisper to her.

She pulls off my shirt and brushes her lips across my bare shoulders, sending a thrill down my spine. I unbutton her dress, discovering her small breasts again, welcoming their return. Sometimes I think about Rowie's breasts and nothing else for, like, hours. I reach around to unhook her bra.

"Hold on," she says, pulling back. "I—I don't know. I just—I wish we could be alone together all the time." She puts her face in her hands and sits back on her knees with the covers fully enveloping her; I sit the same way, propping up an impromptu tent with our heads, protected in our confidence. It's getting colder too fast; we're bundled under a sleeping bag and two blankets now. Rowie smuggled out an ancient space heater, but we can't leave it on too long without risking a fiery tree-house death.

"What's eating you, kitten?" I ask tentatively, unable to see her face. My eyes begin to adjust to the dark, but the scent of her fear is thick, distracting.

"Today just freaked me out. Did you have anything about us in your notebook? Did she see it?"

I take a breath. "Calm down. She didn't see anything. But it scared me, too."

"It's like, I started thinking about what would happen if my parents ever found out about us. If all of Holyhill found out."

"I mean, I can see where you're coming from in terms of your dad," I say. "But would your mom really bug out that hard if you were—with a girl? She seems so feisty and smart to me."

"She is, but all my parents want is for me to get into a good school and eventually to end up with a nice Bengali boy," Rowie insists. "They're always talking about a son of some family they know who's going to Princeton next year. Fuck it."

I choose my words carefully. "What do you say?"

"I say I have to go do homework, which is probably what they want to hear anyway."

"And then?"

"That's it. They're never long conversations. We don't really have those."

"I wonder what that would be like, that kind of family conversation," I speculate. "Pops and I just beat the emotional shit out of everything until we're too tired to talk anymore."

"Humph," she harrumphs. "White people are so into talking about their feelings."

"Oh, sure," I tease her. "Make it racial." I stroke her hair. "MashBaum really got to you today, didn't she?"

She cracks a grin. "I think *you* really got to *MashBaum* today."

I grin back. "Bitch had my heart in her hands. I didn't stop to think."

"Whatever," she says dismissively. "I really don't want to talk about it. I just want—to feel something else." She buries herself in my shoulder, and I wrap my arms around her, and we hunker down into the blankets to make a stay against the encroaching cold.

Next thing I know, I look at the clock and it says 5:38 a.m.

"I gotta get, pretty." I trace a map on her back, over the perfect fins of her shoulder blades.

She nods, snuggling down in the covers. Dawn is just breaking, bleak and freezing, drizzling weak light over the frosted grass.

I will myself to leave, yanking on my jeans and sneakers and jacket. "I'll see you at school. Don't forget to go back inside soon."

"Mmm," she grunts in response, already half-asleep. Some nights I come home and she's still trapped in my nose, gardenia and almond and that third fragrance that is, I know now, cardamom.

"Ro?"

"Mmm."

"I think I could fall in love with you."

There is a pause in which I wonder if she's already slipped into a REM cycle.

"Rowie," I whisper. "Don't fall back asleep. You have to get back inside."

As I gingerly lift the door and toe the ladder, I hear her small voice.

"Not a bit tamed," she murmurs.

The morning frost hits me like a cold mackerel in the face; I let out a soft string of expletives as I dig through the damp, dirty leaves, grasping for my bike. My legs are limp as I try to shake enough sleep out of my head to ride. The faint light breaks into morning, accelerating my pace as I race to beat Pops's alarm clock. I swing around Iroquois Circle and offer a silent salute to Tess's waking house, the lights in the upstairs bathrooms just flickering on. As I ride past the high school, a few teachers are starting to arrive in cars far less expensive than their students'. I can't believe I have to show up there in a few hours and stuff my lunch in my locker and hobble through class and pretend the electricity in my gut isn't there and Rowie and me aren't really Rowie and me, the manic sample of us in my head looping *no one knows, no one knows, no one knows*. I walk around with it inside me every day, all the days after the nights we spend in her treehouse, and I wonder if people are starting to wonder why we look so underslept.

Our garage door is old and wicked janky—it's one of those relics that you have to hoist open manually. I sleepily pull it up halfway and duck under it, ditching Priscilla, my bike, in the corner. The door into the kitchen is unlocked. Shit.

Pops is sitting at the kitchen table, whittling a wing as I slink in. Not seeing the point of trying to avoid him, I drop my backpack on the floor and flop into a chair.

"Have you been up all night?" I ask.

He nods slowly, not looking up. "Mmm-hmm. You?"

"Pretty much."

He sets the knife and fairy down. "Where you been, parakeet?"

I shrug and look down, pigeon-toeing. "Out."

"Yeah, I'm gonna need more information than that." He looks up. "You been drinking? Getting high?"

I shake my head and stare at my feet, trying to undo the laces to my Pumas without using my hands.

"Look, Ez, you know I don't want to put a curfew on you. There's nothing you can do after eleven p.m. that you can't do before. But six a.m. on a school night? Three, four times a week? I gotta know what's going on here. I'm worried."

My head snaps up. He knows I've been sneaking out and hasn't said anything?

"You don't have to be worried."

"Yeah, parakeet, but the thing is, I love you and I don't know if you're out turning tricks on the streets while I'm trying not to invade your privacy. I'm worried. I just need to know where you've been and if you're okay."

"I was over at a friend's," I concede. "And I'm not turning tricks, for Christ's sake. Do you really think I'm, like, standing outside the Holyhill Community Center hitching my skirt at passing midlife-crisis-mobiles?"

"I don't know, Esme," Pops says, throwing up his hands. "You never tell me anything anymore. Whose house were you at? Is it someone I know?"

Pause. "Yeah."

"Well, that's fine if you were sleeping over at Marcy's, but why didn't you tell me?"

"I, um, wasn't at Marcy's."

All of a sudden, new understanding breaks across his face. "Esme, are you — seeing somebody?"

I squirm uncontrollably, literally writhing in my chair.

"You could say that."

Dad looks like he's just been given a free pass out of hell. His face dissolves through relief into a big smile.

"You know, I can't believe I didn't think of this before, but it's so nice not to be afraid you'll get pregnant."

"*Dad*. Ew."

"I mean, it is, a—you know, right?"

"Is *girl* the word you're looking for? Yes. It is a girl. Have you ever thought about how ironic it is that *I'm* the gay one? I mean, you build fairy houses, for Christ's sake."

"Don't turn your little poison darts of wit on me, missy. I'm impervious."

"Christ on a bike. I was just saying it's funny."

"To avoid talking about your love life."

"I have to go to bed. For like, an hour."

"I'm grounding you only if you won't tell me who it is."

"You are the weirdest parent ever."

"Spill it, kidlet."

I take an extremely deep breath. "It's—it's, um. It's Rowie."

Pops makes a little sound, and his face gets all warm and soft and gooey. I begin to pray fiercely that he won't cry.

"Dad. Compose yourself. This really doesn't have to be a moment."

He gets it together, cupping a hand to my cheek. "Rowie is wonderful. Smart and beautiful. Just like you."

"Whatever."

"Uff-da, I just didn't know I had to be ready for this yet. I do miss your mother in these moments," he says.

"I wish you had a woman around to help you with stuff like this."

"Because she always dealt with things so well?" I say acidly.

"She did the best she could, kidlet."

"You let her off the hook too easy."

"It's not that," he sighs. "I've just—made my peace with it, and I'd like to see you do the same. She's gone, and we miss her, and we can't change that."

"Sometimes I don't know—like, *how* to miss her," I say. "I don't feel like I ever knew her very well, or well enough to miss her. And I don't know how to forgive her for leaving."

"Yeah, that's a tough one." Pops rests his chin on folded hands. "Tell you what, though. In Jewish law, it's customary for the children of departed parents to atone for those parents, but not vice versa. So maybe in finding your forgiveness of her, it might be helpful to understand that forgiveness as a Jewish one: it's your sacred responsibility, in a sense, to find forgiveness for her."

"That's a bum deal," I say.

"How?"

"That I have this Jewish responsibility to atone for her when I wouldn't have been Jewish without her in the first place. It's basically all her fault."

"Well, your first responsibility is to figure out the kind of woman you want to be without her help, and I'm sorry for that lack." Pops looks pained. "And you're entitled to your anger at her, but it would be a far better thing, in the long run, to find forgiveness. And love." He gives me a crinkly smile. "So. You and Rowie. Are you happy?"

"I think so."

"Why do you sound so unsure?"

I put my head down on the table. "Shit's complicated." He raises his eyebrows. "She doesn't want anyone to know."

He folds his arms across his chest in thought. "Hmm. That's tricky."

"Yeah. I guess I'm just hoping she'll get past it."

"Well, promise me you'll quit with the sneaking out from here. I want both of us to get a lot more sleep than this. Bring Rowie over sometime, anytime. I'll stay out of your hair."

"We'll see." I haul myself to my feet with great strain, stretching. "Pops?"

"Hmm." He's inspecting the wing again; I guess he's decided it's too late to sleep.

"If you know it won't last, is it still worth it? I mean, losing Mom—was it worth it?"

He looks up.

"That's a complicated question—you know that."
He pauses. "Of course Johanna was worth it for me
because she gave me you. But you need to find your own
love, to give yourself away. Now—you'll only be able to
be this uninhibited once. Don't let it pass you by."

CHAPTER EIGHT
The Goats, or
Who Is Esme?

Halloween at school is even weirder than regular school. Halloween is too confusing to do it at school. Not to be, like, a total buzzkill, but I feel like it's so easy to get way too into dressing up for the whole day, and then you're just the douchebag trying to sit down in a SpongeBob costume in math class. So I always skirt the issue in regular clothes, erring on the side of disdain. Today I'm just wearing a big T-shirt over a black unitard and Timbs. While Rowie and Marcy share my resistance to dressing up for school, Tess, of course, does it with unabashed eagerness. She also never tells anyone what her costume's going to be beforehand; she's into surprises or something. We're shambling into Mrs. DiCostanza's AP English class second period, waiting for Tess to make her grand entrance. Just before the bell, she strolls in wearing a long kind of Laura Ingalls Wilder dress with fake blood all over it, holding a bloody ax under her arm.

"Who the eff are you supposed to be?" I lean over and whisper as she slips into her seat.

"Lizzie Borden. Duh," she says.

"Who the balls is that?" I hiss back.

"You know. 'Lizzie Borden took an ax, gave her mother forty whacks, and when she saw what she had done, she gave her father forty-one.'"

"Sick," I say approvingly. I was actually born late the night of Halloween, during a huge blizzard. It's like one of those back-in-my-day-I-walked-to-school-uphill-both-ways legends: I was born right smack in the icy middle of the Halloween blizzard nearly seventeen years ago. Pops couldn't drive very fast in the midnight hell-snow, so I was mostly born right smack in our 1984 Colt Vista supercruiser, and my birthday's technically November first, which is tomorrow. Marcy always pretends to forget, but she's definitely up to something.

"Ladies, let's rein it in," Mrs. DiCostanza says tersely. Marilyn DiCostanza is no fucking joke. There is absolutely no messing with this woman; she's a Holyhill institution. She's head of the English department and has been teaching AP English here for twenty years. Everyone says that if you can get in with her good enough to ask her to write you a college recommendation, you'll get in anywhere you want, because all the committees know her (yes, these are the titillating urban legends Holyhill has to offer). Some of the other kids talk shit about her because she's so strict, but I secretly worship her. She's supersmart and sometimes she even throws things. In HolyHell, where parents will drop a lawsuit quicker than you can say *jumpin' Jehosaphat,* throwing things at your students takes some serious ovaries.

"Hey, Mrs. D." The four of us sidle up to her. "Can we talk to you for a second?"

"Make it quick," she says, ordering some papers.

"Would you be the faculty adviser for our new student group?" Tess asks.

She looks up and smiles. "Ah, yes, I remember my ill-timed entrance into your attempt to convince Ross Nordling about this. Remind me of the particulars?"

"It's, um," I say. "It's a gay-straight hip-hop alliance. Called Hip-Hop for Heteros and Homos."

"Excuse me?" Marilyn DiCostanza says.

"It's not as crazy as it sounds, I swear," Marcy says. "Nordling tried to make us sign that racist hip-hop policy, so we decided to form a combination hip-hop/gay-straight discussion group to prove that people can learn from hip-hop. We want to talk about gender and race and culture and stuff."

"It sounds a *little* crazy," Mrs. D. says, "but I must admit I thought making students sign that policy was ludicrous. Let me know when your next meeting is and I'll come learn more?"

"Mos def," Rowie says.

"What?" Mrs. D. asks.

I giggle. "We'll definitely let you know."

"Ah," she says. "Well. Super. Now take your seats, please.

"In honor of Halloween," Mrs. D. begins as we sit, "I have made the ambitious decision to spend today's class discussing Christina Rossetti. Who would like to begin by reading the poem 'Goblin Market'?" A pointy witch hat sits on her desk.

"We're not going to read 'The Raven'?" Tess asks eagerly, her hand popping up. "I *love* 'The Raven.'"[42]

Mrs. D. cracks a smile. "I left Poe off the list because I thought it was a predictable choice, but if 'The Raven' sets your heart on fire, Tess, we'll try to squeeze it in at the end. Oh, and also, the little ghost in the back is my daughter Johanna. Her school is closed today, so she'll be joining our discussion."

The name makes me start; Johanna is my mother's name, after the Bob Dylan song, or that's what Pops told me, anyway. I turn around to see a small besheeted figure wave shyly at us. Seeing Johanna makes me wonder what

---

42. Ultra-stealth text from Marcy: *I'd know she quotes Radiohead on her Facebook profile even if we weren't friends.*

would happen if I ever met my mother on the street, randomly, a meeting I've both fantasized about and feared. How would I know she corresponded with me, her body with mine? How would I recognize her? Sometimes I don't remember what she looks like. Looked like. Would she recognize me?

Tess leans over and whisper-sings the White Stripes' "Little Ghost" in my ear. Though the sheet makes it hard to tell, I'd place this Johanna at about eleven or twelve, and think that she's younger than a child I'd imagined someone of Mrs. D.'s stature having.

"Will someone volunteer to read the poem?" Mrs. D. asks. I raise my hand. She nods at me. "Thanks, Esme. Whenever you're ready."

I begin to read; the poem is long, lyrical, more than a little sensuous, rhythmic, and riddled with graphic fruit. It seems to be about two sisters walking through this surreal bazaar where sketchy goblins try to sell them evil fruit. One sister, Lizzie, is the good, virtuous, cautious one, and the other one, Laura, is too curious for her own good:

" 'No,' said Lizzie, 'no, no, no;
Their offers should not charm us,
Their evil gifts would harm us.'
She thrust a dimpled finger
In each ear, shut eyes and ran:

Curious Laura chose to linger
Wondering at each merchant man. . . .

Laura stretched her gleaming neck
Like a rush-imbedded swan,
Like a lily from the beck,
Like a moonlit poplar branch,
Like a vessel at the launch
When its last restraint is gone."

I look up. Mrs. DiCostanza smiles expectantly.

"So—first impressions? Where do we start with this poem?"

I love the dead silence that always follows open-ended questions like this, especially when they're about poetry. We're all word nerds, the Sister Mischief cohort, so I'm just waiting to see who jumps on it first.

It's Marcy, hot on the buzzer. "The metric structure is pretty complex," she answers. That's my girl, finding the beats in everything. "It mostly alternates between iambic tetrameter and trimeter, but a lot of the lines stop short at dimeter."

"Can someone translate that into English?" Anders Ostergaard quips from the back. What a genius.

Johanna DiCostanza lifts up her ghost face and smiles helpfully at him. "It means that the emphasis is on every second syllable, and that there are alternately three and four poetic feet per line. And that some of the lines stop at two feet."

"Oh, *snap!*" I hoot, raising a snicker from the class.

"Yo, Mrs. D., your kid is like crazy smart," Elijah Carlson, another of the white hats, contributes. I see Johanna kind of shrinking in her chair and remember viscerally how much it sometimes sucked to be the smart kid.

"Yes, my kid is smart," Mrs. D. says. "Nicely observed, all of you. So what's the thematic content of 'Goblin Market'? What kind of narrative does it enact? And why did I choose it for Halloween?"

"Because it's about goblins and it's creepy as fu—?" Elijah offers another insight.

"Watch yourself, Mr. Carlson," Mrs. D. responds swiftly.

Tess raises her ax. "This poem feels really sexual to me. Like, kind of violently sexual. This is a really intense sister relationship."

"Can you push that a little bit harder?" Mrs. DiCostanza asks.

Tess continues. "It kind of feels like a fight with seduction. Like, Laura's the greedy sister, the curious sister, and she gets all up in the market, but Lizzie's a little more prudish, a little more wary. And the goblins are all after them in this sort of rapey way."

"Do you think we're meant to interpret this poem

as an allegory?" Mrs. D. asks. "Is this a cautionary tale about girls and sex?"

"No," Rowie pipes up unexpectedly. "It starts off wanting to make you think that. But it ends up being more like the sisters vanquishing the goblins, outwitting them at their own game." She pauses. "As a whole, this feels to me like a poem about love between women."

Rowie's pupils dart around as if she's being followed. Mrs. D. nods.

"I like that interpretation very much, especially considering it's ultimately Lizzie's love that saves Laura from ruination and death. Can we unpack the significance of fruit in the poem a little bit more—"

Mrs. D. still has her mouth open to continue her sentence when she is abruptly cut off by a whoop in the hall, followed by the fire bell. She hangs her head, having taught too many Halloweens to feign surprise. Resignedly plunking her witch hat onto her head, she ushers the class and Johanna toward the door.

We squeeze out the door with no preparation for what we're entering. The hall is a scene of unbridled sensory chaos. Everyone's pressing their ears and squinting against the jangling bell and flashing alarm lights, but, even more jarring, the central cafeteria floor is covered in a tempest of wretched shit—there are suds everywhere, suggesting that soap is one of the ingredients to this liquid disaster, and there's gobs of something thick and shiny that looks a lot like Crisco mingling with the bubbles. I hear Wu-Tang's "Shame on a Nigga" pumping, but I don't know where it's coming from. As we gape from the doorway, various stained people run by: two guys chortle as they slick the slime off their vintage North Star hockey jerseys, and a short girl weeps as she realizes her suede skirt is ruined. I clap a hand over my mouth, awestruck.

"This ish is bananas," Rowie says. "B-A—"

"Cheese and rice!" Mrs. D. exclaims as shrieks begin to erupt from all the other classes emerging into the storm. "Come on, we're taking the north stairs." She snatches Johanna and marches our class toward the exit, but we move reluctantly, rubbernecking at the administrators who have begun to enter the scene.

People are catapulting into the bedlam, slipping and sliding around the lunchroom, veering and falling amid the teachers' hapless protests. The white hats are all bat-shit trying to push each other down in the goop, and a group of burnouts form an impromptu blissed-out dance circle near the windows, obliviously gyrating in the muck. Coach Crowther tries to make his way over to break up the party—which I have half a mind to career over and join—but totally eats it on his third step into the slippery lunchroom maw. As he writhes in the goo, I notice Marcy smirking like she knows something we don't.

"Aren't you going to help him?" I ask.

"Naw, I'm pretty sure they covered this in basic

training. We should get moving," she says, chuckling. "It's about to get worse."

"How do you—?" Rowie manages before the first water balloon hits, taking Lauren Wilshire down like she were made of Styrofoam. Shrieking, we scurry out of the line of fire as the ammunition descends like a hailstorm.

"NASTY!" Tess screeches as we try to run down the stairs. The banisters are covered in the same lardlike substance as the cafeteria floor, but mercifully, the terrorists have spared the stairs. Holding our hands up like hostages, we make our way down to the exit. There isn't any more order outside the school: teachers don't get training for emergencies like these, I suppose, and half the students have already started migrating over to the parking lot and driving out through the bus entrance on the other side of the school.

"Marce, you wanna fill us in here? I assume you have sources on this," Tess says.

Marcy snorts and motions for us to draw back from the AP English crew a little, leaning in.

"Look, all's I'm saying is I heard a little chatter about the hockey team trying out some new initiation strategies. I think the new guys had to come up with a prank that'd get everyone out of school early on Halloween," she says.

"Oh, Lordy," Tess says. "I hope Anders wasn't up in this."

"So why are we still here?" I say. "I say we follow the parking lot migration."

"Won't we get marked absent for the rest of the day if we bail?" Rowie says worriedly.

"Ummm," Marcy says, "I think Project Mayhem here may have the fire alarm set to go off every fifteen minutes for the rest of the day." The fire trucks roll up just as the alarm goes off again. I look over and see Mrs. D. on her cell phone, fighting with someone. The little ghost is fastened close to her side, taking in the anarchy around her with wonder. *Wow,* I think, *some people have moms at times like these.*

"They've already started to leave, Ross," she argues, yelling into her BlackBerry speakerphone like a Hollywood agent. "You have to notify the parents so they can pick up kids who don't have cars. You'd also be well advised to do so before the press gets wind of this."

"Marilyn, I can't close the entire goddamn school because some little asswipes decided to unleash a holocaust of—of—*slop* all over the building," the voice of Principal Ross Nordling warbles hysterically from the other end of the speakerphone.

"Ross, you can't expect kids to learn when they're knee-deep in *bullshit.* I just heard there are animals loose in the school. It isn't safe. I'm telling my class to call their parents." Mrs. D. ends the conversation, pitching her phone in her purse.

"Animals?" Rowie asks.

"Tess, can I see your iPhone for a sec?" Marcy's got that impish look in her eyes again.

"Where's your phone?" Tess asks suspiciously.

"I need interwebs," Marcy replies, grabbing the magic gadget. She clicks on it for a minute,[43] then gives us a thumbs-up.

"Fuck all y'all, Holyhill."

"What did you just do?" I arch an eyebrow at her.

"Direct-messaged the KIND-11 Twitter tip line." Tess snatches her iPhone back and reads us the tweet.

"You said the school's under attack?" Tess's jaw hangs agape.

"The school *is* under attack. Sort of." She hangs up, grinning at us.

"Oh, man," Tess says. "Darlene would hit the roof if this was what I wore for my local TV debut." She giggles and taps on her iPhone.[44]

Marcy gets on her own phone and dials.

"Yo. No, *you* piss off, I *know* you're at work. That's why I'm calling. Look, just do me a favor and check the Twitter tip line. Naw, we didn't get bombed or anything, but you're still gonna wanna haul it over here. Dude, I am

43. Marcedemeanor DM @ KIND11Tips: *If you guys have anyone near Holyhill, the high school's been attacked. #holyhillholocaust*

44. TheConTessa @Marcedemeanor: *All hell's breaking loose at Holyhill High. #holyhillholocaust*

not trifling. Just grab whichever Botox Barbie is on duty and a camera and come here. Okay, bye." She hangs up.

"Rooster?" I ask.

"You know it." She grins.

"LADIES AND GENTLEMEN," the megaphoned voice of Principal Ross Nordling reaches us. "SCHOOL WILL BE CLOSED FOR THE REST OF THE DAY." A cheer rises from the crowd. "PLEASE MAKE YOUR WAY TO THE PARKING LOT. YOUR PARENTS WILL BE NOTIFIED AND BUSES WILL BE ARRIVING SHORTLY FOR THOSE OF YOU WHO DO NOT DRIVE TO SCHOOL. IF YOU HAVE ANY INFORMATION ABOUT THE PERPETRATORS OF THIS INCIDENT—"

In a turn of events that can only be described as absurd, Principal Nordling is interrupted by a chorus of bleating. Turning around to face it, I see several goats trying to cross the street between the school and the track, where everyone who hasn't already busted has gathered. More goats begin to appear at the exit doors of the school, looking pleadingly at us through the glass. I meet their gaze and understand how they feel down to their bleeding marrow. They can't get out by themselves.

"Save the goats!" I scream, hurtling into the street to rescue the lost goats from the impending fleet of arriving buses.

"Save the goats!" Rowie squeals with equal fervor, dashing into the street behind me. The poor animals have Crisco all over their hooves. I hope it's not, like, the guts of anyone's cousin or anything.

"Here, you're cool. Crunch on some munchies over here," I soothe my new cloven-hooved homie, leading him over to the grass. "Keep an eye on him," I tell Tess and Marcy. Rowie's already back up at the school, springing the other goats from the building and steering them toward us. I run back to help her herd them across the street; there are two, four counting the ones we've already guided to safety. Rowie and I both have this animal instinct. I think it's a Hindu thing for her; I'm pretty much just a dirty hippie. Two of the goats are covered in red liquid that appears at first to be the carnage of a senseless goat slaughter but upon closer inspection reveals itself as either fake blood or red Kool-Aid.

"These guys are a mess," says Tess, stripping lengths of lace from her dress to tie around the goats' necks as makeshift leashes. One of the goats has already started nibbling at his lead, and another bites a chunk out of her tattered hemline. Still holding the ax and her iPhone,[45] Tess looks like some sort of nightmare shepherdess from a pastoral landscape gone horribly awry.

"Did you know goats are actually very smart?" Rowie asks as she nuzzles noses with one of the girl goats and

45. TheConTessa: *WTF is going on #holyhillholocaust*

pulls her phone from her back pocket.[46] "Much smarter than sheep."

"Poor little guys," I say, stroking their heads. They baa in pleasure. "Where do you think they came from?"

"I don't know, but I can tell you they're not leaving with me," Marcy kicks back.

"Let's just walk them up to the north lot to calm them down some." Rowie follows Marcy as she walks toward her car.

"What do you mean, calm them down? They look fine to me." Marcy nods at the quartet of goats, who seem happily affixed to Tess's decomposing Lizzie Borden dress.

"Dude. They're freaking out." Rowie strokes a pair of ears as we walk.

"They're straight chilling! You're the one who's bugging." Marcy unhooks her keys from her belt loop.

"We can't put them in the car like this." I watch the Kool-Aid drip from the goats' bellies.

"*Oh hell* no. No goats in the James," Marcy says. "The goat stroll ends here."

"But we can't just *leave* them here. That's just like giving them up for goat meat." Rowie looks distraught.

---

46. WowieWudwa @Marcedemeanor @TheConTessa: *what kind of sick fuck drags farm animals into this? #holyhillholocaust*

"I'm not making myself party to goat slaughter unless there's a spit-roast involved," I say. Rowie looks at me, stricken. "I mean, um, say no to roadkill."

"Look the eff out!" Tess throws her body against all of us as a KIND-11 van wheels narrowly by us; it seems to have entered with some urgency through the parking-lot exit.

"Hey, local media! Wrong way!" Marcy yells, waving her arms. "Over here!"

The van screeches to a stop, and a stringy-haired guy in sunglasses — Rooster Crowther — pokes his head out the driver's side window, grinning. "Where's the fire?"

"More like the apocalypse," Tess calls back. A woman in a fuchsia power suit appears on the other side of the van and gives us a harried smile.

"Do you girls go to school here?" We nod.

"That's my little sister," Rooster says, pointing at Marcy.

"Precious. Then could one of you be a doll and clue us in as to what exactly the story I'm here to report is?" Her tone turns slightly snotty.

"Whoa, angry," Marcy mutters.

"Shut up and let's get 4H on TV," I hiss at her.

"Are you effing serious?" Rowie blurts out.

"Hi, I'm Esme Rockett, I'm a junior here at Holyhill," I introduce myself, sticking out a hand to the reporter.

"Brenda Banacynzki." She grasps my hand briefly

between fiddles with her lapel mike. "Are you afraid of cameras?" the reporter asks.

"Not particularly," I reply. The goat covered in red refuse next to me bleats. Brenda and Rooster regard it, exchange glances, and shrug.

"Ready when you are, Bren," Rooster says, hoisting the camera up to his shoulder.

"Kid, you're our first interview on the scene. Do you think you can tell us what happened?" she asks me, dashing a final mist of powder on her nose.

"Uh, I'll do my best," I say, reaffirmed in my gladness that I didn't wear my costume to school today.

"Darlene's going to be even pisseder than that time Ada got arrested." Tess frantically smooths her hair, leaving a red streak in the front.

"Smile!" Brenda Banacynzki says.

"Great, Ez, you're on in five-four-three-two—" Rooster points a finger at the reporter.

"Good evening, I'm Brenda Banacynzki, reporting live from Holyhill High School, where unknown attackers struck today, disrupting classes and terrifying students. I'm speaking to Esme Rockett, a junior at Holyhill. Esme, can you tell us what happened?" She thrusts a microphone in my face.

"It's hard to sum up," I say into the microphone. "Basically some kids covered the floors and banisters in soap and Crisco and inexplicably set a whole bunch of goats loose in the building, and the fire alarm has been going off every fifteen minutes."

Brenda Banacynzki looks slightly taken aback, but recovers. "What's the mood at Holyhill today, Esme?"

It's my moment. "Well, Brenda, I think a lot of Holyhill students are sick of the administrative hypocrisy that allows nonsense like this to go on while prohibiting activities that are actually conducive to academic dialogue."

"Can you tell us more about that?" Brenda asks, a smile permafrozen on her face.

"I'd be happy to," I say, snatching my chance amid her confusion. "Holyhill calls itself one of the safest communities in America, but the truth is it's only safe to be rich, white, and straight here. The Holyhill administration announced earlier this year that it would not permit any hip-hop music, or really anything associated with hip-hop culture, to exist on campus. I think that policy highlights the need for a safe space at our school, a space where music and lifestyles that some consider controversial or alternative can be discussed freely, without needless threats and disruptions like what happened today. That's why my friends and I"—I glance over at Rowie and the girls, who are gaping at me with dumbfounded mouths—"that's why my friends and I are petitioning the administration to add a hip-hop gay-straight alliance to the list of recognized student groups."

I can't believe Brenda Banacynzki is going along with this, but she totally takes the bait. "Are you saying that what happened today was a Holyhill hate crime?"

Marcy steps in and grabs the mike. "Uh, hi. Marcy Crowther, captain of the Holyhill Fighting Loons drumline. No, I don't think the incident today was a targeted attack. But students here do need a safe space, and we'd like that space to be one where students can feel free to examine the culture around us, including hip-hop and sexuality. We've spoken with administrators, but our application for school recognition has been denied."

"What do you call your group, and why do you think your application was rejected?"

"Hip-Hop for Heteros and Homos is a name that playfully describes our purpose of sexual and musical inquiry," I say. "But to discuss hip-hop, we'd need to be able to listen to it, and school policy currently prohibits that, so the administration has told us that we can't meet on school grounds." Rowie and Tess edge in next to us.

"Are you implying that the Holyhill administration is unable to maintain order at school or unwilling to protect the rights of all of its students, regardless of personal beliefs or sexual orientation?"

Tess's shoulder interrupts my thought as she lunges to grab the mike from Marcy. "Hi there. Tess Grinnell. I wouldn't go that far, Brenda. I think it's more that Holyhill has been a little slow to acknowledge the presence of students who are interested in this kind of frank discussion. And especially as a thinking Christian, I think that should change."

"Last question, girls—who's your four-legged friend?"

"I'm Rohini Rudra," Rowie says passionately, "and this is one of the goats that was brought into the school and brutally endangered today. Whoever was responsible for this incident set this poor animal free in a cafeteria that was covered in, as far as I can tell, soap and Crisco, and then pelted him and others with water balloons filled with fake blood or Kool-Aid or something. When the administration can't prevent cruel antics like this, I don't understand why they think they can violate our First Amendment rights by censoring the music we can listen to on campus."

Brenda Banacynzki nods with fake TV-reporter compassion. "That's quite the paradox. Well, girls, we're out of time. Reporting live from Holyhill, joined by girls and goats, I'm Brenda Banacynzki, KIND-11 News."

"And, we're out," Rooster says, lowering the camera.

We all begin to laugh and scream, still in the zone, pumping Brenda Banacynzki's hand. Pops is going to flip out when he sees this.

"You girls are good talkers," Rooster says, palming me his business card. "If the administration tries any other bullshit, give us a call and we'll do a follow-up story."

"Rooster, did you actually just give me your business card?" I mock-sucker-punch him in the ribs. "It was cool of you to show up, though."

Rooster smiles wanly. "Keep your head up, Ezbones. There's life after high school."

"Thanks, man," I say, pocketing the card. "Really. Thanks."[47] We give a last wave as they retreat back to the van.

"You are un-fucking-real," Rowie says, shoving me. I feel like her hand makes a permanent impression on my shoulder, like I'll take off my shirt tonight and see her handprint. "You have absolutely no shame."

"Dude, Holyhill is *fuuuucked,*" Marcy sings, doing a little jig. "There's no way they can reject our application after that rant. Not to mention the fact that we were, like, right."

"What are we going to do with Faithe?" Tess asks.

"Who's Faith?"

"This is Faithe, with an *e.*" Tess pats one of the goats' heads. "And these are Prudence, Penitence, and Chastity."

"What does that make you? Promiscuity?" Marcy teases her.

---

47. SiN, later: *Someday I will be Rooster's age, and I have to remember to tell some other lost, angry teenager that high school isn't the end of the world.*

"*Mais non.*" Tessie grins.

Mrs. D. appears. "Was that KIND-11 News I just saw driving away?"

"Mrs. D., it was so cool!" Marcy explodes. "We totally stuck it to the man."

Mrs. D. does that grin-suppressing thing she always does in the presence of irreverence, like she knows she's supposed to disapprove but can't quite. "Then it's probably best that I know absolutely nothing about what just happened. Can I take the farm animals off your hands? You girls should get out of here before this gets any worse. Do you have a ride?"

"Yeah, Marcy's car is over there," Rowie says. "What are you going to do with the goats?"

"We're pretty sure they came from a petting zoo in Waconia. My husband's coming with a truck for the trip." Mrs. D. sighs. "And we never even got to 'The Raven.' I've taught through twenty-seven Halloweens and lived to tell, but this one dwarfs them all."

"Well, thanks for volunteering to take them," I say, handing over the lace leash. "And hey, Johanna, you were really smart in class today. I was impressed. Sorry if anyone was a jerk to you."

Johanna beams. "Thanks. I like your shoes."

I look down at my Timbs. "Thanks! Hey, Mrs. D., is Johanna named after the Bob Dylan song?"

Now it's Mrs. DiCostanza's turn to beam. "I had no idea anyone your age still listened to Dylan. Yes. She is."

"My mom was named Johanna after the song too," I tell her, a little surprised that I'm telling her. "If I ever have a daughter, I'm naming her Ramona."

"Like *Ramona Quimby, Age 8*?" Johanna pipes up excitedly.

"Dude, totally," I tell her. "Beverly Cleary is the shit. I mean, uh—yeah."

"We're gonna take her home and wash her mouth out with soap," Marcy says.

"Have a nice Halloween, you girls." Mrs. D. chuckles, shaking her head, and she and Johanna take two goats each, receding.

"We can go to my house," Rowie says. "My mom's been asking about you guys anyway."

"Okay, but can we run by the SA first? I need a Diet Coke and there's never anything chemical to sip on at Dr. R.'s house," Tess says, jumping into the front seat. "Shotgun!"

"Sold," Marcy says. "Oh, we missed lunch—that's why I'm starvacious. Call Priya and tell her to put, like, twenty-five samosas in the oven."

"Okay, bossy," Rowie mutters, dialing her phone. "Mom. You're not going to believe why, but we're on our way over."

"Let's get the eff out of here," I say, rolling down the backseat window and gazing back at the empty, sudsy building. "Figure out how to *really* drop some bombs on this place."

CHAPTER NINE
Halloween 2

Marcy takes a long, roundabout way to Rowie's house, savoring the freedom from school, still high from our local media victory: a Diet Coke–and–gas pit stop at SuperAmerica, a gratuitous roll around Lake Harriet and the bandshell, anything to prolong the slanty yellow afternoon sunshine before the later-day clouds gather. Marcy's car feels like the only square footage in Holyhill that really belongs to us. I cast a deliberately nonchalant arm over Rowie's shoulders; to my surprise, she lets me. Tess turns around and regards us.

"This is going to sound super weird, but you guys would make a hot couple," she says, squinting. "I don't know, you just kind of look like a good hot mess together."

Rowie squirms and lets out an uncomfortable laugh.

"Yeah, man," I play along, "we'd be the hottest interracial gay MC couple in the Midwest."

"Seriously," Tess hoots, clapping. She shoves Rowie, who's blushing furiously. "That would be so nutty."

"Yeah," Rowie manages. "Nutty."

"Can you guys tell if we're good girls or bad girls?" Tess prattles on. "I can't tell anymore. Does our flipping off Ross Nordling on KIND-11 make us bad?"

"I think—I think we might be good girls who maybe like the idea of being bad girls, but aren't that good at being really bad," Rowie says.

"Yeah," Tess says. "I guess I just never thought about being a bad kid until now."

"I mean," Marcy says, "we never really had a reason not to do what everyone told us to do until now. Or at least you didn't."

"I know," Tess says. "I'm not that used to it yet."

"Maybe that's what growing up is," Rowie says. "When you can't be who you are and do what everyone's telling you to do at the same time anymore."

"Preach," Tess says.

"Do you guys know where you want to go to college?" I say. "I think good kids know by now."

"New York City," Tess says.

"Any Big Ten school that'll pay for me to go there," Marcy tosses in.

"I have no idea where I want to go. Does that make me a fuckup?" I ask. "I know I want to go to a good school,

I guess, and that I don't want to go anywhere where the people are going to be lame. The idea of a women's school sounds all right, but is that too predictable?"

"Quit spazzing. We're only juniors," Marcy says. "Just think how much easier beer and weed will be to find in college."

"True. The whole Where and Why question just freaks me out. Ro, what about you?"

Rowie sighs. "Ambivalent. My dad just wants me to apply to the Ivies and Madison and Minnesota. He says if I can't get into an Ivy League school, it's not worth paying out-of-state tuition."

"I sort of see where he's coming from," Marcy says, "but that's mostly bullshit."

"You'll get into one of the Ivies," Tess assures her.

"Is that where you want to go?" I ask. Fire-colored elm and maple trees shed a hail of leaves on the windshield as Marcy turns onto the lakeshore drive.

Rowie looks at me with a wide expression of surprise. "I guess so, if they're better than everywhere else."

"Who says they are?" Marcy says. "Rich people, that's who."

"I mean, maybe they are the best," I say. "But maybe you should tell everyone to go fuck themselves and go where's best for you."

"Easy for you to say," Rowie says. "Your dad would let you go to clown college if you wanted to."

"My mom didn't go to college," Marcy says. "I guess her dad didn't think girls needed to."

"My mom was up in some activist shit in college in India, but she never talks about it," Rowie says.

"Yeah?" My ears perk up. "What'd they do?"

"Vague. All I know is that it had something to do with banned books. Like I said, she doesn't talk about it." Rowie says.

"My mom was in a sorority at the U of M," Tess says.

"Sororities are for bustas," I say.

"Hey, cranky." Tess flicks my nose. "Got some opinions?"

"I didn't get that much sleep last night," I mutter. "Makes it harder to turn down the volume on my internal monologue."

"Okay, since you brought it up," Tess says, "can we talk about your *Twilight* look of late? I swear the dark circles under your eyes are starting to take over your face."

"Aw, thanks, hon," I say sarcastically. "You sound like my dad."

"Hate to say it, dude, but blondie's got a point," Marcy says. "You fall asleep in Precalc a lot these days."

"Like that's news?" I say, electrically aware of Rowie's prolonged silence and backpack-digging. "I always get a second wind at like eleven, and then if I don't make myself go to bed by midnight I end up dicking around until like three. I'm nocturnal is all. Like raccoons, and bike thieves." I'm rambling.

"If you say so," Tess shrugs, giving me a last lingering look of suspicion.

"Did your mom go to college?" Rowie says.

"Yeah," I say. "Berkeley. That's where she met my dad."

"What'd she study?" Tess asks gently.

"I don't know." I shrug.

"Do you remember anything about her?" Rowie brushes my shoulder with the back of her hand.

"Only, like, a snapshot here and there," I say. "I have this memory of her wearing a green sundress, eating chunks of pineapple out of the can. I was trying to get her attention with one of my weird art projects, but she wasn't taking the bait. She just sort of stared into space. I think it was around then that she left." I pause, watching the joggers and strollers lap the lake. "Fruit cocktail still makes me kind of anxious."

"Have you heard anything from her since then?" Rowie asks.

"She sends me a letter on my birthday every year," I say.

"From Israel?" Tess asks.

"Yup," I say. "Who knows, maybe this year's is already in the mail."

"Did you guys hear some parents wanted to give Halverson a talking-to about his moon rocks?" Marcy says. "Because they're older than Genesis. The rocks, not the parents."

"Yeah," Tess says. "I think Mary Ashley's folks were probably behind that."

"Seriously?" Rowie says. "I mean, really? It's a public school, for Christ's sake."

"I think it's ridiculous," Tess says. "I believe in God, and I believe He's intelligent, but I don't expect teachers to teach that at a public school."

"Are you actually saying you believe in intelligent design? That's pseudoscience!" Marcy says.

"I *didn't* say that, and why do you care even if I did? I'm not asking anyone else to believe it. I have a right to believe what I believe." Tess's tone grows heated. "They're all theories."

"This is what I don't get about you, girl." Marcy pounds the steering wheel. "You're so — *smart*. And yet you believe this shit."

"See, this is why it was easier sometimes to hang out with the church kids," Tess says. "There are things about them that I don't agree with. But they never thought having faith made you dumb. Believing what my family believes, feeling like I have a relationship with an entity that's greater than I am — that doesn't make me an idiot. I believe in a world in which some things can't be reasonably explained." She takes a breath, molding her last bullet. "Your reason isn't better than my reason." A hush falls across the car. For a moment, at a just-so angle, we can see the downtown Minneapolis skyline across the lake.

"I don't think you're an idiot," I say. "I wish I felt what you feel. Sometimes I think I might."

"I don't think you're an idiot, Tessie," Marcy says, softening. "You're just — you're better than the ones you hung with. MashBaum and her cronies think it's, like, their God-given mission to shit on me."

"Yeah, well, I haven't been that impressed with Mary Ashley's interpretation of what it means to be a Christian lately," Tess snaps. "Or Holyhill's. And your painting us all with the same brush is just as hypocritical as them trying to ban hip-hop or say gay kids shouldn't have a safe place at school. So lay off."

"I know. Sorry, dude," Marcy mumbles.

"Are you a Christian because your mom is a Christian?" I ask Tess.

"What do you mean?" Tess cocks her head to the left.

"I don't know. I just feel like my mom never stuck around to teach me how to be a Jew, so I don't know what I'm supposed to believe." I look out the window at the arc of the abandoned lake beach. "But I wouldn't be a Jew without her, so where does that leave me?"

"Well," Tess says, "where do you think you've learned what you do know about being a Jew?"

"From her books, I guess," I say. "And Pops, and the ABCs of Minnesotan Jews: Al Franken, Bob Dylan, and the Coen brothers."

"The Minnesotan Jew," Rowie say. "Shit's complicated, huh?"

"Sort of," I say, putting on MC Paul Barman's *Paullelujah!*

"Oh, my God, you are so into nerdcore," Marcy groans.

"MC Paul Barman is *not* nerdcore," I inform her.

Tess smiles and smacks Marcy lightly upside the head. "Shut up. Maybe you should just keep reading, Ez. You seem to find something divine in words."

"Maybe you're right." I watch the lake recede as Marcy turns onto France Ave. "I thought I was mad at God when Mom left. But I think maybe I was just mad at Mom. And I'm still trying to figure out how not to be."

"I think you're allowed to be," Rowie says.

"Yeah," I say. "I know. But I want to forgive her. I just don't know how." I take out my notebook.[48]

---

48. SiN: *Almost seventeen, I'm angry, young and green / I'm so pissed off at God that I think I'm gonna scream / My moms packed up and peaced to go and chase some crazy dream / She left me decent genes but damn, she weaned me mean / I'm gonna cause a scene, can't get out from in between / Moms, you're the reason God and me can't get clean.*

"The funny thing about forgiveness," Tess says, "is that if you want to feel it, it'll come on its own."

"Dude." Rowie cuts her off, gaping at her Black-Berry. "Check it. KIND-11's already got a teaser of the interview with us up on their website. The headline says: Holyhill Students Speak Out Against Hypocrisy by School Administration."

"OMG," I say. Tess lunges for her iPhone.[49]

"Whoa," Marcy says. "Shit just went public."

"We're gonna be so Googleable!" Tess screams in delight.

"How long do you think it'll take for Nordling to call another meeting with us?" Rowie says, snickering.

"At least until tomorrow," Marcy says. "The six o'clock news hasn't even aired yet."

"I don't know, man." Tess shakes her head. "I posted the link on my profile literally thirty seconds ago, and five people already like it."

"OMG squared," I say. "This is gonna be huge."

Marcy rolls down Iroquois Lane, Rowie's copper door in sight.

"Maybe we should think about finding an agent." Tess unbuckles her seat belt as Marcy parks. I tuck my notebook back in my bag and tumble out after them.

---

49. TheConTessa @Marcedemeanor @WowieWudwa @pockettrockett: *Holyhill Students Speak Out Against Hypocrisy bySchool Administration.*

"I'm *starving*." Rowie slams the car door behind her, then gives an impish flash of her eyes to Marcy and Tess, who seem to be in on something I'm not.

"Go!" she cries.

The three of them scramble to the front door and slam it in my face, giggling. I knock, confused.

"Guys? Was it something I said?" I call.

I can hear them gobbling like a brood of turkeys on the other side of the door. It flies open.

"SURPRISE!" They're standing around Rowie's mom, who's holding a birthday cake with candles and everything. I know it's for me because it says HAPPY BIRTHDAY, ESME in big loopy red-frosting letters.

I'm stunned. "But it isn't until tomorrow," I manage.

"No matter, come in, come in!" Dr. Rudra crows, ushering me inside. I'm holding back that rising feeling again. "We were going to have it tomorrow, but when Rohini called, I just hurried up the frosting a little bit. Happy birthday, pretty girl." She puts the cake down and hugs me, and I can't say anything because I know if I do, I'll cry at how nice she's being and at feeling so guilty that I was breaking and entering in her basement twelve hours ago. Rowie's mom does all the things that moms are supposed to stick around and do.

"Thanks, Dr. R.," I whisper as we embrace, willing the words not to catch in my throat. Rowie's eyes meet mine over her mother's shoulder. She smiles, and means it, but that still, persistent distance is there in her eyes again; lately, it almost never goes away.

"Come into the kitchen. We'll have cake with lunch. Why not?" We follow Dr. Rudra and the cake. Rowie tugs at my wrist, letting the others go ahead of us.

"Too much birthday hoopla?" she asks. "It was Marcy's idea. Was I wrong to tip Mom off? She, like, loves you."

"No," I say, shaking my head fervently, "just enough hoopla. Thanks." I go to kiss her on the cheek and she makes a face, flinching, but lets me.

"So what's everybody going to be for Halloween?" Priya Rudra asks as she sets out fresh fruit and silverware next to the samosas, roti, curries, and cake.

Marcy raises her hand. "Missy Misdemeanor Elliott."

I cackle nostalgically. "That's hardly a costume. Do you remember the firestorm you set off at Plainview Middle School when you started dressing like a honky baby Missy at age, like, twelve?"

"Whatever, that warm-up suit was fierce, and it still is." Marcy looks satisfied. Dr. Rudra looks confused.

"Remember when we didn't get what Halloween was?" Rowie asks her mother, diving into the buffet.

"Oh, my gosh, I remember." Tess laughs, close behind. "You showed up at my house in this super fancy sari, and I was all 'Who are you supposed to be, your mom?' I guess you sort of were."

"There's, like, a cultural gap between Indians and

Halloween," Rowie explains, a little embarrassed. "The closest thing we have is Diwali, which is sort of like Halloween on steroids with fireworks instead of costumes, but you get presents."

"I thought I could just dress her up nicely." Dr. Rudra shrugs matter-of-factly. "I used the clothes we had around the house."

"Wow," I say. "That's kind of—fraught."

Rowie dips a samosa in ketchup and pops it into her mouth, shrugging. "Just another Midwestern desi girl with identity issues."

"So, Miss Esme." Dr. Rudra claps her hands. "Tell us all about your seventeenth year. What are your dreams for the next three hundred sixty-five days?"

"Well," I say, thinking, "hmm. I have a dream that . . . Sister Mischief gets to play a live concert in Holyhill."

"Holla back," Marcy says, pumping a fist in the air.

"And I want to write more rhymes with my girls."

"Check, check," Rowie says, chewing. "On that."

"Worthy dreams." Dr. Rudra nods thoughtfully, and I notice that she and Rowie have that same speaking tick, the one-bullet modifier: *vague, worthy.* She pauses. "Is there anyone special in your life?"

I freeze, and Rowie looks like she's going to choke on her paneer. I wonder, for a flash, if there's any chance that Dr. Rudra has any idea what's been going on between me and her daughter. She can't. Or could she? Could she know and let it go on? I wonder if she could be offering an opportunity, a litmus test for how everyone might react. Then I look over and see the black panic in Rowie's eyes, begging me not to do it, and I remember that she isn't my opportunity.

I smile calmly. "My homies are super special. They threw me a birthday party."

"Yes! And it's better that way." Dr. Rudra pats me on the elbow. "You girls have enough to worry about, between making excellent grades and working on your music. Rohini never lets me hear any of it, of course, even though I'd like to." She looks meaningfully at her daughter, who doesn't respond.

"I'll rap for you, Dr. R.," I say shyly. Rowie's head jolts up like she's been electroshocked. "Don't worry, Ro, I'll keep it PG. Mostly. Marce, can you drop me a beat?"

"Oh, good!" Rowie's mom claps again, looking delighted. "I'm so curious, and Rohini won't indulge me."

"Unbelievable." Rowie hides her head in her hands.

"I know just how you feel. Okay, be warned that this is, like, a super rough draft. SheStorm?"

Marcy beatboxes a mid-tempo backbeat. I take out my notebook and open it to the new lyrics I've been toying around with. *Go, I will myself.*

"When I was just a young one, my papa told me
'Girl, you gotta be your own girl, wield your words
    like guns
You gotta keep it peaceful but you gotta play it tight
Gotta treat your people like you see what's wrong and right
You gotta be a smart girl, best be erudite
Ain't no one gonna tell you how to be your own light.'

Then my mama up and left me
When I was teeny-weeny
When I asked my daddy why
He said she needed to be free.

We all gettin' free, gettin' free, been gettin' free since
    ought-three
I got my bitches in their niches and we all be gettin' free
I got this open can o' whoop-ass and a fire in my eye
So I gotta ask my mama, gotta ask her why
She couldn't stick around and couldn't realize
That I was driving sideways and needed her to guide,
    fighting eyes open to a mama gone blind

And I say hey mama, hey mama, why you up and fly?
I'm seventeen now and I don't know how to cry
Don't know how to grow or how to prettify
How to clarify, verify or bear this burden till I die."

There's more, but I'm so keyed up and out of breath that I have to stop.

Dr. Rudra is looking at me with a strange expression on her face. She reaches out and takes my hand. The girls are silent.

"I think that sometimes you don't think that anyone is listening," she says very slowly, "but you must believe that we are listening. You have something to say, and we are listening."

"Girl, is that some new flow?" Rowie asks, her intoning all the same shades as her mother's. "I don't think I've heard it before."

This is all getting kind of heavy now. It's so much easier being a smartass.

"Yeah, it's just some shit—oh, fuck, sorry—some stuff I've been dicking around with." I wish everyone would go back to their lunch.

Rowie smiles a little mournfully; there's something faraway in her voice. "I didn't know you could do that shit without me."

Dr. Rudra says something rapid and snappish to Rowie in Bengali. Rowie mutters a word or two back and shuffles in her chair, crossing her arms. She cracks a grin at us.

"She told me to watch my mouth."

We laugh. "Rowie's got some bad influences on her," I say. "*Dangerous* American hussies."

"Yo, Ezbones, we should lay down some beats to what you were just spitting," Marcy throws in. "It was—that was real."

"Couldn't help but notice you hadn't gotten to a chorus by the time you stopped," Rowie says with a smirk.

"All we have to do is pull a hook and some vocals into it," Tess adds. "Those lyrics've got a heartbeat if we can give them a skeleton. That was really beautiful, Ez. I've never heard you write about your mom before."

"Okay!" I cry brightly. "Would you look at that, it's subject change o'clock again! Getting a little hot in hurr."

"No, dude, it's time to make this track happen," Marcy insists. "This is the next song in our arsenal. If we can get it together, that means we'll have, like, a good three or four songs down hard for our concert."

"Our *huh?*" Rowie stops her. "Since when are we having a concert?"

"Well, after 4H's celebrity turn on the six o'clock news tonight, people might be more curious about what we have to say, don't you think?" Tess reminds us.

"Are we talking about Sister Mischief or 4H here?" I ask.

"Does it matter? At a concert, we could charge for admission and make some money for real equipment," adds Marcy, getting excited.

"We could bring back the telegenic goats," Tess says.

"Would someone care to fill me in here?" Dr. Rudra asks. "I still haven't heard the details of today's disaster."

"It was so ridiculous. Basically some hockey morons got together and decided to cover the school in soap and Crisco and let a whole bunch of goats loose so we could all get out of school early on Halloween," Rowie explains.

"*Goats?*" Dr. Rudra drops her fork in disbelief.

"We saved them. And then KIND-11 News showed up and Esme told them that the administration had no right to prohibit hip-hop on campus when they couldn't control cruel antics like that."

"Point well taken." Dr. Rudra nods. "This is America, isn't it? Isn't freedom supposedly why we all came here in the first place?"

"*Damn* straight," I say, pounding the table. "Pardon my Bengali."

"So," Rowie continues hesitantly, "we're starting a student group to listen to and discuss music and, um, culture and sexuality. Because shouldn't we be able to study what interests us? What's relevant to us?"

"*So,*" Marcy interjects, "this is the perfect moment to make our Holyhill debut. Then they really won't be able to ignore us anymore. We have to put on a concert."

"Sometimes I think you have no idea how much you are like me." Dr. Rudra looks lovingly at Rowie.

"Always curious. Always stirring up trouble." She smiles. "It is good to question. To demand to know." She gets up and begins to clear the table. "Go work on your new song."

"We can help you clean up!" I say. "You made such a nice birthday lunch."

"No, you have important things to attend to. And it's Halloween. Go enjoy yourselves. Write big songs. Go." She shoos us out of the kitchen and we trot downstairs to Rowie's room. Rowie's mom is the best mom I've ever had.

I brush my fingers along the tapestries hanging above the stairs as we thunder down to Rowie's room and they leave a fine mist of dust on my fingertips. I'm getting too tangled up in Rowie's house; it's getting too tangled up in me. Going downstairs and seeing the treehouse out the window is like walking into a church where people are talking too loud.

Tess ambles over to Rowie's piano, sitting at the bench with purpose for her warm-up. When she lifts the cover off the keys and opens her mouth to sing, I understand anew what it is about her voice that makes church ladies twist in their seats. The voice — hers — is gritty, mettlesome, riven with glittering edges. She sings her favorite hymn, and it chills me; when Tessie sings, I *believe* her:

"My life flows on in endless song:
Above earth's lamentation,
I hear the real, tho' far-off hymn
That hails a new creation."

Marcy whips her laptop out of her backpack and makes a few hasty clicks, then softly introduces a back-beat into the hymning. A wide smile spreads over Tess's face, but she doesn't miss a beat. I notice something strange happening: Rowie is singing, faintly, along with Tess. For all of us, the singing territory has always been firmly ceded to Tess. But the way Rowie's singing right now, it's like she doesn't even realize anyone can hear her. Her face is like a chick's first peck out of the eggshell, as raw, as vulnerable. In the vector of her closed eye I see the subtle birth of a tear, a tiny groundswell from dry brown earth. Her face is like she's singing because she doesn't have a choice.

"Through all the tumult and the strife
I hear the music ringing;
It finds an echo in my soul—
How can I keep from singing?"

My throat closes; the breath catches. Carefully, so gingerly, I reach out and place my hand on hers, not asking for a reciprocal grasp, just touching. Her eyes spring open, stung, caught, but she stills her hand and holds my gaze for a moment, toeing the border of a smile. Not knowing what else to do, I smile back, willing the song not to end. With her hand in mine, I look at Marcy and Tess and wonder what would happen if they knew. Tess's eyes are closed, and Marcy hunches over the computer, pulsing with the beat; neither of them seems to feel me watching. If they really love me, I think, if I trust them enough to tell them all about my mom and something that might be faith, what could possibly happen if they just knew?

The song does end. I knew it would. Tess gives a layered-arpeggio flourish at the end, working hand over hand up the keyboard, and Marcy seamlessly concludes the percussion. Collectively, we take a breath; a beat passes. Marcy puts on Jay-Z's "Roc Boys" and grins. Tess claps the cover back onto the piano.

"Birthday dance party!" Marcy hollers, grinding up behind me.

My friends begin to dance around me; I dance too, and watch them. Tess dances in a series of poses, more like a flip book than a movie. Marcy just sort of hulks to the beat, and Rowie tosses her head back and forth to the music, her arms like commas above her head, fluid, possessed, opaque. Watching her, I realize that this is the best birthday I can remember.

CHAPTER TEN
The Critical Mass

A few days later, Rowie blows up at me before we've even gotten to school. I guess it's getting too hard not to sleep and too cold not to fight.

"Stop saying you want a *chai tea*," she snaps at me in Caribou Coffee. Marcy picked us both up for school at Rowie's this morning, under the guise of an elaborate story about a Chem problem set that took us all night. Really we fell asleep in the treehouse again and woke up in a freezing panic at six thirty this morning, so we're both tired and cagey. "Chai *is* tea. And this chai tastes like fucking feet."

Marcy and I exchange raised eyebrows.

"Can I have a caffe latte coffee, please?" Marcy orders. Rowie scowls.

We shamble into school, parting ways. It's Election Day. It feels important, but my mind is foggy, overtired, elsewhere. I plunk down in AP American History to loll through an instructional video about the immigrant surge to America in the late nineteenth century.

"Some immigrant groups encountered intense discrimination upon their arrival to Staten Island and the New World," the somber voice-over informs us. "Italian, Irish, Jewish, Hispanic, and Asian newcomers faced a harsh welcome to the United States, where many were forced by economic necessity to perform backbreaking labor in factories and fields. . . ."

Jews exist in a kind of weird in-between space in the American ethnicity spectrum, I ponder while nodding off, but being first-generation Indian would be a lot different from being just another overeducated pseudo-Heeb. Shit, Rowie's parents were born in a whole other country, and I never even had a bat mitzvah.[50] Marcy and Tess and me were never the kid whose house smelled like spices no one recognized; none of us grew up in the only brown family on the block.

The thing is, Rowie is the realest thing I've ever felt; just the sound of her name in my head makes me wake up a little. She makes it sound like Indians just aren't allowed to be gay, but how is that possible? There's like a billion people in India. If ten percent of the population is

---

50. Text to Marcy: *If I decided to have a bat mitzvah now, would u throw down some beats while I rapped the Hebrew monologue? Temple Beth Israel would <3 it.*

gay, that means there are at about 100 million gay Indians in the world. I don't get it. I don't get why we can't just be together. I think Rowie is mad at me for not understanding it. She's sad and I want to hold her sadness.[51] But no matter how many times I promise not to tell, she still won't look at me when other people are around.

The bell rings. I zombie-shuffle to the girls' bathroom to splash some water on my face before gym class, and while I'm washing my hands I see it scrawled on the mirror: *Rowie + Esme.* I rub my eyes in astonishment and look closer; it actually says *Rudi + Eddie,* but it still takes me a minute to recover. I see our secret everywhere. In gym class, Ms. Strybel decides to show *Bend It Like Beckham* as a "fun introduction to our soccer unit." There's desi-honky love floating in the ether all around me, and it's making me *crazy.*

"So Perez Hilton is saying M.I.A.'s preggers," Tess informs us as she digs up the gossip on her iPhone at lunch.

---

51. SiN: *I'm 99.9% sure I gave Rowie an orgasm last night. She finally told me that she'd never had one, which I kind of knew already, and I've been a woman on a mission ever since. When it finally happened, her whole body seized and she had to muffle her own face with a pillow to keep down the sound. I looked at her face afterward and there were little tear-streaks on the sides, where glasses would be if she wore glasses.*

"That's the news you're checking on Election Day?" Marcy carps.

"Who's the baby daddy?" I ask.

"Hmm, let me see." Tess scrolls down. "Apparently she's engaged to some guy named Benjamin Brewer."

"Sounds like a cracker name to me," I say, looking pointedly at Rowie. "I wonder if that's, like, a problem with her family."

"Her dad is a Tamil Tiger." Rowie rolls her eyes at me. "I think he's got bigger buns in the oven."

In AP Chem, Halverson's droning numbingly about nuclear chain reactions, and I'm buried in Mom's copy of *Portnoy's Complaint*. Marcy stealth-texts me;[52] I respond.[53] As I struggle not to laugh out loud at my book, the term *critical mass* wrests my attention away long enough to jot down the following notes:

CRITICAL MASS:
fissile (reactive) material

$$k = f{-}I$$

52. Marcy to me: *Mos def to hip-hop bat mitzvah. U look like shit. Do u ever get any sleep anymore? Story??*

53. Me back: *Dbag, this is just what I look like.*

CM = the lowest possible amount of fissile
material required for sustained
nuclear chain reaction

KABLOOEY

It's a formula for my life, I realize with a sinking feeling.

I spend my last-period art elective intently building a papier-mâché sculpture of a two-headed girl with four hands.[54] I find some random Lincoln Logs lying around and paint them into sticks of dynamite, gluing them along the spine of the body I'm sculpting.[55] I paint NOT A BIT TAMED onto one stick and set it aside. I slice open the chest and carve a window into it. I'm gluing a small parrot onto one shoulder when Ms. Mayakovsky comes over to examine my work.

"That's a powerful piece," she says. "What are you going to put inside the chest cavity?"

"I don't know," I say. "I'm thinking some hanging jewels and maybe some more dynamite."

Ms. Mayakovsky studies me and my monster, nodding. "Hanging jewels would augment the suspense of the piece—that's a good idea. I'm getting strong erotic

54. Text from Rowie: *Still coming over for dinner tonight?*

55. Me to Rowie: *You bet.*

energy from this sculpture. Failed separation, and crisis. An ominous thing in the distance. Do you have a title?"

I peer at the two-headed body. *"The Critical Mass."*

After the interminable school day ends, I drag myself home and head straight for the couch, where Pops already has his TV tray set up in front of CNN. I plunk down my backpack and almost knock over the aviary he's carving.

"Nice birdcage." I steady the TV tray and settle in, leaning back and closing my eyes for a second.

"It's a butterfly cage," he informs me. "How was your day?"

"If a birdcage is an aviary, what's a butterfly cage?"

"Hmmm. A lepidopterary?"

"Hm." I nod, scribbling.[56] "Probably not in the dictionary, but decent guess."

"I'm glad you approve." He cuffs my cheek. "You look beyond tired, parakeet. Don't think I don't know your nights haven't gotten any earlier."

"We don't really have to talk about it." I put my notebook away and close my eyes again.

---

56. SiN, later: *Can't find lepidopterary / in the Oxford English Dictionary / I dig big words, but they can't help me carry / The weight of a gay interracial literary / Mate rhymes with date / Baby, why you gotta hate / Why you say we gotta wait / We're at a gay stalemate / Can't equivocate and date / I hate the hook but not the taste / of how my heart dilates when I swallow your bait.*

"Yeah. That's gonna work," he says with a snort. "Look, it's not like I'm trying to slap a chastity belt on you."

"Ew, Pops. Don't say *chastity*." I grimace.

"Calm down. I just want you to get enough sleep to be able to function. This has got to stop. You can't get zero sleep and feel good about life. You look depressed. You're going to get sick."

"Okay, okay, I'll get more sleep." I flip the channels uselessly; the polls aren't even closed yet, and Herb Baumgarten is leading by fourteen percent. I feel tired of the same old conflicts.

"Quit appeasing me—you're not fooling anyone." He puts down his knife and goes into the kitchen. "Something's stuck in your gullet. What is it? Rowie?"

I sigh dramatically. "I don't know."

"More specifically?" He piles Town House crackers and cheddar jack on a plate. He knows I'm powerless before cheese.

"I guess—it's like, are Rowie and I together? Like, actually dating, or just equivocating? Clearly I can't even really call it *dating*."

"What does *dating* mean? Do people still do that? I read in magazines that no one in your generation does."

"I don't know." I shove my hands in my hoodie-pocket, flummoxed.

"Is Rowie—out?" he asks, slicing cheese.

"No," I say. "I don't even know if she thinks she's gay. Or one-hundred-percent gay, or bi or whatever. I don't know what to call her, and I don't think she wants to call herself anything. God, why is it harder to know what to *call* things than it is just to do them? Like, if she's different, and I'm different, can't we just decide to call ourselves different the same way?"

Pops smiles sadly at me from the kitchen door. "It's like—what do you call a secret that wants to change its name?"

I open my mouth to say something, then realize he said it. "Yeah."

He motions to me to move the lepidopterary off the TV table and sets down the snack platter.

"Listen to me, little Rockett," he says, feeding me cheese. "I don't know everything. But I know questions like these are better considered after a regular amount of sleep. Take a nap now, and will you please just spend the night in your own bed sometime? Is that really so much to ask if you know you both can stay here?"

"Noof." I work on a hunk of cheddar jack. "Noof, it issnot." I swallow.

"Does Rowie know you told me about the two of you?"

"No," I say. "I promised her I wouldn't tell anyone."

"Really?" he asks. "How long can that reasonably last?"

"That's the question of the hour," I say. "I'm going over there for dinner later, though. Dr. R invited me."

Pops looks mildly hurt. "But I was making coq au vin. And we were bonding."

I lay my head on his shoulder. "I'm hearing you. I just don't want to renege on a nice invitation from Dr. R."

"Fine, go ahead, abandon me and my chicken." He smooths my hair, planting a kiss on my crown. "It'll be better tomorrow anyway. Take a nap on the couch now, while I work."

And we sit there on the couch for two hours, him whittling, me dozing, with the blare of news that isn't really news yet in the background, seeping into my dreams.

Arriving at Rowie's at six, I raise my fist to knock on the door, but before I strike, Lakshmi opens it.

"After dinner, do you guys maybe wanna freestyle for a while?" she blurts out.

"Um," I sputter, trying not to laugh in her face. "Maybe."

"My mom cooked a *ton* for you," she says. "She's a really good cook. That's why my dad married her."

"Really?" I ask. I notice how much more makeup Lakshmi wears than Rowie.

"Yeah." She takes my arm and leads me down the

hall into the kitchen. "You should ask them about it—they really like telling the story."

Before I can solicit more information, we're in the kitchen, where Dr. Priya Rudra has assembled the most awe-inspiring spread of food I've ever seen—all kinds of meats and vegetables bathing in a spectrum of aromatic sauces: green, yellow, orange, oranger, red. Seeing me, she throws down the basket of naan she's holding and comes to embrace me. Raj is sitting at the table, watching us from a short distance.

"Esme!" She squeezes my shoulders. "I hope you came hungry."

"Sure did." I smile, masking my cheddar-jack regret. "Where's Rowie?"

"Ah! She's downstairs trying on a beautiful new sari my mother sent from Bangalore." She leans down the hall. "Rohini! Come up and show me!"

"Is Esme here?" the voice calls back.

"She wants to see, too!" Dr. Rudra calls back, winking at me. "Come up!" I'm not totally sure, but I think I hear a groan from downstairs.

"Can I do anything to help?" I ask.

"Don't be silly!" Dr. Rudra insists. "Sit down." I obey, planting myself at Raj Rudra's right hand.

"Glad you could join us," he greets me. "Chicken?" He offers me a piece of chicken from a pile he's working through.

"I'm good, thanks." I eye his half-masticated wing. "So Lakshmi tells me you married your wife for her food."

He bristles slightly. Lakshmi has an impish look on her face. Did she bait me? Priya turns around with a look of surprise.

He clears his throat. "My younger daughter likes to tell stories." He smiles sternly—I didn't know such a thing was possible, but he does—in Lakshmi's direction. "Yes. It is true. The first time my wife cooked for me, I knew I could not marry her sister."

The story sounds juicy but is interrupted by a flash in the door: Rowie. She's swathed in the most breathtaking sari I've ever seen: deep cerulean, with sequin-patches of aqua. She looks stunning, much older than I've ever seen her look, and much more, I don't know, Indian.

"Aha!" Priya spots her, bustling over to adjust the length of sparkling fabric draped over Rowie's shoulder. "It fits!"

"It's too girly. I'd rather just wear the salwaar kameez Dida sent me last year," Rowie whines. She sees me at the table and blushes. "Hey, dude."

"Hey." I try hard not to blush. "You look—God, you look amazing. Who's Dida?"

"My grandmother," Rowie says. "It's Bengali."

"My sister's daughter is getting married in January," Priya explains, and—do I imagine it?—looks at me queerly. "My mother sent this to Rohini for her to wear to the wedding. And I don't see why having a lovely new sari is such a bad thing. You look marvelous."

"Whatever," Rowie says, plunking down at the table. Raj barks something to her in Bengali. Rolling her eyes, she gets up and begins to unwind the length of fabric from over her shoulder and around her waist. I see the curve of her waist between blouse and skirt gleaming like a violin in the dinnerlight; I struggle not to gasp. She sets the twinkling fabric aside, tucks a napkin into her sari-blouse, and leans back.

"Feed me," she orders her mother.

"Feed yourself!" Priya retorts. "It's all ready. Esme, our guest, please help yourself."

I sidle up to the island and dabble a little bit of everything onto my plate, having a limited idea what I'm eating. Rowie senses my ignorance and appears over my shoulder to narrate the buffet.

"Lamb korma, chicken tikka masala, mattar paneer, aloo gobi, garlic naan, regular naan," she lists, smirking. "She made totally Americanized Indian food for you. She hardly ever cooks meat, and no self-respecting Bengali actually makes chicken tikka masala at home."

"Hush, Rohini," Priya scolds her. "Don't make her uncomfortable, you rude girl."

"I'm just saying, you never cook meat, even when

Dad wants you to." Rowie pops a bite of cauliflower in her mouth.

"It's true, I didn't even know how to cook meat until we came here, really," Dr. Rudra says apologetically. "But here most people eat it, so there, I learned."

"Huzzah," Rowie's dad says through another bite of chicken.

"No, I appreciate it," I say, sitting back down with a heaping plate. "It looks delicious, Dr. Rudra. I'd marry you for your food."

Rowie throws down her fork. "Mimi"—she punches Lakshmi's arm—"you're such a turd." She turns back to me. "She likes to make us all sound like total FOBs in front of unwitting guests."

"Luckily, Esme is like part of our family." Priya smiles gracefully. "I will tell you the whole story. My husband was supposed to marry my oldest sister, Anjali. He was already living in America, and he'd come back to Bangalore to find a wife. My mother told me I had to cook the dinner for when he came to meet her, so I did. I was only eighteen. And then he came and ate with us." She smiles at Raj, nodding for him to continue.

He clears his throat again. "I thought it was the most delicious meal I had ever tasted, even though there was no meat. When I finished, I asked who had prepared the dinner. Her mother said it was Priya, the youngest.

And I said that was the daughter I would marry. But her parents said no, the eldest had to be married first. So I said no, I would not marry Anjali, Priya's sister, and that if they would not let me marry Priya, I would choose a wife from another family. They were offended; they thought I was a very rude dentist to refuse their eldest daughter."

Priya leans forward, her hazel eyes glinting minerally. "But instead, he went back to St. Paul and opened his dental practice and began to write to me. He told me that he was saving money to send to me to come to him. And at first I said no, that I could not disobey my family's wishes for an older man I hardly knew. But then I fell in love with his letters. We wrote to each other for four years while I finished university in India. And then I was accepted to American medical school and I came." She pats his hand and smiles. "It was a love marriage that was the casualty of an arranged marriage."

"So romantic," Lakshmi sighs in wonder. She obviously loves the story.

"Her family did not speak to us for another three years. But when Rohini was born, they relented," Raj finishes simply. I catch my jaw hanging open and snap it closed. He looks back at his plate and resumes eating, scooping up scraps with a hunk of naan.

"Wow," I say. "That's a heckuva story."

Raj's face breaks into a whole smile for the first time. "I love the way people exclaim in Minnesota. It took me a year to figure out how to use *uff-da*."

I crack up. "Yeah, that's a tough one to explain."

"There weren't very many other Indian families in Holyhill when we moved here," Priya says, nodding. "We were like thumbs."

"Sore ones?" I ask.

"Yes." She nods solemnly. "We were the sorest thumbs."

"We still are," Rowie mutters.

"Do you know that when she was six, Rohini told her friends that she was adopted?" Priya laughs. Raj says something else in Bengali; I notice he always admonishes them in his own language. "Raj-ji, it's just a funny story," she soothes him. "I said, 'Rohini, why on earth are you saying that? You are my daughter. I should know. I'm a doctor.'"

"And I said, that's not what *adopted* means. *Adopted* means you were born somewhere else. Like Asia," Rowie says.

"I was so horrified. And tickled," Priya remembers. "I tried to explain that *adopted* means that you were born to one family and raised by another, and that what she was is Indian. And do you know what she said? She said, 'But Mommy, I don't look like anyone but the adopted kids.'"

Rowie gives a strange smile at the memory. "And you said, 'Neither do I.'"

"So, Esme. Are you looking at colleges?" Raj steers the conversation away before I can respond.

The abrupt redirection jars me. "A little bit, mostly smaller liberal arts schools on the East Coast. I'm trying to decide if I want to go same-sex."

Rowie chokes, making a noise so grotesque that her mother immediately gets up and springs into Heimlich position.

"Rohini!" she exclaims. "Are you choking?" She puts both hands to her neck in the universal choking gesture. Rowie shakes her head, getting it together enough to swallow.

"I'm all good," she says, coughing. "Went down the wrong tube."

"I meant—I'm trying to decide whether I want to go to a women's college or not," I offer lamely.

"Yes," Raj responds, his eyes darting back toward Rowie with concern. She pounds some water and mops up the rest of her dinner with her last bit of naan.

"Are you done?" she asks me. I look down at my empty plate and nod.

"Oh, my goodness, look at the time," Priya says. "I have to get to work. Leave the dishes. I can clean them up when I get home." How can Rowie's mom work so much and do so much to take care of all of them? I wonder.

"We're going to go check the elections." Rowie pushes back her chair and rises, dumping her plate in the sink. "C'mon." Her sari-skirt swishes as I follow her out.

"Dinner was fantastic. Thank you so much," I tell Dr. Rudra.

"You're very welcome. Do you want a blanket to take downstairs? I went down to wash some recently and I couldn't find the extra ones that are usually in Rohini's closet," Dr. Rudra says.

I freeze, waiting to see how Rowie will play it, knowing all those extra blankets have been out in the treehouse for at least a month.

"No, we're good," she says. "I know where they are."

"Let's hope we have a state senator who isn't Herb Baumgarten by the time you get home from work," I say, smiling brightly.

Raj says something else in Bengali, but this time he smiles at us. I turn to Rowie.

"What did he say?" I ask.

She pulls the napkin out of her sari blouse, crumples it up, and tosses it affectionately at him. "He said, 'Write big songs.'"

After about an hour of watching TV downstairs, Rowie leads me back upstairs, where I make an audible show of leaving. The door is open a crack in the master bedroom, from which we can already hear the early throttles of Raj's snoring. I walk out the door she holds open, exchanging good-byes, then roll my bike around to the back of the house, hide it, and make my usual labored push through the treehouse door. She brings out her computer to stream audio coverage of the election. We don't talk for a while, processing dinner.

She broaches it first.

"So, you haven't, like, told anyone about us, right?" Rowie asks later in the night.

"No," I reply, winding a little rope of Rowie hair around my finger.

She shakes her head, loosing the strand. Pauses. "Can we not?"

"Can we not what? Tell anybody? Ever?"

"Yeah." She stares at the clapboard wall.

"I mean, yeah, I know you don't want to tell anyone, you tell me that, like, every five minutes. But why are you so hung up on it?" I say, touching her chin with one finger, trying to tilt it back toward me.

"Look, you don't know how it is," she says with an edge of panic in her voice. "There's no way you can understand what it would be like. Kids get thrown out of their houses, just shut the fuck out of their families."

"It's not like that doesn't happen to some kids here."

"But it's not going to happen to *you*."

"It seems like," I say, "it seems like when you say

'my parents,' you mean your dad. And it doesn't seem like your family would turn you out on the mean streets of Holyhill."

She gets quiet for a long time.

"How would you know? Maybe you're right. But you need to know I'm not necessarily—choosing this."

It stings. "Does it really feel like something you chose?"

She slumps over. "No, you're right—it just happened. It chose us. But it's different for you. You don't hate yourself for being—whatever."

"Jesus, Rowie, you shouldn't either." I try to touch her shoulder; she flinches.

"I don't know if I'm actually, like—I mean, I've never—with a guy," Rowie mutters, avoiding me. "You tried it."

I recoil. "Well, I can't help you there, but it's not like anyone's trying to lock you down for life."

"I just never—I never thought this would happen to me. That like, a girl—would happen to me."

"I never thought you'd happen to me either."

"But it's *different* for you," she rasps, whispering as loudly as she can, exasperated. "You knew you wanted it to happen, or something. You were ready."

"Are you kidding?" I cry. She clamps a hand over my mouth, her eyes widening. I try to kiss her hand.

She clenches harder. I give her a conciliatory look with my eyes: *okay, okay.* She releases.

"Rowie, where the fuck did you get the demented idea that I was ready for this?" I hiss. "Are you for fucking real? This is like a fourteen-wheeler careening across the highway of my life. No one could be ready for this."

"I just really don't think I'm all-the-way gay." Rowie rolls over on her away side.

"Call it what you want, honey, but let's talk about it later," I breathe, trying to kiss her neck. Faceless talking heads chatter quietly in the background, tallying counts.

She turns away. "I don't mean it like I'm not into you. I'm really into you. You know that. Maybe if we were in college, or even just not in my *house* . . ." She trails off.

"Maybe what? Maybe you'd be gayer? Yo, do you ever think you might be underestimating your mom just a little bit? Because she's pretty much the most understanding person I've ever met. She disobeyed her parents."

"Fool, you think that means she'd be psyched I'm taking away from SAT study time to hook up on the sly? With a *girl*? Get real."

"Still," I take her hand and put it on the side of my face so she can feel me talking. "Haven't you ever wondered if she already knows?"

"She can't." Rowie shudders. "Look, my dad only has opinions about things every once in a while. But when he does, there's no moving him. And having a daughter with a girlfriend would definitely be one of those times." This is the first time Rowie's ever used the word *girlfriend*.

"Ro, I gotta say, I am so fucking sick of you talking about your parents—"

Before I can finish my sentence, we hear a bark from outside. Rowie freezes.

"Did you hear that?" I say. "It sounded like it's right below us."

She opens the floor door and peeks down into the yard. We hear the bark again. A puggle bark.

"You've got to be kidding me," she moans. "It's fucking Stinker."

"Stinker, you little shit!" I whisper-yell down to the dog. "Why are you always spying on my makeout spots?" Stinker's intrusion brings me back to Charlie Knutsen's Camry, which suddenly feels like a very long time ago.

"Christ," she says. Stinker yaps again, wagging his tail in excitement as he notices us noticing him. "What are we supposed to do? We can't call Tess."

"What do you mean, we can't call Tess?" I snap. "Why would she think it was weird that we're hanging out? Jesus, how fucking paranoid *are* you?"

Just then, we hear a voice in the middle distance. "Stinker! Stinks!"

"Shit," Rowie cusses under her breath, pulling the floor door partially closed.

"Stinker, where are you?" There's no mistaking; it's definitely Tess's voice.

I throw up my hands. "What do you want to do?"

"I don't know," she hisses. "Stay here." She shoves on her shoes and shimmies down the ladder. I pull the floor door open a crack and lie belly-down by it to listen.

"Ro!" I hear Tess shout as she sees her.

"I've got his collar—don't worry," Rowie calls weakly.

"Thank goodness." Tess jogs up to them, out of breath. "I left the door open while I was taking out the trash and he bolted before I could grab him. Stinker, you jerk."

"Stinker, you jerk," Rowie echoes.

"What were you doing out here in the cold?" Tess asks. "Oh, cheese and rice, Stinker, I didn't bring a bag with me—stop pooping."

"Oh," Rowie says. "Well. I was—I had to grab something from the treehouse."

Neither of them says anything for a tick. I suddenly become aware of the audio election coverage still droning from Rowie's computer. I slam the computer shut.

"What was that?" I hear Tess ask. Fuck.

"What?" The crisis in Rowie's voice is audible. "What was what?"

"It sounded like there was a radio or something on in your treehouse, and someone shut it off," Tess says suspiciously. Shit.

"No, it didn't."

"Ro, why are you being so weird? Your hair looks like you just woke up."

"Oh, I mean—I just like to go up there sometimes. To be—by myself."

Stinker yips. "You go outside to sit in your tree-house alone in November?" Tess isn't buying it, Rowie's teetering on the edge of her rails, and I hear it all.

"Rowie, is someone up there?" The edge in Tess's voice is gentle. "Who is it?"

"No," Rowie's voice catches. "There's nobody up there." It feels like a bowling ball slamming into my gut, hearing her call me *nobody*. I only hear muffled noises for a minute.

"Ro, why are you crying? I'm so confused," Tess says. "What did I say?"

This is it; the jig's up. I can't sit here and hide while she cries and feel okay about myself in the morning. I take a deep breath and poke my head out through the floor door.

"Hey, Tessie."

"Ez?" she says in disbelief. "What are *you* doing up there? Why are you guys hanging out in the treehouse at night when it's so co—" She catches herself, coughing, clearing her throat, pausing. I pull a blanket around my shoulders and work my way down to the ground. The moon is out and shining on the tears streaming down Rowie's face.

"Are you guys—uh, I mean, were you guys—?" Tess doesn't finish her sentence again, but doesn't really need to. All she has to do is look at us to know. She caught us and right now all I can feel, at least when I don't look at Rowie, is relief.

"I'm sorry—" Tess says. "I didn't mean to—I mean, I'm sorry I—*fuck*."

"Wow," I say as Rowie's sobs escalate, "I can't remember the last time you dropped a heavy *F*."

"I'm sorry," Rowie heaves.

"What are *you* sorry for?" Tess and I say in unison.

"I don't know," Rowie says, her shoulders slumped. She turns and dashes back up into the treehouse. Tess looks at me, shell-shocked.

"Is she okay? Are *you* okay? Are you guys, like, together? What the heck is going on right now?"

"Listen, Tessie, could we talk about this later?" I say. "I'll explain later. I just want to make sure she's all right, and I don't want to wake up Raj."

"Yeah—" Tess hovers. "Okay. I'll take Stinker home. We can talk later." She turns to go, then turns back in continuing disbelief. "Why didn't you tell us?"

I look desperately at her. "Isn't that kind of obvious?"

"Yeah," she says. "Wow. I mean, go take care of her. I'll talk to you later, I guess. Bye, Ez." She withdraws bumblingly across the quiet lawns, Stinker in tow.

I climb back up to the treehouse. Rowie's quivering like a bomb.

"What are we going to do?" she wails. "This is a disaster."

"You know what, Rowie? This isn't actually a disaster. You really think us being in love is the biggest problem in the whole world right now?"

There is another detonating pause as Rowie and I both digest the fact that the word *love* has entered the conversation, spoken out loud. She stares at the wall, receding. The silence is gravid.

"Tell you what," I explode, too tired to hold it back anymore. "I don't give a fuck anymore. I love you. I am in love with you. I can't help it, and I don't want to. And I'm sick and fucking tired of sneaking around and acting like I'm ashamed of something I refuse to be ashamed of. I would—we could tell people together. It couldn't possibly be as bad as you think. I love you and I *want* people to know." Everything is spinning.

Rowie looks like she's about to throw up. "Can you *please* keep your voice down?" Her voice is feeble but trembling with intensity; the moonlight throws a twinkle into the tiny jewel in her nose. She doesn't say anything else.

"Look, Rowie, we've been slinking around for nearly two months pretending this is something we can keep close forever." Fuck. Please don't let me cry. "I can't lie about it anymore. It's—it's too much to ask. Please tell me I don't have to." *Please* don't let me cry.

"I'm sorry." Her voice is the size of a bird's heart.

"Sorry for what? Sorry you don't love me?"

"I didn't—Esme, I didn't say that. God, it's so cold out here. I can't think straight." She shivers.

"Look, Rowie, every time this comes up, this issue of us being out as a couple, you give me some lame excuse about your parents, and frankly, I'm not sure if I believe it anymore. I don't believe your mom would freak out. Maybe your dad would, but you know what? At the end of the day, with something like this, you either decide it's worth the trouble or it isn't, and it's your decision. I get that you don't want to disrespect your parents, and I get that being Bengali is a big part of who you are, and I get that I just don't get it."

"Did you ever think that maybe it isn't my job to help you understand what it means to be Indian, or

227

a person of color, or whatever?" Rowie snaps. "I can't purge your white guilt for you, snowflake. You're right. You just don't get it. You never will. And I've started to wish you'd stop trying."

I recoil, as wounded by that as by anything she's ever said to me. "Stop *trying*?! But Ro—I love who you are. Maybe I can't understand, but—why am I here, Rowie? Tell me why you're so ashamed of this, what it is that happens between us that's so disgusting you can't even tell your family or your best friends. Tell me why I let you in on me if you were this full of shit all along."

She says something I can't hear. I reach out and lift her chin.

"What did you say?"

"I said *I never asked you to*." Her eyes are twin shimmering wells of grief.

"Are you fucking serious?" I can't stop pushing. How can she say this to me?

She throws up her hands.

"I'm not ashamed." Her voice is still faint but her eyes flash. "I'm *not* ashamed. But I can't give you the kind of love you need."

"You mean the kind that other people know about?" I ask bitterly.

She turns to me slowly.

"I don't want to lose you," she murmurs. "I've never been like this with anyone else. But I just can't do it—out loud. I just—I'm not sure enough that this is what I want to fuck it all and be with you. You know who you are, Esme. What you are. What you want. I'm not so certain."

We lay there doing nothing for a minute as the cold sets in. I feel like wishbones are snapping inside me as I feel her abating, one after another coming up short-ended. I break the silence in a final flight of desperation.

"Look, Rowie, or Rohini, whoever you are," I implore her. "Hear me out for one more minute. Imagine what this could be like if we could go on an actual date. Imagine just going out and eating dinner some-where and going a movie together, and making out in the back row of the theater like couples do. I don't want our whole relationship to exist in a treehouse. I want to take you to school dances and have you sleep over at my house sometimes and hold hands in front of our friends and not have you make weird faces every time I try to touch you. I just want to not have to hide this beautiful thing we made together. All I want is for you to be my girlfriend, for real. It's that simple." I suck in some air.

Her hair muffles something else I can't hear.

"Girl, raise up your head!" I sputter, exasperated.

"I SAID I NEVER ASKED YOU TO COME HERE," she bursts, hissing in fierce red tones that liquefy into tearful blues. "You are so focused on getting what you want that you're not listening to me. I'm saying I love you and I can't do this. I *do* love you and it can't stop me from failing you, or you from failing me. I can't be your girlfriend. I'm sorry." She takes a heaving breath. "I think you should leave now."

You.

I'm sweating.

I'm going to cry.

I'm going to throw up.

I'm going to crap my pants.

I need to bolt now with the three shards of pride I have left.

I will leave this treehouse immediately. Forever.

"Okay—" I say, starting to get up. "Look, I'm gonna—"

She starts to cry again and grabs my arm, pulling me down without saying anything. I bury my face in her hair, toppling back over in the mess of blankets as we sob, quiet sirens crying like the lostest of the lost, lonesome together in the severing hour.

"Don't do this, Rowie," I mewl. "You did ask me to come here, the first night we kissed. Please—can't you see it? It could be real."

She's shaking her head *no, no, no.* I feel vague, robbed of victory.

"I can't," she says, two syllables. "You're strong. You can handle it. I can't. Will you please leave?"

You.

There is a buzzing in my ears, a dim din of anger and a deeper disappointment than I've felt since I was five, a hum like the phantom ring you hear the moment after a phone stops ringing. I can't believe she's chickening out, and at the same time, I can.

"Fuck you, Rowie," I manage without dignity. It's a frayed blur as I split, struggling with my jacket, both of us crying, my hair sticking to her face, swallowing. She lets out a strange yelp as I retreat. Her arm is outstretched as though I were a boat pulling away in the night, like longing from a dark dock. I close the floor door to her. I climb dumbly down the tree trunk, stopping my ears to the celebratory racket from the Baumgarten house leaking into the night, and barely prevent myself from screaming as I hurdle toward home.

III.

All true quests end in this garden, where the spilt fruit pours forth blood and the halved fruit is a full bowl for travellers and pilgrims. To eat of the fruit means to leave the garden because the fruit speaks of other things, other longings. So at dusk you say goodbye to the place you love, not knowing if you can ever return, knowing you can never return by the same way as this. It may be, some other day, that you will open a gate by chance, and find yourself again at the other side of the wall.

—Jeanette Winterson, *Oranges Are Not the Only Fruit*

CHAPTER ELEVEN

Mixed Histories, or Don't Call Me That

Marcy and I are testing the ice sheet on the creek with our feet. It's Wednesday afternoon; I hear church bells tossing hollow echoes across the plains.

"Who goes to church on Wednesday?" I ask.

"Catholics, duh," she says.

"Huh," I say.

"Wanna go steal some signs?"

"Eh." I shrug listlessly. "Maybe later."

The wind bites and the winter light clouds over the patchwork of white frost and dead brown earth. Brittle Creek runs through her backyard; it was a source of endless fascination when we were younger, swimming in the summer and boot hockey in the winter. As we probe the half-frozen sheet, daring it to crack under our leaning, I feel an awareness of seasons, of the ache that comes when seasons change.

"Hey, dirtbag. What's with you? Where were you today?" she asks.

"Just wasn't really feeling school. I had some things to do."

"Like building a secret annex and hiding in it? You showed up to like one class all day."

I squirm. "Okay. I have to tell you something and I don't know how to put it."

"Put what? Just put it."

"It's about Rowie."

"What about Rowie? She's been totally AWOL, too."

"Yeah. Um."

Marcy throws a stray rock into the river in frustration. "Spit it the fuck out, Ez."

"We could ice-fish through that hole," I say, misdirecting, pointing at where the rock went through.

"Esme."

Marcy very rarely uses my whole name. We're always just Ez and Marce.

"Mary Marcella, I really don't know what to say. Remember the night we ripped off that joint of Rooster's and smoked it in the treehouse, and you left early?"

"Yeah."

"Well. After you left, Rowie and I were talking and realized that neither of us had ever kissed a girl."

"Why would Rowie have kissed a girl?"

"Um," I say.

Marcy searches my face. "What are you trying to tell me?"

"Um, I guess—fuck. I don't know how to—I mean, I haven't ever really told—oh, fuck all. Rowie and I made out that night in the treehouse, and we've been hooking up on the DL ever since, until last night Tess caught us and Rowie freaked out and I realized that she would never be able to handle being my girlfriend." I start getting choked up and try to wipe the tears off before she notices.

"Holy shit, Ez," she says, looking at me incredulously for a full ten seconds. "Are you serious?"

I nod.

"Is that why you've looked like a zombie for, like, two months?"

I nod.

"Shit," she breathes, understanding dawning across her face. She shifts from standing on the bank with one leg arched onto a rock like a pirate to a flabbergasted sprawl in the snow, her heels resting on the ice.

"Say something," I insist with what little insistence I have left in me.

She drags her heels over the ice, tracing a snow-angel arc on the creek.

"Something, Ezbo," she says.

"Don't call me that." I kick the ice and it cracks like crème brûlée under a spoon. My toe breaks through, dipping into the searing freezing water, and I stumble back onto the frozen bank. "I think I hear my dad calling."

"Bitch, please." Marcy grabs my sleeve, pulling her feet under her. "You can't pull this shit on me. I'm a shitbag with emotions too, but quit with the cactus act and fucking come in for some hot chocolate."

"Okay," I sniff.

Marcy drags me across her backyard and into the kitchen, where we stomp off our shoes and leave our wet jackets in a pile on the floor.

"Is Bob here?" I ask.

She shakes her head as she takes a swig from the milk carton. "Practice." She exhales, wiping a renegade drip from her chin. She dumps the milk into a saucepan to heat up. My phone beeps.[57]

"I'm, um — I'm sorry I didn't tell you sooner," I say. "Rowie, like, couldn't really deal with people knowing about us." I take a breath, still unsure how to talk about Rowie and me to anyone other than Rowie or me.

"Don't trip," she says. "I mean, I understand, or whatever. At least now I know why you never sleep over anymore."

It dawns on me how displaced Marcy must have felt while Rowie and me were — whatever we were. I've

57. Text from Tess: *How are you doing, babe?*

spent so much cumulative time at the Crowthers' over the years that I actually have my own set of dishes here. Me and Marcy were really picky about what we ate and what we ate it on when we were little, so Bob and Luke had to team up and provide full sets of diningware for both girls at both houses to appease us. She hands me my #1 Grandpa mug and I pinch a marshmallow out of the cocoa. Marcy's drinking out of her 1991 Twins World Series Champions mug.

"Are you, like, okay?" she asks abruptly.

"I don't really know," I say. "I guess I just needed to say it out loud more than anything. It was really hard not to tell you while it was happening."

"Yeah," she says. "It was hard not to know why you looked so sad."

"Marce?" I ask.

"Yeah?"

"I know we don't usually talk about stuff like this, but—do you believe in God?"

She takes a long pause. "I do my best to remember that I am loved. The source is less important." For a long moment, I am washed over by a wave of intense love for Marcy, the longest-running female lead in the sitcom of my life. I take her for granted the way I take my ability to read for granted. Not for nothing, we're the only sisters we've got.

"I love you, Marce," I blurt out. "I know we don't

really say that, but I don't know. I guess I need us to say it sometimes."

She returns my long look. "I love you too, Ez," she says. "I can deal with us saying that sometimes."

"I won't tell anyone if you won't," I say, grinning.

"Deal." She grins back.

"I gotta jet," I say, rising.

"To do what?" Marcy scoffs. "I know you're not going to do homework."

I crack a grin. "If I did my homework now, what would I do during the first five minutes of every class?"

"Dude—I don't want to push you or whatever, but when there's no talking happening, there's no sweet beats and fat rhymes happening either. . . ." She trails off meaningfully.

Nope. Not yet.

"Nope. Not yet."

"I'm just *saying,* we got some good momentum going after the LocoMotive, and your on-camera interview about Hip-Hop for Heteros and Homos, and you had that new song you showed us on your birthday, and we were talking about having a concert. . . . Come *on,* Ez. Don't let all this drama get in the way of our dream."

"Give me a little time." I tip my hat on my way out. "Later, homes."

"Minnesota-do-or-die, soldier."

Marcy lives on the eastern border of Holyhill's west

side, near the highway and the big Lutheran church and the old Soo Line train tracks, a ways away from the big houses in the old-money part of town. I plug myself into my iPod and start walking, Black Star trickling into my ears. It's barely four o'clock, but the sun is indistinct, as if afraid of wearing out his welcome. I begin to climb the spiral-ramped bike path up to the bridge over the highway, and a twinge of hunger reminds me I haven't eaten in a while. I look down at the highway: the traffic is thickening as the giant arched streetlights begin their neon flicker into the evening. This was Marcy's and my favorite place to hide growing up, a perch in plain sight that no one can really get a good look at.

Twilight has settled around the cold midday and that frozen-eardrum feeling starts to set in; I don't want to go home, but it's getting time to stop in somewhere and thaw out. My favorite diner, Home on the Range, is a few more blocks north, and my pace quickens as visions of bottomless chicken noodle soup dance in my head. Minnesota: the only place on earth that'll give you free refills on pop *and* soup. The green-and-pink Art Deco sign beckons and I have a rush of hoping I don't run into anyone I know. The bell jangles as I duck in out of the cold.

"Just me," I tell the fifty-something waitress in the white button-down dress, holding up one finger. "I can sit at the counter."

"Any place you want, honey," she says through her gum, ripping off a ticket and slapping it next to my knife. I plop down, seizing in a thaw-shiver as I unwind my scarf and coat. The diner's been alive in Holyhill three times as long as I have and has a pleasant old-timey tone: cue the red-and-white plastic checkered tablecloths, cue the Everly Brothers on the jukebox. The weekday crowd is brimming with young families toting boxy bags of hockey gear and early-bird seniors stirring steaming mugs of decaf. I see a pair of old ladies sharing a spotted cow milkshake and laughing in a booth by the window, and it shoots me through with missing Rowie. Mom took me here for my birthday breakfast right before she left. All I remember is that she had oatmeal with Craisins.

"Somethin' to drink, doll?" Her name tag says *Marjean* and she has what you'd call kind eyes behind her bent wire glasses.

"Can I have a Coke, please?" I reply as she tries to hand me a menu. "No, thanks, I don't need it. Could I just also please have a bowl of chicken noodle soup?"

"You bet. Want some crackers with that?"

"Yes, ma'am. And could you put an orange slice in the Coke?"

She looks up from her pad and smiles. "Sure thing, honey. Back in a jiff."

I rummage around in my backpack for a book. I can't remember what I've got in here today. Catching the edge of something, I grab it and pull out. It's Mom's grimy old copy of *A Tree Grows in Brooklyn*. Eureka! I thought I'd lost it, but it turns out it was just buried in this old bag, which I haven't used in a while. Salt-and-peppery Marjean returns with my Coke and orange, but I barely look up, immersed in my favorite passage of *ATGIB:*

> *It was at Thanksgiving time that Francie told her first organized lie, was found out and determined to be a writer.*

It wasn't until a few years ago that it hit me how obvious it was why I loved books like this and the Annes (Frank, Green Gables) in my early years of loving books: they all had that telltale smack of autobiography, of authors re-envisioning themselves as little girls lost in their imaginations who dream of growing up to be writers. I think it's strange that Francie can't figure out how to tell the truth in writing. I can't figure out how to tell the truth without it. I copy the passage down in my notebook, not wanting to lose it again.

"Soup's on!"

Marjean interrupts my trance with a steaming bowl of luscious noodly broth and whips a fistful of saltines out of her apron. I hear the bells over the door clanging behind her as she sets down the bowl and I thank her. A familiar peal of laughter floats through the entryway, and in the mirror above the grill I'm facing, I see Tess and her little brother, Anthony, stripping their winter gear, the right arm of Anthony's flannel shirt hanging slack beside him. Even though my back's to them, there's no way I can avoid her; she's ten feet away from me. I see her freeze in the mirror as she recognizes the back of my head. I meet her eyes in the mirror, acknowledging that we're both here and we both know it. She takes a few steps toward me.

"Can't stop running into you lately," she says, straining to make it sound like a joke.

"Hey," I reply, not having come up with anything else yet.

"Hey, Esme!" Anthony waves to me with his good arm, which is to say his only arm. "I haven't seen you in forever! How are you?"

I have a serious soft spot for Anthony; I always have. He's thirteen now, in the same class as Lakshmi Rudra.

"How's it going, little G?" I low-five him. "You keeping it real?"

"You know it." He grins. "Come eat with us! We'll get a booth and you can bring over your soup."

Tess and I are caught in silence for an awkward moment.

"Anthony, didn't you say you had to go to the bathroom?" Tess says.

"Uh—yeah. Be right back." He doesn't know what he did wrong, and his face flickers in confusion before he obeys, disappearing. Another moment passes before either of us speaks.

"Join us," Tess says. "I've been thinking about you all day."

"Naw, that's okay," I say. "I've kinda got my own little jam going here." I hold up the book.

"Don't be like that," Tess says. "I feel terrible about busting in on you guys like that last night. I had no idea what was going on, or that it would—blow up so hard."

"I know. It wasn't your fault," I say. "Have you talked to her?"

"Not really," Tess says. "She barely looked me in the eye today." She winces. "Look, I gotta tell you something, and I feel really wretched about it."

My stomach sinks. "What?"

"I—um. I went to Bible study today because I wanted to say a prayer for you guys, and Mary Ashley cornered me afterward."

"And?"

Tess takes a deep breath. "Dude, she told me that Nordling thinks that 4H was behind the whole day of goats and Crisco, that we like did the whole thing ourselves just so we could get on TV, and I was like, that's ridiculous, and she was like, yeah, but how do you know and why are you trying to protect a bunch of lesbians, and I was like, because they're my best friends, and she was like, oh, so you're saying they *are* lesbians? Is that why you were praying for them? And I was like, no, well, and I sort of stuttered, and she just sort of caught me and was like who's gay in your group? Is it Esme Rockett? Who's she hooking up with, it's gotta be either Marcy Crowther or that weird Indian girl, it's so obvious, and I was like, why do you always assume Marcy's gay, it's so narrow-minded of you, and she was like, so it is that Indian girl! And by that time I was so confused that I just paused too long, and she was like, I know it's Esme and that girl Rowie, everyone knows they're hooking up, tell me if it's true and I'll tell Nordling the whole day of chaos wasn't your fault." She runs out of air as I struggle to comprehend what she's telling me.

"So—did you tell her?" My stomach feels like it's going to drop out of me.

"I didn't exactly tell her. She was just talking so fast, and I'm so bad at lying when people ask me direct questions, and she just sort of—*guessed,* I guess."

Home on the Range suddenly becomes as claustrophobic as a beehive, alive with lunatic buzzing. "Jesus. I—look, I'm sorry, but I really can't deal with this right now." I take a five-spot out of my wallet and throw it on the counter.

"Please don't bail," Tess sputters. "Just come finish

246

your soup with me and my brother. There has to be a way for us to talk this out."

"I can't believe you told Mary Ashley," I sputter. "That's like the same thing as just putting it in the newspaper."

"I didn't mean to!" Her eyes start to well up and my need to bolt increases. "Esme, I don't *care* that you're gay, or that Rowie is, if she even is. You guys have been totally distant, and I didn't know what was going on, and I just felt kind of—I don't know, kind of left out in the dark or something. I tried to talk to Rowie, but she just shut down. I was—I was really overwhelmed, okay?" She's red-faced and emotional, and a few curious early birds are starting to watch us.

"It was overwhelming for *you*?" I stammer in disbelief. "I tell you what. Why don't you go back to Bible study and puzzle over other people's lives until you're blue in the fucking face. Because the person I love is gone, and thanks to you and your gossiping little bigot friends, there's absolutely no chance that she's going to come back, and frankly, I really don't feel like talking about it anymore."

I start to huff myself into my coat and scarf, knowing she doesn't really deserve this, pretending not to notice her eyes brimming over with tears. I hear a little boy throw down his fork and whine, "Mommy, why we come here?" Tess doesn't seem to hear.

Anthony returns. He gives us both a searching look. "Are you guys okay?" he asks uncomfortably.

Tess tries a smile for him. "A-train, why don't you grab a booth and order your cheeseburger. I'll be over in a minute."

He pouts. "You guys are acting weird."

"Sorry, kiddo," I say.

"Hey, Esme?" he asks timidly.

"Yeah, Anthony?"

"It sucks to be different sometimes, huh?" I turn, astonished, to him, and regard his empty sleeve.

I sigh. "Yeah, babe, it does." Maybe we don't actually understand things better as we get older. Maybe we understood them more clearly before.

"I don't care that you're gay. And I'm sorry Rowie decided she wasn't."

I gape at Tess. "Even *he* knows?"

"Anthony, go get a table," she snaps.

"Fine," he groans, making himself scarce again.

"I get that you're mad, and confused, and scared," she says. "And I'm so sorry about everything. Just—please don't shut me out like this."

"I'm not," I say dumbly, fumbling to get my backpack together. "I just—I need some time to think. I'll call you." The clamor of the doorbells alarms me as I stumble out into the first snow of the season.

▼ ▼ ▼

The next day at school, it takes me approximately one hour to figure out that the big gay cat is out of the bag. It's like that nightmare where you get to school and realize you're buck fucking naked, like all the locker crowds are whispering your name. Between first and second periods, some mousy girl whose name I don't even know ambushes me in the commons.

"Are you Esme Rockett?" she asks.

"Yeah," I reply hesitantly.

"You're totally gay, right?"

"I don't see how that's any of your—" I run out of words, confounded. Fuck it. "Yes. Will you go away now?"

"Yup!" she cries gleefully, scampering back to her crew of tittering cronies.

Mrs. DiCostanza has been majorly cracking down on cell phones in her class lately, so secret messages have to be conveyed through old-fashioned note writing. Thursday's third period is shitty with them; they're flying back and forth with more audacity than most people usually dare in front of Mrs. D. None of the unsubtle glances in my direction escape me, and neither does Rowie's iron-fixed stare at the whiteboard. Exasperated, I finally grab one of the pieces of paper as it passes from Mary Ashley Baumgarten to one of her minions and read it. It seems to be a collaborative list of sorts, in four different handwritings:

HAVE YOU BEEN MACKED ON BY ESME ROCKETT?

1. *She totally checked me out while I was changing at the Holyhill Pool once.*

2. *She tried to kiss me at Tess Grinnell's birthday party in seventh grade.*

3. *She and Marcy Crowther once asked me if I wanted to go lesbo threesies.*

Everyone's watching for my reaction. I won't give way. None of it's even true.

"Esme?" Mrs. D. asks gently. "Give that here, please."

Not knowing what else to do, I dumbly hand over the note. She reads it, her face tensing.

"Anyone else I see passing notes," she says in a low, seething voice, "is going straight to the principal's office with my recommendation for an immediate suspension. Now, quit it with the emotional subterfuge, girls, and *read*."

The rest of the class passes like a funeral, long and surreal. The bell sounds and I bolt out of my chair.

"Esme," Mrs. D. calls after me. "Hang back for a minute." The bitch clique explodes into a rash of giggles, dashing out as I slump in place. I watch Rowie slide out with her head down and my heart feels like it's being suctioned out of my chest. Tess makes a *call me* motion with her fingers as she walks out. Mrs. D. waits until everyone leaves, then turns to me with the most genuine look of compassion I've seen all day.

"Do you want to talk about anything?" she asks, placing a hand on my shoulder.

"Um." I try to find something to say. "I'm gay."

She nods, not reacting. "How did they find out?"

"I don't know."

"How are you feeling about it?"

I'm at a loss. Like I live in the zoo? Like a girl in a cerulean sari broke my heart? Like God shat on my face?

"Out," I say, throwing up my hands and turning to leave.

On my way out at the end of the day on Friday, I'm pumping my bike through the parking lot when I hear a lilting voice call my name. I look over and see Yusuf and Jane Njaka waving at me from a blue Buick rust bucket, and roll over to their window.

"Hey," I greet them dully.

"How's your day been?" Jane asks sympathetically, like she doesn't really need to ask.

"Oh, well—fucking awful." I look down at my filthy Chuck Taylors.

"Get in, girl," Yusuf instructs me.

"I better get—"

"We weren't asking," Jane insists. "Get in. We're not going anywhere." I lean my bike up against the Buick and crawl in the back. The car stanks of weed.

"Here." Yusuf hands back a bowl.

"I shouldn't—" I start, then fail to come up with a compelling reason why I shouldn't. "Fuck it. Thanks. It's been one of those weeks."[58] He lights it for me and I take a long hit, then cough. I offer it to Jane.

"No, thanks, I don't dabble."

Yusuf swivels to face me. "Hate parade getting you down?"

"Christ on a bike," I marvel. "I feel like this story's already hit the *West Wind*. Does literally everyone know?"

Jane and Yusuf nod in unison.

"Hate to be the bearer of bummers, girl," Jane admits, "but—yeah."

"This is bad," I say, reaching for another toke.[59]

Jane searches my face. "So you and Rowie, huh? I can't believe she started seeing that loser Prakash Banerjee just to convince everyone she isn't gay."

The buzzing takes over my head again.

"What did you say?"

"I said I can't—" The realization of her mistake, the magnitude of it, spreads across Jane's face like

58. Text from Tess: *Girl, where you at??*

59. Another one: *Can we talk?*

gathering clouds. "Oh, my gosh, you didn't know. Esme, I'm so incredibly sorry. I had no idea—I thought you'd heard. I thought you must have heard already. I'm so sorry."

"Rowie's—Rowie's *with* Prakash Banerjee? We broke up, like seventy-two hours ago." The shaking starts at my center, radiating outward like the shock waves of a pebble upsetting a lake.

Jane claps her hand over her mouth. "I'm so sorry. I didn't mean to—"

"I have to go." There's no fight left in me, only flight.

When I get onto my bike, it's starting to snow again and I'm blind all over. Rowie's getting with *Prakash Banerjee?* Prakash of the Magic cards, Prakash of the very Bible group that outed her? It has to be reactionary. I mean, she *has* to be dating him just to convince everyone that she isn't gay, because unless Prakash's packing some major Hindu heat in those khaki Dockers, ain't no other reason to hit that. I don't know how I manage to make it home, but by the time I do, I'm soaked through with snowmelt.

"Kidlet, what's wrong?" Pops asks in the kitchen, seeing my disastrous state.

My vision is blurring. "Rowie's dating some douchebag just because he has a dick," I warble, losing it.

Pops sinks into a chair in sympathy. "Oh, honey. Did you finally talk to her?"

"No. I had to hear it through the fucking grapevine. Listen, I know you wanted me to get a high-school degree and all, but I am *never* going to school again. My life is *over*."

"Calm down," he says, pulling me into a seat and hugging my head as I sob. "Shh. It's gonna be okay."

"No it's *not*," I insist, disintegrating further. "I got busted out of the closet without my consent, and everyone else treats me like I'm a fucking leper. All the girls act like I'm just some big lesbo perv who's going to hell for trying to mack on them all damn day, everyone knows more about my love life than I do, and the only girl I've ever loved would rather date some ugly knock-kneed freak *dude* than be with me in public. Can I *please* go to college now?"

"Baby, you have to breathe." Pops strokes my hair, his chest lifting as he guides me through a breath. "Good. Take another one." Inhale. Exhale.

"How can I go back there?" I whimper. "I'm serious. I can transfer my AP credits to the U and finish the rest of the classes I need for the equivalency test there."

"Let's not get ahead of ourselves," he says gently, sighing. "I was so afraid this was going to happen."

"What do you mean?" I sniffle.

He hesitates, searching for the right way to say it. "Ever since you told me it was her you were seeing, and that she didn't want anyone else to know, I was always a little afraid that Rowie would never be able to love you the way you deserve to be loved, and that you'd get hurt."

"Cool," I say. "It might have been nice of you to mention that before. I mean, if in your infinite wisdom you knew it was all going to turn out shitty."

Pops sighs. "You're in pain, and you're lashing out, and that's okay. It's healthy to let it out, but there's no need to be nasty, babes. You have no idea how awful it is for me to see you hurting like this."

"Women are *bullshit*. Why do they all leave, Pops?" I say. "Why was she ashamed of me?"

"Listen to me," Pops says with gravity. "You are the most beautiful and amazing seventeen-year-old badass I've ever known in my entire life, and no one with half a brain would ever be anything but proud and lucky to love you. Rowie's not ashamed of you. She's afraid of herself. It's not your fault. You deserve to be loved for exactly who you are, and I'm sorry the best school district in the state is full of assholes, and I promise—I *promise* you—that you are going to come out of all this even more beautiful and amazing than you went into it. And then you can go to college. You can't do everything you want to do and be young all at the same time."

"AAAARRRRGGGGHHH," I roar into his waffle-knit shirt.

"Hush, hush, my parakeet." He strokes my head, shushing me. "This will all be better tomorrow, I swear.

And better yet the next day. Oh, hush, love. You are my *child*, Esme. You are an artist. Use all the ugliness you're feeling to make something beautiful. Don't you know that you're the most amazing artist I've ever met?"

"What about the time you met Leonard Cohen in San Francisco?" I mumble into his shoulder.

"Pshaw." He tosses the thought away, rocking me back and forth the way he used to do when I was little and scared. "You are a hundred times prettier than Leonard Cohen, and more talented to boot. You have to just open your mouth and let this all out. You did the most sacred human thing in the world—you fell in love with another human being. I know how it feels to lose that."

I look up at him; his face is blurry through my tears. "How—how did you get over Mom?"

"I'll never get over her. I've forgiven her, the best I can, and I've moved forward, and the only way I've done that is by remembering that love . . . creates things. You were created by love, for one," he says.

"Ew," I respond feebly.

"Oh, get over it," he says, mussing my hair. "But you have to use the love you still have for Rowie to create some things yourself. You fell in love. That's brave. Find the courage it took to do that and use it to write something that makes other people *feel* something. It isn't just about getting everyone's attention, about shocking people and making them laugh. It's about giving people a reason to think about something they've never thought about before, something only you can make people consider. It's about moving people, honey. About telling your truth." He puts a hand to my cheek, his eyes crinkling. "I know you can do it. You move me every day."

"I can't rap without Rowie." It's the first time I've said it out loud.

"You can. And you will. Because you have to give things away. Give yourself away."

I take a big breath. "I don't know how."

"Just try. Try to *make* something out of all of this, and it won't fix everything, but I promise you will start to feel better. Do you understand what I'm saying?"

"I think so," I say. "I love you no shit, Pops."

"You bet your best bunch of bananas I love you no shit. Do you want some tuna salad?"

"Pickles and onions and lots of mayo?" I say, taking another shuddering breath and trying to smile.

"Pickles and onions and lots of mayo," he says, smiling back.

CHAPTER TWELVE

Give Yourself Away

Dear Mom,

For the last few days, all I've been doing is bailing on all the people I love. I guess I probably learned that from you. But Yom Kippur was a few weeks ago, and since then I've been thinking about atonement.

I'm thinking about actually sending this letter.

I'm mad at you. Mad at you for being too nuts to handle anything, for leaving me stranded as a Jew in the Christian heartland, for not even sticking around to tell me how to be a Jew, or how to be anything, really. When you left, it felt like a chandelier crashing from heaven to the ocean floor and taking me with it. The noise it made was people talking. There were crazy rumors: that you'd run off with our gymnastics coach, that Pops kicked you out for beating me, that you died on the operating table during a botched boob job. Only Pops and I knew that the difference between those stories and what actually happened was that in all of the made-up shit, there was an explanation for why you left.

Why am I thinking so much about childhood, about you, about when you used to be here? Did you know I once got attacked by a Canada goose? It was the autumn after you left: Pops and I were taking a walk around the lake, and Make Way for Ducklings was my favorite book. I was mesmerized by this mama goose and her baby goslings, and I kept trying to get close to pet them, giving Pops the runaround as he tried to chase me. I was a pretty fearless kid—maybe you remember that—kind of drawn to dangerous places: the tip-top of the playground slide, the deep end of the pool, too close to wild animals. Anyway, I crept toward the mama goose near the edge of the lake, and she rose up in this big majestic wingspread like a thunderbird, scaring me off for a minute. She had one beady eye fixed on me the whole time, so I don't know why I thought I could sneak up on her, but I got away from Pops and bum-rushed the birds, determined to crash-bang my way into the family. I got within about two feet of the terrified goslings before the

*mama dove for my arm and bit me harder than
I've ever been bitten, even by Marcy. I hollered
bloody murder and burst into tears and Pops
actually kicked the goose. My arm was so black
and blue — the doctor said I was lucky Mother
Goose didn't break it — that we got funny looks at
the grocery store for weeks. That's why I hate birds.
That and I think you liked them.*

*I like being scary a lot more than I like being
scared. But it's strange, you know? Feeling apart
from people all the time.*

*You hardly know any of the people in my life.
You don't even know Marcy. And you don't know
Rowie, but she's the girl who just broke my heart.
Rowie's real name is Rohini and she has beautiful
black eyes and long branch-brown arms and
we're — well, we used to be — MCs together and I
haven't talked to her since we fell out. I don't even
know if she's, like, okay. She doesn't know it, but I
pick up the phone and start to call her every day.
I wondered while I was falling asleep last night
if she'll ever be glad I happened to her. Despite
everything, in a secret sacred place that no one
will ever be able to gossip about, I'm still glad she
happened to me.*

*Rowie and I had, like, a secret relationship and
my friend Tess found out, and from there word just*

got around the way shit does here, a place where nothing ever happens, and the next thing everyone knew, everyone knew. I'm not even really mad at Tess now, even though I was at first. In a weird way, I'm almost grateful to her for doing what I couldn't, whatever it was that Rowie's fear or my own mournful borders kept me from doing.

I'm out. I'm not like the pretty girls, the salon-blond birds hanging out the passenger windows of all the hockey players' trucks, with their indoor laughs and shallow lacquered faces. I'm a lot of things—hardheaded, smart-mouthed, kind of oddly dressed—but I'll never be like those girls. And I'm glad. I needed to get honest about who I am, honest about the fact that I'm not ashamed to be this kind of girl, and I have that gladness now. I wear it like a pendant on a chain. I'm Esme Rockett, foul-mouthed, prickly syntaxed, oddly dressed, and gay.

I can't decide whether being an only child makes it easier or harder for me to reject. Sometimes for a hot minute I hate Rowie, hate her in a heated humiliated way, for always wriggling farther away whenever I wanted to get closer, for telling me I didn't understand the way she was different and never realizing how much she has that I don't: a sister, a mother. Do we all hate the people we love sometimes? Sometimes I imagine *myself breaking up with everyone in my life. (You did that.) I've never told anyone this, but I've always been secretly terrified that all the people I love most privately despise me, that I'm, I don't know, a trying person, a vexacious, snarky, know-it-all brat who can only be tolerated for so long. Maybe I was even worse than I think I am, like really awful, and that's why she couldn't ever be my girlfriend.*

It's funny how experience is made up as much of what we forget as it is of what we remember. I never remember how mean I was to Charlie Knutsen back in August. I do remember every mean thing I said to Rowie the night we fell out. Or maybe I don't. I'm not funny anymore. Or I worry about that. My thoughts aren't really connecting; this has been happening a lot lately. I find myself having to talk myself through things, narrating my own life, having to understand it in words, a lot lately. Pops says I should make things out of what I'm feeling, so I'm making things: making rhymes, making sculptures, making letters. The words hang all around me like hot summer lemons and limes, like suspended jewels hungry for my touch, and I am in love with them, and with the sound of them.

I do feel better when I make things. I remember to feel better. Seeing yourself in a letter is funny, like seeing yourself naked in someone else's house. The whole body business gets really gross by now; you never told me that. Why didn't you stick around to explain any of this shit to me? My boobs are bigger than last year, and I don't know if I'm supposed to be this hairy. No one ever told me having sex makes you look different but only to yourself.

Pops says it's my Jewish responsibility to atone for you. Tess says forgiveness comes if you let it. So I guess my tasks are to atone for your sins to God and forgive you myself. I may be working on that for a while.

Well, Mom, I know this is sort of random and wandering, and I'm sorry. I'm trying to get better at telling people how I feel about them, because I've learned that it really sucks when other people can't tell you how they feel about you. So I'm still mad at you, and I don't even really feel like I know you, but I suppose that I love you, or that I could try to love you if you ever stuck around long enough for me to stop being mad at you. I'll probably just keep trying to figure out how to love you and be mad at you at the same time, while I work on forgiving and atoning for you. Do you miss me, ever?

Sincerely, your spawn,
Esme Ruth Rockett

CHAPTER THIRTEEN
She Can't Get Down

About a week and three or four dodged Chem classes later, I resolve to go to a full day of school, because this is post–9/11 America, after all, and you can't let the terrorists win. The morning goes passably; the hissing in the halls has reduced to a dull simmer. After AP English and the pressure of avoiding eye contact with Rowie, I drag Marcy out for a walk around the school to recuperate after Precalc. She smokes a Parly. I try to breathe regular. We don't talk. I start to feel edgy about Chem, needing a release.

"Can we go to your car and have a dance party really quick?" I blurt out.

"What?" Marcy says. "Now?"

"Yeah, now. I just—I just need to dance really hard for a minute."

"Okay." Marcy shrugs, heading for the James. She reaches in and starts the car. "What's your poison?"

"Your choice," I say. "Just something with a beat."

Marcy cranks Brother Ali's "Forest Whitaker." I reach into my hair with both hands, ratting the curls out into my best Jew-fro, and start to shake my shit sans abandon. I jump around, loosening my arms, dancing from my core. For three minutes, I don't think about Rowie, don't think about school, think only about being in my body. Marcy laughs and busts some moves with me.

"Shake it, girl," she hollers.

The song ends and I'm breathing hard, my heart racing. I throw my arms around her.

"Thank you," I say. "I needed that." I've worn myself out a little bit, and it makes me feel less keyed up. We trudge back to the school entrance.

"Meet me by the gym after last period," she says casually as we throw a what-up to Mrs. Higgiston, the nearsighted attendance lady. She smiles and waves — for some reason, if you're nice to her, she never gives you shit about coming and going at will. It makes me wonder if she's lonely. Maybe she just feels invisible.

"For what?" I ask, stomping dirty slush off my hand-painted Timbos.

"Just something I had cooking while you were AWOL. No bigs."

"Whatever, dirtbag. Later."

I summon my courage, one foot in front of the other, and walk into AP Chem. Rowie's there early, of course, already taking notes from the whiteboard, and she's sitting at our table. Breathe. Breathe.

I sit down and she looks at me as though we've never met, as amazed as if I were a stranger boldly taking the seat next to her on an empty bus. She's wearing all black again. This is the fifth day in a row that Rowie hasn't worn a single color.

"Um. Ez?" she croaks.

"Let's not," I say.

"Okay," she says, looking back down at her notebook.

The bell rings. I look up and realize twenty-six pairs of eyes, including Mr. Halverson's, are trained on Rowie and me. I resist the urge to flip them all off.

I lean forward on the lab space, widening my eyes. *"Boo."*

The room is a tomb for a moment, my crack falling flatter than the drive from Minneapolis to Fargo, until Halves the Calves clears his throat and starts his lecture.

About two minutes after the bell, who should saunter in but Prakash Banerjee in the flesh, and he's walking toward me. The situation rapidly goes from bad to worse. He's standing next to me. He's leaning in—*revulsion*—to tell me something.

"Esme," he trills, "you're in my seat."

You. Have. Got. To. Be. Kidding. Me.

"Are you *for real?*" I fix him with a withering stare. "Isn't Jane your partner? Where is she?"

"She got switched into a special section that's taking the AP test this year instead of next year, and you weren't here, so Halverson reassigned me to Rowie, and you to a single table. Over there." He's practically singing. *You will pay for this, nerd,* I vow silently. *Rockett wrath remembers.*

Halves is clearing his throat again. Navy-blue sneakers today, but no point in noting it.

"Yes, um, Esme, if you'll just move to that table over there, you and I can go over the work you've missed after class," he says.

I can't believe this. Humiliation churns like vomit in my middle as I pick up my stuff and march it over to the single table—the *single* table—on the other side of the room, where I have a perfect view of Rowie and Prakash. I would rather have a million of Chuckles's babies, literally rather be barefoot and pregnant making Tater Tot hot dish in his kitchen for the rest of my *life* than be in this class right now. After a few minutes, I put my head down on my crossed elbows, watching the cracks of light between my arms, breathing in the antiseptic smell of the table. *Maybe I can just hide here for a while,* I think. *Maybe when I look up, it'll all have gone away.* No such luck. I look up and Prakash is leaning over Rowie's notebook just the way I used to; she gives me a guilty look when she sees me seeing them.[60] Miserably, I turn my attention to Halverson's drone, making a halfhearted attempt at taking notes. I'm such a phony. Rowie knows I never take notes.

Ten thousand years later, the bell goes off in a soul-saving scream and I'm on my feet before it's finished ringing. I barely pause at Halves's desk to pick up the pile of papers he has waiting for me and flee, taking third lunch instead of my usual first, because more face time with Rowie is out of the question today.

I merge into the lunch line. All I want is French fries. At the cash register, I grab a handful of ketchup packets and a Coke, and scan the room for a good, removed place to sit and read. God. I haven't read through lunch since elementary school. Some days Marcy would make me play kickball with her and the boys at recess, but most days I curled up against the side of the school and buried myself in a book. I spot an empty corner of the cafeteria and head for it, trying not to make eye contact with anyone.

"Esme!"

I hear my name and have an off-kilter moment of searching for its source. Turning around like a dog bedding down for the night, I finally see Jane waving at me, motioning for me to come sit at her table. I melt in relief.

60. Text from Rowie: *I'm so sorry. We got switched when u weren't here. Super sorry.*

"Hey, dude," I greet her, taking an empty seat. Jane's sitting with Angelo and a senior girl whose name I'm pretty sure is Courteney. "How's it going?" I wave to them. "I'm Esme. Courteney, right?"

"Right." Courteney smiles. "What's good?"

"You know, not a lot right now, but I'm trying to be optimistic," I answer honestly.

"Girl," Jane responds in a rush. "I feel so bad about the other day. I'm so sorry I spilled the beans like that. And then I heard Halverson made Prakash Rowie's lab partner when I switched my section, and I felt like I had probably just ruined your whole life."

I wave her apology away. "Don't sweat it. The lab thing isn't your fault, and as for Rowie and Prakash, I would have found out anyway. I'm sorry I was so weird when you told me."

"Oh, my God, don't even worry," Jane says. "This shit about you, like, will not die. I'm pretty much sick of hearing about it, so I can't even imagine how you must feel."

"Oh, snap, *you're* the one everyone's talking about?" Courteney asks. "Damn, even I've heard that shit."

"Yeah," Angelo adds. "People are saying some crazy shit. I heard you tried to feel up Mary Ashley Baumgarten at a pool party and that you were, like, secretly dating Rowie Rudra."

I laugh for the first time all day.

"Wow," I say. "First part, very false. I did once tell

269

Marcy I wanted to have hate sex with MashBaum, but that was before I really knew what it was. Or what she was."

They laugh, which feels even better than laughing myself.

"Second part, true. But I'd kind of appreciate it if you guys didn't feed the gossip flame too much, if you wouldn't mind."

"No worries there," Angelo chimes in. "You should hear the shit they say about *us*."

"For real?" I ask. "Like what?"

"Okay, you know Mary Ashley's little flat-assed friend Annaleigh?" Courteney launches in. "So I was on the danceline with her for a semester before I realized all those bitches were no-talent white girls — no offense — who'd get laughed out of auditions at my old school, and one time I was at a party with them and this girl Annaleigh, like, got so wasted on Malibu shots that she lost her Tiffany's bracelet with the little silver heart on it, and she accused me of stealing it in front of the whole team. Like, hold up, hide your valuables, we got a Negro in the house. I almost decked her."

"Seriously?" I reply, dumbfounded.

"Welcome to the outside," she says, toasting me with her Diet Coke.

"Yeah, and then there was that rumor that we'd all just gotten out of juvie and our house was like a halfway house," Angelo remembers. "That one was kind of funny until all the white girls started switching sides of the hall when they saw me coming."

"Damn," I say. "That's cold."

"Yeah, especially 'cause we all actually had to get good grades to get into the"—he sighs—"ABS program."

"Dude, do you, like, *hate* that name?" I say.

"Yeah, it's bad," Courteney says. "But you can't let that shit get to you or it'll make you crazy."

"Yeah," I say, not sure if I'm actually agreeing with her or not. "Well. I was gonna ask you guys how you like Holyhill so far, but I guess you already answered that."

"Pssshh, I'm just here because I wanna get into college," Angelo says. "Colleges love A Better Shot. Especially when Holyhill has the best AP program in the state."

"More so if the ABS kid's *in* the best AP program in the state," Courteney teases him. "Some of us are taking one for the team there more than others, friend." She takes one of my fries and looking at me all *Can I take this?* I nod, chuckling.

"Whatever, Harvard girl," Angelo says. "You can tell Cornel West what up for me when you get there. I don't gotta put myself through that shit to get a good scholarship at Madison or the U of M."

"Cornel West's at Princeton," Jane says.

"You already know where you're going to college?"

Jesus, I'm facing all kinds of dragons today. "I have no fucking clue where I want to go."

Angelo jerks a thumb toward Courteney. "I still got a year. She just applied to Harvard."

"And about fifteen other schools," Courteney says, sizing me up. "For you, offhand, I'd say small eastern liberal arts, serious but not *too* serious, maybe a girls' school. Like Vassar, maybe? You'd probably pull down more ass at Smith."

Jane giggles. "You're so snap judgmental. I'm getting more of a Berkeley vibe. You know, smoke a little ganja, talk some lit theory, hit a protest or two, go to class when you feel like it. I could see that working for you."

"That's funny," I say. "Both my parents went to Berkeley."

"Ah." Jane smiles. "That explains it."

"Christ on a bike, you guys are better than the *Princeton Review*," I marvel. "I should be taking notes."

Oh!" Jane claps her hands. "I almost forgot to ask you. Are you going to Marcy's hip-hop thing after school?"

"She told me to meet her after last period, but she didn't say why," I say. "What the hell does that girl have cooking?"

"Oh, no! Maybe I wasn't supposed to tell you." Jane looks worried, gun-shy after her faux pas about Prakash.

"Marcy was trying to get some people together for a meeting of Hip-Hop for Heteros and Homos. We're meeting in the warming house after school today."

"Oh, God." I dissolve into laughter. "I can't believe she got it together for another meeting without me knowing. That girl is something else." As I laugh, I feel a strange edge of tears rising, out of exhaustion, or gratitude again. Thank God for Marcy, that fearless beast.

"Are you coming? I was trying to talk these guys into coming too," Jane tells me earnestly.

"Hold up," Courteney says, waving her hands. "Hip-hop for *who*? What the fuck is going on in the suburbs right now?"

"My friends and me, we—well, we used to—my girl Marcy and me are heavy into hip-hop. She's the beat maestro and I write rhymes sometimes, and a while ago we were thinking that it might be cool to make Holyhill lift its ban on hip-hop by forming a student group to, like, study it and shit. And we sort of worked sexuality in there too, because we're trying to figure out what sex-positivity in hip-hop is all about, and because Holyhill's never had a gay-straight alliance before, and because, well, you know"—I point to myself—"big gay girl here—I guess we're basically just trying to make Holyhill recognize a group about everything Holyhill thinks is taboo, because hip-hop is sweet, and because— because *fuck* them, that's why." It all comes out in a thrill of memory, all the big fat ideas we had together, and it suddenly makes me sad.

"Girl, it's a damn shame you're into women, because I think I'm getting a crush on you," Angelo says. "I'll come if you can find me a ride home."

I throw back my head and laugh.

"I bet Marcy can give you a ride," I assure him. "If you're willing to listen to her diatribe on the douchebaggery of Kanye, that is."

Courteney looks less convinced.

"I don't know. I gotta check how much homework I have tonight," she says dubiously. "I might swing through; I might not."

"No doubt," I say with a nod. The bell rings. "Well, folks, I hope I see you all after school. Thanks for—I don't know. Just thanks." I'm kind of embarrassed by the last part, so I walk away quickly amid their farewells.

My end-of-the-day art elective passes in a gentler drone: I'm working on another sculpture piece, this time of a little girl with a purse in one hand and an alligator eating the other. I got the idea from the first girl I ever crushed on, who I met at some super-hippie Raising Empowered Daughters thing Pops dragged me to in elementary school. Her name tag said *Blue* and her eyes were brown, like these wide oval velvet mirrors, and she sat next to me during one of the boring talky parts doodling all these morbid little girls: a girl sitting on a high branch in a tree, captioned *She can't get down,* a little pigtailed girl half-smiling with a hand on one hip and a BB gun in the other, a girl in a square bedroom with a purse on one hand and an alligator on the other. Blue and her big, sad, blinking brown eyes. She was a sphinxy little minx, and I never forgot her.

The waning afternoon sunlight is casting a drowsy haze over the art room when the last bell finally rings. I strap on my headphones to "Ain't Nuthin' But a She Thing," pack up my brushes and plaster of paris, and join the current of the hallway.

Marcy is tilted against the bust of James P. Waldinger outside the auditorium named for him, crunching on an apple as she waits for me.

"Holla, balla," she calls when she sees me approaching. "What's crappenin'?"

"You old polecat sonuvabitch," I crow, tackling her. "You planned a 4H meeting without me."

"Well, it wasn't like I was gonna get a whole lot of help from your depressed Sapphic ass." She doesn't miss a beat as she twists and pins my right arm behind my back like a girl who grew up wrestling guys bigger than her. We scuffle for a minute, cackling.

"Whoa, *hey*, sexual tension!" Elijah Carlson catcalls as he passes with Charlie Knutsen. "Get a room!"

"Fuck the fuck off, Carlson." I roll my eyes, flipping him off. "Find some new whack-off material."

"Oooohhhh, angry dyke," he says, miming fright. I instinctively stick an arm out to block Marcy from charging him.

"Shut up, Elijah," Charlie says. "You sound like a fucking redneck."

Elijah looks at Charlie, shocked.

"Have fun with your dyke posse, fag," he says with a pout, and disappears.

"Hey, Esme. Hey, Marcy. Just ignore him," Charlie says shyly.

"Hey, Chuckles," I say. "That was cool of you."

"Yeah, whatever." He shrugs, embarrassed. "I've been wondering how you are with all this shit flying around."

"Really?" I ask, surprised. "I'm okay, I guess. It's been pretty wack, though."

"Yeah," he says. "Well, keep your head up."

"Thanks, man." I'm touched. "Hey—at least now you know why I was the way I was back at the beginning of the year, huh?"

He smiles, glancing at Marcy, embarrassed again. He leans in. "It was actually kind of a relief to find out—you know, that it wasn't totally my fault you were so pissed off."

I laugh. "I bet."

"I gotta run," he says. "But I wanted to tell you—I

mean, my brother's gay and he didn't get up the balls to come out until after he left Holyhill. So I think you're really brave." Charlie blushes.

"Yo, Chuck, you should come to our Hip-Hop for Heteros and Homos meeting," Marcy says. "In about ten minutes, in the old warming house."

"I got practice, but thanks," he says. "Maybe another time. Anyway, catch you guys later."

"Catch you later, Charlie," I say, and he blends into the exodus.

Marcy and I look at each other.

"Well, I'll be damned," she says.

"Yeah, what a trip," I say. "Nice to remember that everyone here isn't all the same."

"Thank God for that. Are you ready for our meeting? We should get out to the warming house."

"Born ready," I say, following her.

We walk into the warming house to find a smattering of people milling around, more than last time: Jane, Yusuf, Angelo, Courteney, the theater girls, a few band kids. In the corner, a curly-haired kid is playing a Casio electric piano like the one Tess has; he plays an undulating, sonorous tune that sounds familiar but that I'm sure I haven't heard before.

"Who is that?" I lean over to Marcy. "He's got some chops."

"Oh, yeah, that's Kai," she replies. "I tutor him in the resource room. He's a prodigy, but he can't really read, can't even read music. He just plays all the time, stuff he writes himself and memorizes. Anyway, I told him we were gonna jam on some beats and talk about why Holyhill's so full of tightasses, and he was pretty much sold. Hey, Kai!" she calls over to him.

"What up, Marce," he says, still playing as he looks up.

A tentative knock sounds at the door, and Mrs. DiCostanza pokes her head in.

"Is this"—she looks down at her copy of our application—"Hip-Hop for Heteros and Homos?"

"Mrs. D.!" I cry. "You came! That's so cool!"

"I reminded her we were meeting today," Tess says, emerging from behind Mrs. D. "I hope that's okay."

"Score!" Marcy says. "Thanks for showing up, Mrs. D."

Marilyn DiCostanza smiles. "Well, I'm interested to learn more about what you all hope to accomplish with these meetings, and I wanted to show some faculty support for the idea of a gay-straight alliance at Holyhill. You all just conduct this meeting as though I'm not here and let me listen to you."

"Word," Marcy says. "Let's get started, then."

My heart melts a little at the sight of Tess. I go over and wrap my arms around her, planting a big sloppy kiss on her cheek.

"I'm glad you're here." I squeeze her. "I'm sorry I've been an a-hole. I know it wasn't really your fault."

"I understand," she whispers back. "I wish Rowie would've let me talk her into coming. Or into talking to her." She smiles wanly. "Sometimes people just need a little time, I guess."

Marcy coughs. "4H, let's come to order. If you were here for our first meeting, welcome back, and if you weren't, welcome. I specially want to welcome Mrs. DiCostanza, who's maybe going to be our faculty adviser." A few people clap awkwardly.

"Pretend I'm not here," Mrs. D. says, motioning down the applause. "Just talk like you normally would. Hell, we're not on school grounds or school time, right?" She gives us that irreverent grin I'm beginning to feel so fond of.

"Maybe we should spend part of the time talking about gender and sexuality stuff, and part of the time talking about hip-hop, and part of the time talking about them in relation to each other?" Tess suggests.

"That sounds—shockingly organized," Marcy says. "What do you guys want to talk about first?"

"Okay." Emma Fazzio raises her hand. "I have a question."

"Shoot," Marcy says.

"So, why do guys, like, *love* bi girls?" she asks, then cracks her gum in the silence that follows the question.

"What do you mean?" I ask, glancing over at Mrs. D., who maintains her poker face.

"I mean, so—like, I feel really comfortable in this room right now, so I'm going to tell all of you that I'm"—Emma's dramatic intake of breath arrives—"I'm bisexual, and even though I've never really, like, *dated* a girl, sometimes, like, at parties, I end up making out with other girls, and I just really want to know why guys are always so *into* it, when it doesn't, like, involve them."

"It's not that complicated," Yusuf says. "Making out with a girl at a party just to get the attention of some guy doesn't make you bi. But if two girls get together in private, on their own time, just for each other, that counts a lot more."

"I agree, I think," I say. "That's an interesting, like, sexual scorecard."

"Didn't we say last time that we were going to talk about our favorite female MCs?" Jane asks.

"Yes! Yusuf and I made an all-girl supermix just for the occasion," Marcy says.

Even though I didn't know there was an iPod hookup to the dingy CD player Marcy brought, Yusuf wordlessly whips a cord or two out of his pocket and, fifteen seconds of dextrous rewiring later, music plays.

"So the first song is by Invincible, who's like my biggest hip-hop crush right now," Marcy says. "She's a white girl from Detroit, and she's a sick lyricist, really political and smart. This song 'Sledgehammer' is blowing up the underground."

"Why aren't there any girls who rap?" Michelle asks, not making herself sound any smarter than at our last meeting.

"I wouldn't say there aren't *any* girls who rap," I say. "I mean, we're listening to one. But the question of why there aren't more is really important to what we're trying to do here. Why do other people think women are so outnumbered in hip-hop?"

"Hip-hop is all about machismo," Angelo says. "It's like, if you wanna have street cred, you have to have a certain image, and bling and bitches are part of that image. No offense, ladies."

"Instead of women creating their own images, which is, I think, what's starting to happen now," I say.

"Yeah, but for a long time Queen Latifah, Roxanne Shanté, MC Lyte, and Lil' Kim were almost the only female MCs anyone knew about, and then Lauryn Hill," Kai says.

"And Missy," Marcy adds. "I think it's important to look at when they emerged, which is like the late eighties and early nineties, when women were just starting to gain more power in a lot of professions," Marcy adds.

"That's a good point," Mrs. D. says. "Carry on — just had to add that."

"When white women were starting to gain power, you mean," Courteney says.

"Yeah, but another thing I think you have to take into account is that hip-hop is one of the only industries in the world where black women emerged first, and white women had to measure their success against black women's instead of the other way around," Jane says. "That's something to talk about too."

All of a sudden we hear a strange commotion outside the warming house.

"Christ," I moan. "Tell me we're not about to be ambushed by goats."

Just then, the room goes dark. I hear Emma and Michelle shriek a split second before the Roman candle goes off, illuminating the two—I squint, thinking that after the day I've had, I might be seeing things—yes, the two Boy George masks behind the spray of light. Everyone's ducking and screaming and trying to get to the light switch, and the laughter coming from behind the masks sounds terrifying and disembodied, the laughter of assailants too chickenshit to show their faces. A bunch of people try to dive for cover under a bench as Angelo dumps water on his jacket and throws it onto the geyser flame. Tess and I spring to the doorway, and in all the flash and darkness, I can see two male-looking figures sprinting away into the dimming late afternoon, leaving a crackling trail of tiny noisemakers behind them, snapping like evil little turtles. I contemplate running after them, but they've got too much of a head start and disappear into the woods before we get it together to follow.

"Is everyone all right?" Mrs. D. rushes to turn the lights back on, the firecracker dying under the smoking weight of Angelo's coat. The light reveals Marcy hovering in a protective stance over Yusef, her arm around his shoulder.

"Those motherfuckers burned my arm!" Jane wails, rushing to the fountain to douse it in cold water. "Who the hell *was* that?"

"Are you kidding me?" Marcy goes ballistic. "Was that a fucking hate crime? Was Holyhill's first gay hip-hop alliance actually just *firebombed*?"

"Is anyone else hurt?" Tess asks. We look around; Jane's arm and Angelo's coat appear to be the only casualties.

"We'll file a report," Mrs. D. insists. "This is not in any way acceptable."

"No," I say. "No, it isn't." I wonder if most people can pinpoint the worst day of their lives so clearly; I lift the smoldering coat off the site of the explosion and shake off the ash, noting the exact moment when the dark matter inside me morphed from sadness to anger. I feel everyone's eyes on Marcy and me.

"Let's continue our meeting," I say, livid. "We can't

let some cowards who don't even have the guts to show their faces stop us."

"Dude." She brushes ash off her sleeves, boiling. "How?"

"I'm going to get out my notebook," I growl. "And we're going to make a plan."

CHAPTER FOURTEEN
B-Girls Will Be Girls

After the firebombing incident, Marcy, Tess, and I demand another meeting with our old friend Principal Ross Nordling.

"The problem is, girls," Nordling wheezes, sounding weary and asthmatic, "the administration can't protect meetings that are happening off campus."

"Principal Nordling," Tess protests, "you can't pretend you didn't *suggest* we meet in the warming house back in September. We had an agreement with you that if we could prove that this group had a purpose and that other people were interested in it, you'd recognize it."

"Yes, Miss Grinnell, but I never formally *approved* it," he sniffs. "You might remember that not one of you signed this year's code of conduct, which was the second part of our deal."

"So let me get this straight," Marcy says. "You're saying that you're reneging on our agreement and that school groups Holyhill ignores don't deserve to have safe meetings?"

"Even if I knew who was behind this alleged assault, Miss Crowther—"

"*Ms.* Crowther," she corrects him icily.

Nordling stink-eyes Marcy for a second, then continues. "*Ms.* Crowther, even if I had any way of determining who set off those fireworks, what would you suggest I do with them?"

"Report them to the Holyhill Police?" Tess says. "Principal Nordling, this was a hate crime. Fireworks aren't even legal in Minnesota, which means our assailants must have trafficked contraband in from Wisconsin. What would you do if some guys in Boy George masks firebombed a Bible study meeting?"

"If anything, what happened at your meeting proves that this kind of music incites violence," Nordling says. "Violence that the administration was trying to prevent by banning it."

"How can you argue that we're the ones inciting violence when we were the victims of it?" I explode. "*You* might remember, Mr. Nordling, our contacts in the local media."

He sighs. "All right, ladies. Let's level with one another here. I have it on reliable information that your little organization facilitated the Halloween incident in order to promote yourselves on the news. Are you sure this alleged attack isn't just a follow-up story?"

I can feel Marcy fuming.

"I have a problem with your referring to Mary Ashley Baumgarten as reliable just because her dad is a state senator," she says. "And if we intended to stage an attack on our own meeting, why would we invite a Holyhill faculty member to be there?"

"I've spoken with Mrs. DiCostanza, and she does corroborate your claim," Nordling sneers. "But I can't help but wonder if you invited her expressly so she would offer that corroboration."

"Principal Nordling," I seethe, struggling to contain myself, "we take the integrity of our group very seriously. We submitted an application. We've met with you about that application. We've recruited a faculty adviser. What we have not done is invent an attack on our own meeting."

Nordling sighs. "Let's call a truce. You and I both know that after the, ahem, Halloween incident, I don't need any more bad press. If any media organizations get wind of this, I'll have no choice but to suspend all of your group members from all student activities. Ms. Crowther, I know you don't want to be kicked off the drumline."

"This is straight crap," Marcy snarls. "We didn't do anything wrong."

"Other than smearing Holyhill's good name in your little impromptu news appearance," Nordling replies levelly. "I also can't help but notice that Ms. Rudra isn't here in support of this group as she was in the fall."

I strive to resist punching him in his smug, pink mouth. *It's your fault she couldn't handle being with me,* I think, fuming. *You and all the assholes like you.*

"Look, you kick me off drumline and this becomes a story," Marcy threatens, losing ground.

"Then if you don't want that to happen, I'd recommend for both of us that you discontinue your meetings," he returns. "The choice is yours."

"*This* meeting is over," Marcy says, rising.

"I agree," he agrees with maddening serenity. "I think I've made myself clear."

We all stand up and walk toward the door. I open it, and Marcy looks behind us to get in the last word on our way out.

"You haven't seen the last of 4H." She throws him the 4H sign as we exit. "B-girls will be girls, buster."

We hold our breath and tongues all the way to the hallway.

"We're launching a counterattack," I pronounce.

"*Hell* yes," Marcy replies in a rush. We fist-pound. It's on.

▼ ▼ ▼

We start small. First, we get all the cats who were at the last, ill-fated 4H meeting to stage silent protests. Marcy and me and even Tess start wearing big saggy jeans every day, and after a few days Angelo, Jane, Yusuf, and the theater girls, who look completely ridiculous with jeans hanging off their skinny asses, follow suit. People start to get creative with their apparel of resistance: Kai shows up one day wearing a white T-shirt with the lyrics to "Fight the Power" hand-scribbled on it.

I have to wonder how Chuck D would react if he knew how meaningful his words are to a bunch of suburban high-school kids, but, hey, I also have to believe that Chuck D and I are on the same side of the freedom-of-speech argument. With a few well-planted seeds from us, word flourishes about the attack on 4H and our response to it, and all of a sudden, to our massive surprise, all kinds of fellow misfits we don't even know are baring their underpants for our common cause. A few even get their hands on Boy George masks at Party City and start wearing them with the baggy jeans, which is one of the more surrealist acts of protest I've seen. Soon the butts are coming out of the woodwork: band kids are going saggy-pantsed, some debaters, ABS kids, goths—even the weird formerly homeschooled kids are panties-out with us. We must be freaking Nordling out a little bit, because, at least for the moment, no one gets reprimanded.

Gaining momentum, we start making hip-hop mega-mixes and blasting them from the warming house during track practice, audible on the track and in the parking lot, thanks to Yusuf and Marcy's clever rewiring. At first we get a lot of dirty looks, but after a few days, a strange, gentle camaraderie builds: even the track stars pick up their pace when we blast the beats.

"I wanna see those knees up *high,* boys! This one's for our principal!" Marcy crows at the team as Gang Starr's "Same Team, No Games" bumps and grinds. "All are welcome at today's 4H meeting! Listen to what you want! Love who you want! Come join the least recognized group at Holyhill Hiiiiiiigh!"

Yusuf examines the PA speaker perched in the corner of the warming house. "If I could get into the main office soundboard for ten minutes, we could totally hotwire the entire sound system to a motherboard out here," he says.

"No shit?" I marvel.

"Yeah, dude," Marcy says, drumming on the side of the house. "And if we really dug in there, we could record anything we wanted too." I see Yusuf beam at her. It's cute how Marcy thinks none of us know she and Yusuf are totally hitting it. Cute, and totally exposing.

For the first time in a long time, I actually look forward to going to school. There's some backlash, of course—

someone scrawls DYKES in lipstick on my locker; a rainbow bumper sticker mysteriously appears on the James's rear window—but for the most part people seem psyched to have something new to chatter about. It's a relief to feel like I'm contributing to the flow of social information instead of just being the object of it. I am becoming the author of my own chaos.

I'm working on new lyrics, too—nonstop. The song I started writing a while ago and performed for the girls and Rowie's mom starts to grow into a longer piece; for the first time, I'm writing for one voice, for a performance without Rowie. Our wave of revolution almost makes me forget how it feels to see her and Prakash together at school. I've developed a unique talent for holding my neck still in Chemistry so I don't have to look at them.

"But that's why *Battlestar Galactica* is the best show of the last twenty years," I overhear him saying to her as I spot them down the hall. "It's all about dynasty."

"It's not that I don't think it could be good," I hear her reply. "It's just never what I want to—" She sees me passing, and stops, dropping his hand. He reaches out and tries to hold her hand again, looking straight at me, but she dodges it. It gives me a sick kind of satisfaction. I duck out of their path and into the girls' room, but I don't look down.

Every time I see his ugly little larper hand on her, I

get this vommy feeling. In the handicapped stall, I lunge for my notebook and start scribbling; if I'm writing, at least I don't feel as paralyzed.[61]

There's this recurring dream of an unrehearsed performance that I've been having a lot lately. It's always a different performance: sometimes a dance recital, sometimes a play, sometimes a concert where I have to play an instrument I've never studied, like the bass clarinet or the harp. I fumble through the performance for what feels like days, faking it as best I can, the faces in the audience vague and hazy with light-blindness, the sweat of the effort beading on my neck, and, as though I'm finding a muscle memory I'd forgotten, I begin to get the hang of it, dancing or playing or speaking freestyle, no longer conscious of the stakes or anyone else, feeding off the energy of the shadowy crowd in a gallop of adrenaline—and then, just as I begin to let go and enjoy it, I wake up. It's nothing like the dreams I used to have about Mom, the ones in which I saw her face more clearly than I can ever visualize it in waking. But it makes me wonder what that second movement must feel like, the one where I start to just ride it, do or die.

61. Scribbled in Notebook: *Die, nerd, die, better recognize / You may of got her hand but I got her voice / I know Ro's flow through alla your noise / So save your show 'bout boys being boys.*

292

"So I've been really getting into hip-hop these days," Pops tells me over his famous bacon-wrapped beef tenderloin one night at dinner.

I choke in laughter, spitting out a bite of steak.

"Yeah?" I sputter. "You're so hip with the kids, Pops. Next are you going to get on Facebook?"

"I'm serious!" he insists, looking a little injured. "I'm really digging that Young Jeezy song. You know the one where he talks about his president and his Lambo being black?"

"His Lambo is blue, Pops." I say. "And you're, kind of freaking me out."

"Well, I think you should be proud that you're encouraging people you know to listen to things they might not have listened to otherwise. You have such a good critical mind. Without you, I would never have known how much I love Beyoncé."

I give him a suspicious look. "You know that Beyoncé's a singer and not a rapper, right? And that you're, like, the weirdest dad in the history of the world? I mean, you don't give me a curfew, you don't try to stop me from going out and hooking up—with *girls,* no less—and now you're encouraging my guerrilla gay hip-hop movement? Aren't you supposed to, like, try to stop me from doing all those things?"

"Would you rather I did? Wouldn't that just make

you want to do them more and be dishonest with me?"
He slurps his wine.

"Hippie freak," I mutter, shaking my head as I tuck
back into my bacon steak. "Why aren't you a vegetarian?"

"Why don't you ever read me any lyrics you're working on? Have I not done enough to make this feel like a
safe creative space for you?"

"No, Pops, we're the safest creative space on the
block." I roll my eyes. "Do you seriously expect me to
rap for you?"

"Yes!" he says, dropping his fork for emphasis. "I
completely do expect you to rap for me. I gave you life.
Now I want to hear a song."

"Are you drunk?"

"No! Aren't I allowed to just want a little rhythm
with my dinner?"

"You are a fucking nutbag."

"I'm taking your steak until you give me some
rhymes." He snatches my plate.

"This is child abuse. I'm calling the authorities." He
starts to take a bite of my steak. "Fine fine fine fine." I
dig my notebook out of my purse. "Are you ready?" He
nods eagerly. I take a breath.

"I got all this hysteria, maybe it's uterus lunacy
I'm defective and restive, gotta find a way to get through to me

And all of these haters, all the shit that they do to me
We gotta get positive, find a cure for this prudery.
Who says that the white girl can't come to drop bombs?
And who says I gotta dress like these Botoxed white moms?

My girl DJ She and me got some anthems to dance with
We wearin' low-riders low and we got plenty of bandwidth
To transmit these messages you best not be messin' with

We got ladies in the house, ladies first, ladies wicked
We ride to get high, Minnesota-do-or-die
We talk shit and kick it, our bidness is the shiznit
So holler out our name, we're the illest Sister Mischief."

He's got that mushy look on his face again. Jeezy creezy.

"Esme! You're so—*good!*" he squeals. "Are you going to perform that?"

I shrug. "Marcy and Tess and me might have something in the works."

"What kind of something?"

"I don't know," I say casually. "Maybe something—at school, or something."

"How are you going to pull that off? Please don't get kicked out—that's all I'm asking. I really can't afford to pay the property taxes here *and* send you to private school."

"Come on, Pops. They can't kick us out for performing our songs, or for forming a hip-hop-friendly gay-straight alliance. The ACLU would spit-roast Ross Nordling over a First-Amendment bonfire."

"Are you sure?" he asks skeptically.

"Look, we're not definitely doing anything yet. Why don't you just not worry about it for now."

"Yeah," Pops snorts. "*That's* going to happen. Just let me know what you're planning when you are definitely going to do something. And for God's sake, think it through."

I squint at him. "What do you mean, exactly?"

"I mean do your homework, girl. Whatever you plan, make sure you're within your rights, make sure you have other people standing with you, and whatever you do, never, ever give away the cameras. And if for any reason the cops get involved, don't say *anything* until you have a lawyer present."

"Jesus, Pops, I'm not going to get *arrested*. All we want to do is stage a sneak-attack performance."

"Just do it right—that's all I'm saying." He pushes my plate back across the table. *Never give away the cameras,* I note silently. Pops has this way of being smarter than me.

The tension's building at school. Angelo and a few other kids get called into the office, but all the administration does is ask them to pull up their pants. Mary Ashley Baumgarten and her creepy little mini-me Stina actually spit at me as I pass them in the hall; MashBaum's been preening around the halls like she's fucking royalty or something since her dad won the election. Marcy and I start to mix up beats under my verses on the weekends. We copy more flyers, neon ones with lyrics this time. Choosing which lyric chunks to paper the school with takes us hours of debating and scribbling. We find snippets of MC Lyte (*I may come on strong but that's what you like / You like a female MC who can handle the mike. . . . / So that's why I'm here, don't mean to make a case of it / This rap here, well, it's just for the taste of it / I write the rap to make the whole world sing / And I'm the type of female, well, I like to swing*) and our hometown boys Atmosphere (*As a child hip-hop made me read books / And hip-hop made me want to be a crook / And hip-hop gave me the way and something to say / And all I took in return is a second look*) and we plaster the girls' bathrooms with them, stuff them in lockers and under classroom doors, pin them under windshield wipers in the parking lot. It's like we're getting into the fray of hip-hop. We're picking a fight and it's coming for us.

The biggest windfall for our movement arrives unexpectedly, though, when an anonymous op-ed comes out in the *West Wind*, the school newspaper. It makes the front page, and the editor's note indicates that it was submitted to the paper from an anonymous e-mail address. For me, seeing it erases any shadow of a doubt that the administration is going to have to respond to the homo-hop revolution before too long. The headline is "Censorship Reigns at Holyhill High." My mouth falls open as I read:

Holyhill High School enjoys its status as one of the nation's best public schools—and its administration is so busy enjoying it, maybe, that it seems to think it can implement intolerant and unconstitutional policies without its students noticing, and prioritize the comfort of some students over the safety of all students. This fall, a clause prohibiting "loud, violent, heavily rhythmic" music, and apparel associated with the culture of this music, on Holyhill High's campus appeared in Holyhill's code of conduct.

This policy is an obvious gesture at hip-hop, which many consider one of the most important artistic and cultural movements of the last half-century, as well as a major force in modern African-American and multicultural empowerment, an instrument of social justice and critical inquiry, and a contributor to the movement behind Barack Obama's victory in the 2008 presidential election. To prohibit students from participating in the discussion surrounding hip-hop is not only to deny this almost inarguable importance; it is to censor and restrict the First Amendment rights of Holyhill's students. The administration's refusal of school recognition to a student group dedicated to the study and discussion of hip-hop affirms its willingness to tamper with its students' right to freedom of expression.

More egregiously, the administration recently failed in its responsibility to maintain a school in which its students are protected from harm. The student group in question, Hip-Hop for Heteros and Homos, also advocates for the acceptance of Holyhill's GLBT students, combining its analysis of hip-hop with an examination of sexual identity similar to gay-straight alliances at many other high schools. At a recent gathering of the group, witnesses reported that several figures attacked the meeting by storming the room, shutting off all the lights, and setting off a series of illegal fireworks. One student sustained injuries, yet instead of prosecuting or even seeking to identify the attackers, the Holyhill administration encouraged the 4H student group to discontinue their meetings.

The fact that many people in the Holy-hill community justify blatant homophobia by claiming it as a Christian value only under-scores the point that the administration must do more to ensure the safety and freedom of all its students. As a public school, Holyhill High cannot align itself with those tenets of religious conviction that reject or demean homosexuality, nor is it empowered to designate any peaceful intellectual inquiry as illegitimate or off-limits. It is the responsibility of the school to guarantee freedom from discrimination for every Holyhill student, and to protect our rights as Ameri-cans to discuss, examine, or explore whatever we please, provided we do so without engaging in or promoting violence. At Holyhill, the stu-dents who disobeyed Holyhill's hip-hop policy to exercise this right were the victims, not the perpetrators, of violence, yet under the cover of their own discriminatory policy, the administra-tion did nothing. The students of Holyhill High School demand a repeal of the ban on hip-hop, as well as the addition of Hip-Hop for Heteros and Homos to the roster of recognized student groups. Anything less would be contemptuous to the quality of a Holyhill education.

▼ ▼ ▼

Marcy and I share a moment of gaping at the power of the article. All around us, everyone looks decapitated, all the faces obscured by copies of the paper.

"WTF does *egregiously* mean?" I overhear someone ask. "I don't know like 90% of these words."

"So let's be real here," Marcy says. "There are only like five people in the entire school who can write like this. Let's eliminate some. Did you write it?"

I wobble my head. "Wish I had, but it waddn't me. Did you?"

"Nope." She takes a loaded pause. "Did you notice—?"

I don't need to wait for her to finish. "That the author seems to know a whole damn awful lot about 4H?"

"Yeah."

"Yeah. I think that list is pretty much narrowed down."

"It had to be her," she says, watching me for a reaction. "Well, the administration's going to have to respond, and that's what matters. We gotta figure out how to make this concert happen, and soon."

I stuff the paper into my backpack. Marcy and I keep mixing beats and tinkering with my rhymes, but both of us know that the synergy of the group has been altered, still not weathered through the split in the ground. I'm writing for one voice, but I don't know how to swagger without Rowie's slink by my side.

"Yeah, all I'm concerned with is figuring out what

our next plan is." I turn back to her. "Let's make a list. What do we need?"

"You and your lists. You can't itemize the world, freak."

"One. Portable mikes."

"Preloaded beats on tape. Speakers."

"New sunglasses."

"An air horn."

"Cameras. Never give away the cameras."

She smirks. "Are we seriously going to call in the media? What about Nordling?"

"Fuck Nordling. But if he's serious, you could get suspended from drumline. Are you willing to take that risk?"

"I'll take the hit if I have to," she says. "Yeah, we're calling the media for *damn* sure."

A grin spreads across my face as I tick another notch of the list off on my fingers.

"We need big humongous ovaries."

She snickers. "We need distaste for peace and quiet."

"And for Principal Ross Nordling."

"And Holyhill."

"And for MashBaum!"

"Ez." She catches her breath. "Do you know what else we need?"

"What?"

"We need more backup."

I nod slowly.

"I know. I'ma gonna call some in."

She nods back. "Just let me know where rehearsal is and when." The bell sounds off, and everyone scurries back to class, trailing a carpet of newspapers in their wake.

CHAPTER FIFTEEN
Doorbells and Corners

It's dark by the time I finish dinner and screw up the courage to face the bitter wind and bike over to Arapahoe Hills, where some of the houses are swathed in twinkling garlands of early Christmas lights; in the windows, I see moms finishing dinner cleanup at the kitchen sinks, families moving into homework and TV and settling in for the night. The black ice is slick on the steep curve of Tess's driveway, and Prissy skids a little as I muscle up it. I toss the bike into the bushes, narrowly missing the left headlight of Darlene's Lexus SUV, and stomp my snowy feet on the super-Lutheran "Living Is Giving" doormat as I ring the doorbell.

An indistinct female figure approaches through the beveled glass and pulls open the door. To my surprise, it turns out to be Ada, who must be home for Thanksgiving.

Because Tess's the only one of us who has an older sister, and because Ada's eight years older, she was impossibly cool to us growing up: beautiful, talented, a little wild. Always had a boyfriend, always getting in trouble and charming her way out of it. She studied musical theater at NYU, and she's been an actress/waitress in New York since then; I think we've all had fantasies of running away to New York and showing up on Ada's doorstep panting *Teach me,* or at least I have.

"Esme!" she greets me. "Come on in. Was Tess expecting you? She's upstairs."

"Thanks." I step across the threshold, entering the warm Glade cookie aroma of the Grinnell house and its multiple chandeliers, its sweeping spiral staircase, its huge black-marble kitchen and wine cellar downstairs. "Naw, I just decided to stop by," I say. "Girl, you gotta tell me about New York. Is it, like, amazing?"

"It's—it's, yeah, it's still amazing. I mean, it wears on a body a little. But it's so much fucking better than here." She laughs, the freckles on her nose dancing; she's holding a glass of white wine exactly the corn-silk color of her hair, Tess's hair. "Are you thinking of applying to any schools in the city?" OMG, she just calls it *the city;* she doesn't even have to specify *what* city.

"Balls, I don't know. All I know is that I want to go someplace really far away from here."

She nods, her side ponytail bobbing. "Honey, I've

been there." She takes a pregnant pause. "Look, Esme, I really hope you won't think I'm being nosy or anything, but Tess's told me some of what's been going on, and I gotta tell you, I've been"—her hands flop over each other as she gestures through her train of thought— "I've just been feeling for you, wondering how you are."

"Um. Thanks, I think," I say.

"I'm just saying that—fuck." She looks around. "Jesus, this house makes me feel like I'm *choking*, do you know what I mean? Come out to the gazebo with me."

"Um. Okay." I trot after her as she throws on a black leather bomber jacket, her side ponytail fanning on its shoulder, and Tessie's blue Ugg boots. We sneak through the living room and out the sliding glass door in the kitchen to the backyard, to the gazebo where I got drunk and came out for the first time. It feels like years ago instead of months; nostalgia takes a swallow of my heart as we trudge through the snow. We track snow into the gazebo and perch on a bench, trying to place as little of our butts on the frozen wood as possible. She takes out a Lucky Strike filter, holding it between black-nailed fingers, and lights it.

"I started smoking these because I liked the way the pack looked. Isn't that stupid?" she tells me. We both study the red-and-white bull's-eye of the Lucky package. I wait for her to tell me what I'm doing here.

"You know what's funny?" I shake my head. She

takes a drag and exhales speaking, the smoke indistinguishable from her breath. "No one tells you how hard it is." She offers me the pack; I decline.

"How hard what is?" I ask.

"All of it. Growing up," she says.

"Yeah," I say.

She turns to look at me. "So were you in love with her?"

"Yeah." I don't face her, keeping her in my peripheral vision.

She turns back to the house. "Then let people say what the hell they want. You gotta get yourself into a city. Things are easier to handle in the city."

"Ada, what were you trying to say before?"

"Fuck, I don't know." She sucks in through her teeth. "I guess it's like this. Tess was never the fuckup in the family. That was my job. I fought with Mom; I snuck out; I got arrested; I didn't go to the school I was supposed to go to. Tess never had any room to push boundaries until one day she woke up sixteen and nothing made sense anymore. And until I wasn't around to steal all the attention."

"Yeah," I say, not sure what she's getting at.

"You're a good friend for her." She shivers, then laughs. "Why the fuck did I drag you out here, anyway? Look, I gotta tell you this one thing. When I was at Holyhill, I was with this guy for a while, and one thing led to another, and we ended up having sex, and neither of us meant for it to happen, but I got pregnant."

"Whoa," I say. "Really?"

"Really," she says, shuddering at the memory. "And there was no way I could have a baby, so I decided—not to. I got a friend to take me to the doctor and I didn't even tell Tess or my mom. But then one way or another, someone found out, and before I knew it, everyone had heard *everything*."

"Oh, my God," I say, trying to keep my mouth from hanging open. "That must have been awful."

"I think you know exactly how awful it was, even though, you know"—she takes a long drag—"even though that wasn't your situation. Anyway, I guess what I'm trying to say is—two things. One, there's, like, a high-school line in the sand between girls who have had sex, gay or straight, and girls who haven't. And the girls who haven't want to know *everything*, and that's why they talk about you the way they do, like, incessantly. Two, the things that feel like the biggest deal ever in high school—no one knows about them after you leave, which is awesome, escaping the gossip and everything. But the thing is, once you escape, you don't have the people who knew how it changed you to go through whatever you went through, either. Do you kind of know what I'm saying?"

"I think so," I say, trying to keep up. "I mean—what exactly are you saying?"

"I'm saying that girl in there, she's your *girl*. She's good people. She prays for you every night, and she's always going to know about these things that happened to you, the things that made you who you are. You aren't going to have a lot of people in your grown-up life who knew you when you were just a teenage dirtbag. I know you're anxious to get the hell out of here. But don't fast-forward your life away, and even though you have every right to be pissed off right now, don't destroy all the reasons to ever come back. And if you don't have your best girls, you don't have shit. Do you kind of know what I'm saying now?"

"Yeah." I nod more confidently. "Do you mind if we go in now? It's cold as tits out here."

She laughs. "I'm right behind you."

"Ada, you're—" I hug her awkwardly when we get back into the living room. "I don't know. You're really cool. Thanks for—sharing that with me."

"You're gonna be all right," she says, mussing my hair. I part ways with Ada and climb upstairs in pursuit of another sister.

I hear her and Roy Orbison in her room; when I peer through the cracked-open door, her back is to me as she gracefully lifts her arms in sweeping arcs, a free weight in each hand. The song, "Dream Baby," strikes me as a little doleful for a workout, but that's Tess, ever her own disciple of paradox. Gingerly, I knock, wanting to startle her as little as possible. She jumps, shrieks, drops a weight, and turns around. Her face cycles through surprise, confusion, embarrassment, and finally something like relief as she sees me standing in her doorway.

"Tessie! What in the name of the Lord's tarnation was that?" Darlene's voice intrudes from the master bedroom.

"I just dropped a free weight—don't worry," Tess calls back. Under her breath, she continues, "Keep your panties together, spaz."

I muffle a giggle. "Hi."

"Hi," she says. "I thought I heard your voice there, but then it disappeared."

"Ada and me were out in the gazebo for a second."

She sits down on her bed and takes a sip of water. "Ah. Was she telling you all about her fabulous New York life and chasing men with guitars and industry parties? Talking about how much cooler her life is in New York is kind of her MO this decade."

"I mean, it does sound pretty sick," I admit. "So you're—sweating to the oldies?"

She smiles bashfully. "I want Michelle Obama arms."

"Dude, that woman is a grade-A badass," I say.

"No joke," she says. "So what's up with you?"

"You know, the usual," I say. "Moving, shaking, balling. No big deal."

She laughs at me in this way that I know she's laughing *at* me. "You're so full of it."

"You could say that." I take a step back and flop cross-legged on the floor, leaning back on the door until it clicks shut.

She looks at me. "Ez, what's up?"

"I'm on my way to Rowie's. I needed a pit stop for courage."

"Gotcha." She nods, sniffing the air. "Have you been smoking? You smell like Mystic Lake."

"You can blame Carrie Bradshaw down there for that," I say, jerking a thumb toward where I last saw Ada. "She was trying to, like, tell me about life and I think it kind of stressed her out."

"I knew she was smoking again. It's her fault I hate it when Marcy smokes; it just reminds me of all the fights between her and Darlene that I had to mediate when I was little and Ada was in high school." Tess sighs. "So you're going to talk to Rowie?"

"Yeah," I say. "I mean, if she'll let me."

"I wanted to tell you," she says. "I don't know why, but I wanted to tell you that I sort of—I sort of always knew you were into her."

"What?" I say, alarmed. "What do you mean, always?"

"Do you remember the time last summer when

we stole the wine from my parents and went out to the gazebo and you told us you like girls?"

"Hazily," I say.

"You all thought I was asleep later on," she remembers, "and I was totally incapable of moving or talking, but I wasn't actually asleep. And the last thing I remember before I actually did pass out was you saying this one thing over and over, going, *Rohini, married to the moon, Rohini, married to the moon.*"

"Really?" I ask. "I don't even remember saying that out loud then."

"Yeah. You're not as good at keeping a secret as you think you are."

"Don't tell anyone," I say, giving her a good-natured shove. "Yo, did she write that op-ed in the *West Wind* or what?"

She smiles. "Come on, do you really need to ask?"

"I knew it." I say. "It probably wasn't as obvious to everyone else as it was to us. But the massive vocabulary and intimate knowledge of 4H kind of gave her away."

"Yeah, figures," she says. "I wonder what made her do it."

I peer at her. "All right, since we're making confessions, there's something I've always wondered."

"Shoot."

"Why did you stop being friends with Mary Ashley and start being friends with us?"

"Hmm." She extends one leg and pulls at her toes, stretching. "I guess it's like this. I used to think that Mary Ashley and all them—I used to think that they spent so much time doing church stuff because they really cared about finding the truth. And I studied the Bible because I did too, because I liked to study and I wanted answers. About, like, how we're supposed to be. But hearing them say that it's somehow wrong to be gay, that it's dangerous or something, it just didn't sit right with me. When I started hanging out and talking to you guys, for the first time I realized there were other people who had a lot of questions about what we're taught to believe when it comes to sex and stuff. And that you guys were looking for the truth too, but you were looking for it through art, not religion. Then when you came out to us, and when I saw what you went through at school after people found out, I realized—I realized that there is no Christian way you can reject gay people, and that it's just not possible if you love a gay person. Which I do." She smiles, taking a breath. "Look, you guys taught me that we all have to think for ourselves and decide what we think is right. And I think love is love, and love is good. God made love. So love who you want. I do."

"It's weird," I say, "how I feel like the time you started to question your faith for the first time sort of coincided with my deciding I had faith for the first time. I think I do believe in God. Not a Jewish god, or a Christian god, but just some being out there somewhere who knows more than I do, an x-factor in how life plays itself out. You know?"

"I mean, just think of it this way," she says, raising her palms up flat like the Bird Girl. "The foundation under the three major world religions, all it is is a really good book. I'm not saying all word nerds have to believe in God, but if you believe language is sacred in some way—well, it's not that much of a stretch."

"You are the best possible combination of Jesus freak and word nerd." I grin at her. "And a good sales-woman, too."

"I know."

"I gotta split, girl," I say, checking the time on my phone: 10:18. "I've got a reconciliation to make."

"'God was reconciling the world to himself in Christ, not counting men's sins against them. And he has committed to us the message of reconciliation,'" Tess quotes. "Second Corinthians five-nineteen."

"It still freaks me out how you can do that on command," I say. "But it's beautiful when you do." I peck her on the cheek and pull on my coat. "Later, gator."

I push back out into the cold, debating whether it's too late to make my next stop, noting the irony of the fact that I showed up at Rowie's house no earlier than ten p.m. three times a week for two months, stayed until the blue light of morning, and now I'm feeling like I'm breaking curfew just because I was imagining myself knocking on the front door this time. I plug in my headphones for some pump-me-up jams to fight the fist of anxiety tightening in my stomach as I roll toward Rowie's. I put on Tess's favorite White Stripes album, and I enjoy it, knowing how Marcy would taunt me if she could hear. "My Doorbell" has a kicking backbeat, I think as I careen around the dogleg in the road.

There is Rowie's driveway, looking prone and open-hearted under the streetlights. I scan the windows for movement, hoping everyone isn't asleep already. Sure enough, I see Priya in her study, reading under a green desk lamp. Collecting all my moxie, I toe up the stone steps and rap lightly on the door, seeing Priya's head twitch at the noise. She ties her robe and comes to the door.

"Esme!" she exclaims, pushing open the glass door and motioning me inside. "What are you doing prowling the cold streets so late? Get in out of the winter!"

"Oh, just restless," I say. "How are you, Dr. R.?"

"Oh, Esme, I'm fine," she says, hugging me. "How are *you*?" The look she gives me suggests that she knows what she's asking.

"I'm—" I don't finish. "I've missed you."

Rowie appears in a yellow nightie at the top of the stairs behind her.

"Well"—Dr. Priya Rudra watches us watching each

other—"there's chai on in the kitchen if you girls want some. I'll be reading. Don't stay up too late." She begins to say something else, then stops. "It's lovely to see your face, Esme. You're always welcome here." Her petite feet recede, padding down the hall.

Here are Rowie and me, confronted with each other, no escape to be had.

"Hi," she says.

"Hi," I say.

"How are you?" she asks.

"I'd be better if I had some chai tea," I reply, making a bloodless attempt at a smirk.

"I can do that." She looks more at ease with a task to perform, and I follow her into the kitchen. For a moment we don't talk as she lifts the wire tea strainer out of the pot and pours two mugs of tea. Except for us, the kitchen is asleep, off-duty for the night, streetlight glinting off the little spoons in the spice bowls. I sit in the breakfast nook with my steaming mug. When she sits, it's half in the shadow.

"So," I say.

"So," she says.

"You're probably wondering why I'm here," I begin carefully.

"A little," she says, blowing on her tea.

"I'll just put you out of your suspense now. I don't totally know why I'm here."

"You don't have to," she says. We look down in our cups for a second, silent.

"I feel—I feel like there are some conversations we never finished," I decide.

"I do too," she says, and it shoots straight through me.

"You do?"

"I mean, I didn't really think I'd never talk to you again." She pulls back a step.

"Yeah, but I gotta be honest—I don't really know what to say right now." My heart is pounding. An icon of Rama and Sita hangs above Rowie's bare, winking shoulder. The fridge clicks on, rupturing the velvety silence. My eyes dart back to Rama and Sita, his blue face and her serene gaze, and I feel suddenly ashamed not to know anything about their story. I point.

"What's the deal with Rama and Sita again?" I ask her. "All I know is that they're, like, Hindu star-crossed lovers."

She tips her head right, craning to search the portrait behind her. "It's just like all the other precolonial love stories," she says with a shrug. "Native empire and divine right and women being sold for land and power. There's, like, this really long, complicated plot about Sita being the daughter of the king of Videha and Rama being blue and divine and winning a contest to marry her and ascend the throne, and then Rama's evil stepmother wants her son to marry Sita instead, and Rama has to go through this long, complicated pursuit of her after she's kidnapped, and there's a lot of deer and birds and forests and fire and questions of purity." She takes a breath. "It's, like, no one ever asks the chick what she wants in these stories. No one asks them if they want to be auctioned off and chased through forests. I mean, maybe she doesn't even really like him that much. Maybe she just wanted to kick it casual. Maybe she doesn't want to deal with all that hassle. Or something."

I don't know how to respond, so I take a blind swing at the elephant in the room.

"So what's up with you and Prakash?"

Her eyes flash at me: she meets mine in a gaze of shock, then shifts her sight out the window. "I don't know. It just feels—uncomplicated."

"*Un*complicated?"

"Please don't start."

"Because he's Indian? Just because he's an Indian dude?"

"Yes," she snaps, lowering her voice, "Okay? Yes. It's just easier. Fuck, Esme, I get dressed in the morning and I'm disappointing my parents. They were sad when I never wanted to go back to India with them. They were sad the first time I talked back to them like an American kid. They were sad when I never wanted to introduce them to my friends because I was afraid people would laugh at their accents. It's—it's just *complicated*."

"And Prakash just magically understands you because he's had some of those experiences? He understands you because he makes more visual sense as the other half of the picture? Are your parents even happy you're dating? I thought they didn't want you to."

"They're not unhappy," she says.

"Yeah?" I shoot back. "Well, are *you* happy, Rowie? Guess what. This is some postcolonial shit right here. This is the part of the story where someone asks you what *you* want. All you do is talk about what your parents want. So what is it *you* want, anyway? I mean *really* want, like a fist-in-the-gut kind of wanting, what do you really, really want?"

"How in the hell can you expect me to know the answer to that question?" she hisses through gritted teeth, her voice clouding. "Don't you get it? This thing with Prakash, whatever it is—it buys me time. It's going to be different in a few years, like college and not living with my parents and—time, you know? Time and space. For whatever."

I let her words set in for a minute. We don't talk.

"Do you ever wonder—what it is we're all making college out to be?" I ask slowly. "It's like, this great escape, the way we're all looking at it, this magic time when we can be whoever and do whatever we want. I'm just wondering, kind of, why we can't be who we are and do what we're gonna do now."

"Because we're sheltered." She shrugs.

"I guess," I say. "But that isn't really good enough, is it? I mean, everything moves so *fast,* and yet not fast enough. Do we really have time to wait to be— ourselves?"

"Ez," she says quietly, "I'm not you. I don't think I'm as much like you as you think I am. I don't think I'm your—the same as you, or something."

"Do you really think that?" I ask. "Or do you just think you're supposed to think that? I really don't think we looked so bad together."

"How do you know?" she whispers. "No one ever really saw."

The wind kicks up outside; I hear my bike topple over. I don't know how to respond to her: if a tree comes out to an empty forest, is the tree still gay? And where is this empty place, anyway, this place that no one sees, this place where things crash but don't resound into all the other places? The crash happened; I *know* it happened; questioning whether it happened or not this late in the game makes me feel insane.

"It's the same old impasse," I observe, wanting to feel colder about it than I do.

"Yeah," she agrees. "It is."

"I don't want to pursue you beyond the point that you want to be pursued."

"Yeah." She takes a slow breath. "There are other things that I want, you know."

"Like what?"

"Like to make music. To write lyrics again. Maybe to be a part of you and Marcy's little Holyhill revolution."

"We don't take maybe members," I say haughtily. "I didn't mean that. I'm sorry." I stop myself. "You're really hard to get at sometimes, Rowie."

"Sorry," she says. "Look, I know. And I'm really sorry. For—everything. With us. I just wish things could be like they were before. Before everything got so messy."

"Love is messy," I say. "There's no love without the mess of it."

"Serious," she says. "But we used to be able to—pound out the truth somehow. Writing and performing with you made me feel better about things."

"I loved being onstage with you, you know," I tell her. "It made me feel invincible. It made me feel like we were charting a course and the world just had to suck it up and follow us wherever we wanted to take them. But I think part of that was feeling like we had a secret, like we knew something they didn't. Like we had a secret chemistry."

"I think we'll always have a secret chemistry," she intones. "Or, like, we'll always be MC Rohini and MC Ferocious together."

"We rhyme," I say, because it's true. "There's—there's this song I've been working on. That's sort of, about you, or whatever."

"Yeah?" she says. "Can I hear it?"

"I guess so," I agree, feeling nervous. "I mean, it's not done, and it needs a chorus. It's just a bunch of verses right now."

"Yeah, 'cause you suck at writing choruses," she says, grinning.

"Yeah." I say. "Okay, here goes." I begin to rhyme in a low voice.

*"I'm MC Ferocious, throwing down some gorgeous
Flows into motion, I'm gonna make a potion
Of women and words, brimming with nerds
So get primed for some rhyming like some shit you've never heard
Unearth your dirty words, cause it's gonna get absurd.*

*This one time I tried
Getting with a guy
I tried it, didn't buy it, couldn't fly on a lie.
He was a cramped backseat and an indie rock blare
It was so hard to believe I was supposed to be scared.*

*'Cause I've spent my whole life trying to be bigger than one
Like I could up and make the earth revolve the sun*

322

Something 'bout that wanting makes a girl feel invisible
Divisible: is it, though?
I wanna get physical
With an unfuckwittable
Visible mistress who
Feels my kind of blue
Listen, I don't care who
Let's screw through curfews
Show me who it is soon, is it you, is it you?
Girl of my dreams, cool as the moon
You gotta come soon 'cause I wanna get with you, boo.

There's a girl who gets me all raucously nauseous
Ferocious is audacious but my object is cautious
Still, when this girl blushes
It twists me up in thrushes
All flustered and hushing
Up in the lushness of lusting
What a rush, I wanna touch
All her luscious erupting
God, her flush gets me gushing
I'm loving like busting
We're hushing, and she's blushing, and I'm mushy on
  crushing."

I can tell that Rowie's face looks a little melty by the
time I finish, but neither of us can hold eye contact.

"That was super emo," she says, trying for sarcasm but failing to conceal a sniffle.

"I know," I say.

"It would—it would make me really happy if we could rhyme together again," Rowie says. "Even if we can't do—all the things we used to do. Sister Mischief was, like, the best thing I've ever done. And 4H."

"Yeah." I nod. "That would make me happy too. It's funny how at least for me, I started off more interested in pissing Holyhill off than anything else, but all of a sudden we had this queer hip-hop *movement* that I really cared about, and you were a big part of that."

"I've been thinking a lot about what *queer* means," Rowie muses. "Maybe I could help you come up with a chorus for that song you just showed me. I'm thinking we could do something with *queer* as the central rhyme."

"Yeah? I like that."

"You know, the story I told you about Rama and Sita—it's only part of the story of how Hinduism conceives gender. It's actually a lot more complicated. There are sort of different interpretations, but a lot of the gods are neuter or even female."

"That's really interesting," I say. "But what's your point? I mean, why did you just tell me that?"

"I don't know." She shrugs. "I just think it's interesting that I come from someplace where the divine—can be as ambiguous as real life. It's just something else I've been thinking about a lot lately. Trying to figure out how I feel about—everything that's happened."

I pause. "I've really missed you, Ro."

"I've missed you too," she says. "Ez, I'm really sorry I couldn't—I'm just really sorry is all."

"I know," I say. "I think we should just try being friends. And you better suit up *right*, girl, because 4H is about to go balls to the wall."

"*Ovaries* to the wall, motherfucker," she corrects me, hinting at a grin. I smile for the first time in this kitchen. The reconstitution of our rectangle—because Sister Mischief was never, ever about squares—makes me feel like things are making some kind of sense again: our fourth corner is back on board.

"Nice editorial, by the way," I say with a smirk.

"Oh." She looks embarrassed. "Yeah. That. I guess— it was my way of contributing to everything you guys were stirring up. And, like, apologizing, maybe. Actually—my mom helped me polish it up."

"Well"—I lower my voice to fill her in—"just wait until you hear what we're rigging up next. This shit is about to fly off the chain."

CHAPTER SIXTEEN

Hellzapoppin'
Hip-Hop for Heteros
and Homos

The reckoning week is upon us. The council of Mischief is united again, and we're feral with anticipation, foaming at the mouth for a fight: Ez and Tess and Marce and Ro. We're ragged from reuniting all weekend, practicing a cumulative mastermix of old and new verses that we're going to drop until they grapple the mikes right out of our hands. Tess even talked us all into getting, like, outfits, which took some doing with old kicking-and-screaming antigirl Marcy. 4H has been going full throttle in the warming house, which has been turned into a chaos factory of sorts, our fracas laboratory.

"So Nordling's called an all-school assembly for next Tuesday afternoon," I announce as I come into the 4H preparation meeting for Operation Sister Mischief and throw my backpack on the chair. "On the hip-hop policy."

"Did anyone see you come in here?" Rowie asks me, looking over my shoulder at the track. It tugs: of *course* Rowie's the one who asks me that. I shake my head, closing the door.

"Why's Nordling calling the assembly now?" Angelo asks. "I mean, what's the sudden motivation?"

"Parents, duh," Tess answers knowingly. "The 4H stuff's been going on long enough that the parents have started to hear about it, and that means he has to deal with it."

"Deal with this," Marcy declares, spreading out a complicated diagram. "With the combined efforts of Rowie, Jane, Yusuf, and myself, we've pretty much laid out a hostile takeover of Holyhill's entire sound system, from the PA system to the soundboard in the auditorium."

"And it's all routed back through the warming house," Yusuf adds proudly. "We can totally have everything ready by Tuesday." Yusuf and his marginally shady supply of sound equipment, or parts that have been hacked together to create sound equipment, have been vital to our plan.

"Damn," Kai says in awe. "How'd you pull that off?"

"Just a little creative technology and a lot of hardcore nerding out," Rowie responds with a grin.

"So with a tap of a button here and a flick of a switch there," Jane adds, "we can not only manipulate but record anything we want in the school's sonic infrastructure."

"It's like—a mechanical metaphor for our entire mission," I breathe, squinting at the blueprint. "That is the most beautiful fucking thing I've ever seen."

"In order to form a more perfect sonic union." Marcy fist-pounds me.

"Who's in the final mash-up?" Yusuf asks.

"Oh, man, our sample list is sick," I say, glowing. "There's a lot of homage to chicks on the stick—M.I.A., Invincible, Bahamadia, Queen Latifah, Lauryn Hill." And a ton of other shit too, like K'naan, some Twin Cities reppers like Brother Ali and Slug, DJ A.P.S., this bhangra-hop dude, and some Bay Area hyphy shit, this homohop group Deep Dickcollective. We didn't know homo-hop, like, existed until recently, but they've got this bomb-ass queer rhythm."

"Donations from Kanye were strictly prohibited," Marcy says.

"I managed to sneak in a little indie rock," Tess pipes up. "Jack and Meg, MGMT, Passion Pit. And Vampire Weekend." She blushes.

"Tess gets all hot and bothered by cardigans," I explain, rolling my eyes. "I think they look like Ivy League dandy boys." Everyone laughs and returns to touching up the final plan.

"Damn," Yusuf says. "This is gonna be some hellzapoppin' hip-hop for heteros and homos."

"Better recognize," Marcy says.

I look over at Rowie splicing wires, and even though we're as good at pretending things are all good as we ever were, I still feel like collapsing in a dead heap after seeing her, overwhelmed by the effort it takes to front at being cool with the fact that she's still sort of with Prakash.[62] Rowie was the kind of love that just walks into your life one day and then walks out the next, I guess.[63]

We're looking over a precipice in our becoming the Sister Mischief cohort, and the pitch of the tension leading up to it is deafening. Part of me is afraid that everyone will laugh, that I'm a caricature of myself, of a hip-hop-loving suburban whitegirl. But the tenets of Sister Mischief and 4H have given us something to stand behind, a kind of credo surrounding our clam-jamming, ruckus-making pursuit of sexual and musical justice. I wake up in the morning and I feel like I was put on this earth to do this.

"I better run." On Tuesday morning, I throw a hoodie on over my T-shirt and jeans, hunting around for shoes. My real outfit is already packed in my book bag, along

62. Text from Tessie: *she and prakash aren't really spending that much time together, u know. caught u looking.*
Response, while glaring at her: *it's cool or whatever, i don't need to know.*

63. Tess back: *you don't have to front. i was just saying.*
I respond: *sorry. i want to hate her, but i can't.*

with a few other key elements of today's periodic table: an extra copy of the preloaded beats on tape, my new hipster shades,[64] *Anne Frank* and *ATGIB* as little talismans of luck, the last picture of Mom and me, the one of her in the green dress, tucked inside the diary.

"Hey. Big day," Pops says, looking dangerously close to a pep talk.

"Big day," I say, refusing to sound nervous, because I don't feel nervous at all—no, sir, nope.

"I want you to know that I think you're totally crazy and I love you no shit and I will absolutely bail you out of jail if need be," he says, "and that I am the proudest dad of a queer teen queen MC that there ever was."

"I want you to know that I think you should have your head examined," I say, kissing the bald spot on top, "but I love you no shit, and thanks. Try not to be too conspicuous sneaking into the back of the auditorium with the video camera, 'kay?"

"Wait," he insists, dashing into the kitchen. "I want to take a picture of you."

"Pops, I have to go," I whine.[65] "I'm going to be late to my own coming-out party."

"You'll thank me later for documenting this." He

---

64. TheConTessa @pockettrockett @Marcedemeanor *if you "forget" the sunglasses I got you, you're dead. #wackassembly*

65. Text from Marcy: *Where are u?? I'm outside. Can't u hear the honking?*

snaps a picture of me flicking him off. "I have only two parting words to give you."

"And they are?" I pull on my coat, poised to depart.

He puts his hands on both sides of my head and pulls it toward him, planting a kiss on my forehead. "Be somebody."

When we sludge through the first hours of the school day, it's another one of those days where everyone knows that something's coming, but we've kept the lid on our plan super tight, so no one knows exactly what.[66] After Chem, I dash to the second-floor girls' room to suit up, feeling like I've had about twelve Diet Cokes. It's like we're at the eye of a tornado about to trunk down on the plains. The assembly is scheduled for after third lunch, which will be over in twelve minutes; they're probably hoping all the kids will be in food comas. All Nordling said in his announcement over the PA system (which, by the way, Yusuf got on tape for our tasty sampling enjoyment) was that he was calling an assembly to discuss "maintaining safety and a positive learning environment for all students." Repeat after me: when I say *no-talent,* you say *ass-clown.*

"Hollerrrrrr," I whisper, dancing into the bathroom to find the three of them twitching at the mirror.

66. Marcedemeanor @TheConTessa @wowiewudwa @pockettrockett RT #4H4life #wackassembly *Get ready.*

"*What* are you wearing?" Tess grabs my wrists, shaking me. "Get changed *now.*"

"Down, psycho." I twist free, whipping out my outfit and stripping. We've all got leggings—except Marcy, who categorically refused to wear anything but her marching band pants—and slouchy T-shirts, with various bling and accessories. Marcy's got her brass-knuckles necklace, and Rowie's got her heart hoops, and Tess's laced up these ridiculous over-the-knee streetwalker boots with gold chain. As I pull off my shirt, Rowie and I lock eyes for a moment. She looks down, searching her shoes.

"Did you drop this?" Marcy bends over, retrieving a small gold chunk and looking at it incredulously. "Shut up. Is that—?"

I cackle, rinsing the prosthetic gold tooth off in the sink, then popping it into my mouth and grinning. "You like?"

"Lawd ha' mercy, you do beat all, Esme Rockett." Rowie tosses my sweatshirt at me, shaking her head, and moves toward the door. "We gotta go."

The four of us hustle through the halls and station ourselves in the catwalk overlooking the stage in the auditorium, hooked up to the warming house via walkie-talkie. None of us ate lunch, and the rumblings in our bellies are pumping a crazy energy into our preparations. Rowie begins to dry-heave quietly in the corner as Tess rubs her back and taps on her iPhone at the same time.[67]

"All systems go. Over to B-girl, all systems go," Yusuf's voice crackles softly over the walkie-talkie. "Operation Sister Mischief waits for your go signal."

"Copy that, B-boy," Marcy whispers back. "Stay close by your trigger."

"I think we gotta get a huddle in here quick," Tess says, gently pulling Rowie back toward us. I hand her the Nalgene.

"FaSHO," I reply. "Quad up, bitches."

We crouch together, glancing down as the auditorium floods with students. Principal Nordling and his cronies below us are adjusting their ties and pacing onstage, looking nervouser than Rowie.

"Who's gonna do the honors?" I ask.

"All you, Ezbo." Marcy chucks my shoulder. Rowie nods, rubbing her upper arms and rocking slightly back and forth.

"Well, ladies," I begin, "what can I say? You are my wickedest mischievous sisters, most beloved friends of my mind, baddest bitches this side of the Mississippi. It

67. TheConTessa @4H4life #wackassembly *free concert in waldinger auditorium in five minutes.*

333

all got a little dramatic for a hot minute up in here, but what matters right now is that we *throw* the fuck *down*. I love you women no shit, and I am proud to share this stage and every stage with your fine asses. What we have today is the opportunity of a lifetime—we've got a captive audience of fifteen hundred Holyhillers, a bitch-ass administration that can't kick us out without making themselves look bad, and the illest illicit sound system this school has ever known. So this one is for our crew, but it's also for all the weird girls and word nerds, for all the in-the-middle wickeds and queers and misfits and hell-raisers. For 4H." I put my hand palm-down in the space between us; they layer theirs one by one on top of mine. "We're Sister Mischief, motherfuckers. Gotta be somebody."

"Be somebody," they repeat solemnly. We hear a series of thuds as Nordling taps his hot mike to start the program. Homeboy has no idea what he's about to get hit with.

"Signal: begin recording, B-boy," Marcy murmurs over the W-T.

"Copy that," B-boy crackles.[68]

"Ladies and gentlemen, please find your seats," Nordling booms over the mike. "Quiet down now, please."

---

68. Fusuy @4H4life #wackassembly *introducing sister mischief: live at holyhill.*

The entire Holyhill student body is packed into every nook and cranny and farthest reach of the auditorium, rustling restlessly in the theater seats and aisles. Our post in the catwalk allows us to reach the stage by climbing over the crowd and dropping down a ladder on stage right. It's the kind of maneuver you can't pull off in a skirt.

"Ladies and gentlemen," Nordling begins skittishly, "we have convened here today to hold an all-school discussion of the recent activity surrounding Holyhill's policy regarding inappropriate music and attire." The crowd titters. "The administration has become aware of a number of infractions of this policy, and from this point forward, will be detaining or suspending any student who chooses to ignore it."

Sounds of protest kindle across the crowd, and upon closer inspection, I see they're coming from Jane, Angelo, Courteney, and a sizable troop of other 4H sympathizers near the stage. At the back of the auditorium, I spot two camera lenses glinting under the lights: Pops's and KIND-11's. Those Crowthers are so reliable. From the podium, Nordling tries to press down the agitation with his hands, shushing everyone like unruly kindergartners.

"We will be taking questions from the student body very soon," he says in an attempt to soothe the unease.

"First, we'd like to review some of the thinking behind this policy and express our regret for not having done so sooner."

"What about your regret for the students who were victimized by the attack on a queer hip-hop discussion group?" Jane stands up and calls out, balls-out. "Do students who disagree with you not deserve to study in safety?" Her comment elicits some whoops and applause from our contingent and a few dismissive moans from the haters.

"Okay," Nordling sighs. "Maybe in the interest of getting you back to class before the end of the day, we'll take questions now. Miss Njaka, of course we value the safety of all our students, irregardless of their opinions, and that's exactly why we take the need to keep the music associated with a culture of violence out of our school as seriously as we do."

"*Irregardless* isn't a word!" Angelo cries.

"We aren't the violent ones!" Kai adds with passion.

"This shit's about to fly off the hook." Marcy scrambles to collect our equipment and starts across the catwalk.

"Let's do this thing." I scuttle up through the crawl space above the lights.

"Ro, you gonna make it?" Tess grabs her hand.

"I'll get it together. Get moving." Rowie takes several deep, wheezing breaths as she readies herself.

The four of us move cautiously over the long span

above the audience, struggling not to make too much noise. We're all shaking. My knees grind against the metal grate of the catwalk. Marcy reaches the ladder first and takes it real slow on her way down, toeing each rung, finding her footing. One by one, we drop to the floor and unpack swiftly. We don't seem to have been spotted from the stage yet. Marcy ducks under her sweatshirt with the walkie-talkie.

"B-boy, stand by for cue one," she hisses. "Come in, B-boy."

"Confirmed," we hear. "Sister Mischief is a go for all operations."

"Are there other questions?" Nordling's voice reaches us from the stage, asking for it, just *asking* for it.

"See you on the flip." I slide on my shades, switch on my mike, and hurtle onstage before I can think myself out of it.

"Yo, Mr. Principal," I say into the mike, setting off a domino-snake of hubbub in the audience. "I got a question for you."

"Miss Rockett"—he looks at me, astonished—"what exactly are you doing up here?"

"Can I ask a question or not?" I shoot back, not really believing my own nerve.

"Miss Rockett, I'm going to have to ask *you* to get off this stage right—"

I don't have time for him to finish.

"My question is—we're about to get scandalous; Holyhill, can you *handle* this?"

The downbeat of our opening backbeat drops, followed by the whine of Nordling's own voice, looping *safety and a positive learning environment for all students* while my three compatriots bound onstage with their mikes behind me, the boom box balanced on Marcy's shoulder, all of them moving to the beat like it's our business to be here. The row of teachers seated on stage left recoils in shock, except Mrs. DiCostanza, who's clearly suppressing a smile. Rhythm pounding, the four of us make our way downstage of the principal's podium. I'm up.

"I'm MC Ferocious, throwing down some gorgeous
Flows into motion, I'm stirring up a potion
Of women and words, brimming with nerds
So get primed for some rhyming like you ain't never heard
Unearth your dirty words, 'cause it's gonna get absurd.

I got this hysteria, maybe it's uterus lunacy
I'm defective and restive, ain't no way to get through to me
And all of these haters, all the things that they do to me
We gotta get positive, find a cure for this prudery.

So I wanna tell the world what it's like for this girl
Wanna shake off the weight of all these diamonds and
*   pearls*

While I ignite this light and crazy drama unfurls,
'Cause I'm a girl who loves girls who love girls who
*   love girls.*

We got ladies in the house, ladies first, ladies wicked
We ride to get high, Minnesota-do-or-die
Talkin' sticky shit and kickin' it, our bidness is
*   the shiznit*
So holler out our name, we're the illest Sister
*   Mischief."*

All four of us hit the *illest Sister Mischief* hard as we launch into the chorus, banked from the back by Tess's belting—she's going for those eagle-dare high notes like I've never heard her go for them before, and nailing every one to the wall. Marcy sets the boom box down on the stage and suits up in her proudest invention yet: the portable turntable, strapped to her torso with the drumline's over-the-shoulder harness for snares in the marching band. She scratches a tattoo or two and people start to lose it, hooting in a way that I think is meant as encouragement. I say a silent prayer for Rowie as Tess finishes her solo: *Please, God, help her get through her verse without vomming.* She starts a half-beat late but recovers:

"They say that I can't spit rhymes full of violence
That the way to the truth is inquiring silence

But I gotta find knowledge with a hard look through
   my lens
Gotta get up with my girls and get people behind this.

I'm bringing beats from the East and pleading for peace
Got SheStorm's piece heaving heat like a beast
Rohini and Ferocious drop R-H-Y-M-Es
To stop the intolerance, why aren't more of you hollerin'
How it ain't right to be collaring the folks who love color in
Music they appreciate for art and for harmony
Got a girl army comin' that's all armed in belief in
A Technicolor dream of a country that leans in
To hear what we're saying when we're young and we're
   feelin'
Like there's gotta be hope and be change and belief in
A system of government that speaks out for freedom."

   Rowie and I are downstage center, rocking back and
forth together, beaming through the first chorus:

"We gonna cause some drama like President Obama.
Yeah, we gonna cause some drama like Barack Obama.
This school needs some leaders who respect the mamas,
So we gonna cause some drama like President Obama."

   I glance around for a few beats, trying to see if
Nordling has forcibly dragged any of my friends offstage

yet or if the cops've showed up. I spot Chuckles in the crowd and he gives me a shy thumbs-up. Shockingly, a few members of the teacher keychain seem to be *enjoying* our performance; a few are even bopping back and forth and clapping in time to the beat, which is maybe the whitest thing I've ever seen. When I look into the audience, the only people I can see who aren't having the best assembly of their lives seem to be Mary Ashley Baumgarten; her creepy doppelgänger, Stina; Anders Ostergaard; and—you guessed it—Prakash Banerjee. Tools! I fling out my second verse, creeping to the front of the stage.

"I've spent my whole life trying to be bigger than one
Like I could up and make the earth revolve the sun
Something bout that wanting makes a girl feel
   invisible
Divisible: is it, though?
I wanna get physical
With an unfuckwittable
Visible mistress who
Feels my kind of blue
Listen, I don't care who
Let's screw through curfews
Show me who it is soon, is it you, is it you?
Girl of my dreams, cool as the moon
You gotta come soon 'cause I wanna get with you, boo.

So who says the homos can't come out and drop bombs?
And who says I gotta look like these Botoxed white moms?
MC Ro and me got anthems to dance with
Wearin' low-riders low and we got plenty of bandwidth
To transmit these messages you best not be messin' with.

So I'm still early on in the journey called rhyme
But I can't stop from rhyming, got no love for paradigms
I got red blood and word floods, and mad love for bad thugs
I got TC reppers, yer boys Ali and Slug
But in this verse I gotta nurse this little purse of sisters who
    subvert
And immerse their minds in different kinds
Of diverse rhymes across the universe
So you heard it here first, female verses are the curses we
    reverse."

Rowie smiles at me as we bound together for the second chorus, one she wrote for me after my super emo rap at her house:

"Get up and cheer
Listen don't hear
Been too many tears
So say it sincere
She's a little bit queer, and he's really queer
She queer, and he queer, and we all clearly queer."

All four of us throw the 4H signal down with the detonation of the final beat: four fingers on the left hand, crossed by one on the right, pressed to the breast. We sashay off stage right, knowing that right now, no one, *no one* in the suburbs has swagger even remotely like us. We're sweating and panting backstage like we've just sprinted a marathon, and I realize that this is the only part of the plan that we haven't choreographed within an inch of its life—what the hell happens when we finish our song? I don't think any of us expected that they'd actually let us finish. Contemplating this, we breathe in and breathe out once, twice, three times, before we hear the dumbfounded silence erupt into cheering.

I peek around the curtain with my mouth agape. The crowd is on its feet and hollering full tilt, cheering like teenage banshees as the teachers still marooned on stage left exchange what-now glances. Nordling returns to the podium, but a full minute passes before the screaming begins to dwindle, during which he's left standing there looking like a puppet on strings, waving his hands, mouthing words that no one can hear. I notice that Mrs. DiCostanza and a few of the other teachers have bowed their heads together and seem to be scribbling something on a notepad.

"What the eff do we do now?" Rowie hisses.

"Let's just see what homeboy does next," replies

Marcy, chewing her fingernails in anxious glee. "I don't want to miss a second of this."

"I must insist—" Nordling tries to interject, cut off by a few final whoops. "I must insist that all of you compose yourselves. Miss Rockett, Miss Rudra, Miss Crowther, and Miss Grinnell"—he points at us—"you will report directly to my office at the conclusion of this assembly." This elicits a scattered, rising boo from the audience, lowing like cattle in disapproval. "As I stated before this disruption, violations of any policy outlined in Holyhill's code of conduct will be met with serious consequences. Now, I'd like everyone, beginning with the senior class, to collect their things and return to afternoon class—"

Nordling gets cut off again—poor fool can't even finish a sentence up in this glorious mess—but this time by Mrs. D., who hands him a sheet of paper and whispers something in his ear. He steps back, cupping a hand over the microphone, and they swap words for a hot second, then he throws up his hands and motions exasperatedly for her to take the podium. Mrs. D. reads from the paper in her hands.

"In light of the authentic intellectual curiosity evidenced by 4H's application for school recognition, and by these young women's unique and remarkable performance, the faculty of Holyhill High School moves to amend the policy prohibiting hip-hop music on school grounds"—a preemptive roar begins to spring from the crowd but is squashed by one withering glare from Mrs. D., that titan—"the faculty moves to amend this policy in order to permit hip-hop music and culture to be studied and discussed and urges the administration to guarantee that all future 4H meetings will receive the administration's full support and commitment to safety."

"YEAH!" Marcy lets loose, hooting and jumping up and down along with everyone else. "Mrs. D. speaks, mofos!"

The world is full of surprises like this, I suppose, but this madcap campaign has recruited the scrappiest mess of encouragement from unlikely places, and I guess that moves me, this showing of support from people it might have been easy to mistake for haters. It gives me a strange kind of faith in people, this jackpot we've struck after we laid our cards out on the table and let go our truth for the whole school to hear. I wonder if this is what everyone will remember about me now, five, ten years from now. It's exactly the legacy I've always wanted.

"Please return to your classes," Principal Nordling announces weakly. The teachers and administrators dispel into the audience, prodding everyone back to class and reality and the rest of this game-changing day. As he walks toward the exit, Nordling turns back to us and waggles a come-hither finger in our direction, reminding us that we're not off the hook yet. Giggling, decompressing, coming down from the rush, we pick up the electronic pieces of our sonic revolution and start toward the office, racking up a few backslaps and props along the way.

"Yo, I didn't know chicks could rap like that," a scrawny sophomore tells us excitedly. "That was badass." Some assorted other people we don't know echo the kudos, and we try to conceal our bafflement as we make our way through the sea of people. Marcy's walkie-talkie beeps.

"Mission accomplished," Yusuf's voice comes in. "That was some wicked-ass shit, Sister Mischief."

"Over and out." Marcy grins into the speaker. "B-girl signing off."

Swiveling back to take one last mental picture of the scene, I see Pops near the exit opposite us; he gives me a smile and a 4H sign and retreats, chatting with Rooster and the KIND-11 team. *Everything I know about protesting*, I think proudly, *I learned from that man.*

Our shoulders slump a little as we gear up to face the music, kind of literally, in the principal's office. We all stop just short of the front desk, not ready to let go of the high. I turn to my girls.

"Look, whatever happens in there," I declare, "we did ourselves proud today."

"For real," Tess echoes, nodding. "If they expel me, I'm glad it was for this."

"For real," Marcy agrees.

"For real," Rowie completes the thought. Marcy and Tess start to slink in, but Rowie holds me back.

"Hey, Ez?" she says.

"MC Ro?"

"Thanks."

"For what?" I ask, incredulous. "You did that shit on your own."

"I know," she says. "But I wouldn't have done it without you."

I feel myself blushing: after all this time, not so much time really, she still has this effect on me. Maybe she always will.

"No doubt," I say. "Let's get this over with."

Hesitantly, Marcy knocks on Nordling's office door. A strained "Come in" resounds from inside. We enter.

"Please sit down," he says, kind of overly gracious. We do.

Tess speaks first: "Principal Nordling, we realize that our performance was disruptive to the assembly you had planned, and we're prepared to accept the consequences for that. All we'd ask you to consider is that ours was a thoughtful and, we think, well-founded act of protest."

He nods slowly, putting his fingers together in a little steeple over his mouth.

"That was quite a stunt you girls pulled," he observes neutrally. "It was uniquely intrusive, completely inappropriate, and clearly premeditated."

"Yes, sir. It was," I agree.

"You threatened the authority of my position, and my credibility in maintaining order at this school." He's oddly calm, and it's kind of creeping me out.

"Yes, sir, we did," Marcy says. "But we ask you to take into account that our actions were in response to a hateful attack on us and our beliefs."

"Yes, Miss Crowther, you've made that abundantly clear," he responds with a little less patience. "And that, along with all four of your excellent academic standings, is the only reason why I'm not going to expel you."

We let out a collective rush of relieved sighs.

"Thank you, Principal Nordling," Tess begins to answer him.

"I'm not finished," he says. "Let me tell you what's going to happen here. The unrest your apparent displeasure with Holyhill's policies has caused stops right now. There will be no more apparel campaigns, no more flyers, no more flirtation with the local media at my expense, and absolutely no more surprise performances."

We nod skeptically, waiting to hear what else he's got.

"If you immediately ratchet all of your antics down a notch, the agreement I'm prepared to make with you is as follows. You will all be suspended from school and all school activities for one week, including"—he looks at Marcy—"including band and drumline, and that suspension will appear on your permanent records." We all pale a little but hold our poker faces. "However, in light of the surprising amount of support you managed to conjure from the faculty, I am also willing to reconsider my decision not to add 4H to Holyhill's roster of recognized student groups, if you can promise me that your group will not in any way disturb the positive learning environment I'm trying to uphold here. Do we have a deal, ladies?"

The four of us look at one another, realizing that, all things considered, this is a pretty sweetheart deal. Three nods answer my questioning eyebrows. I stand up and stick out my hand.

"You've got a deal, sir," I say. "I think you'll find that our group will enrich, not disturb, Holyhill's learning environment."

He rises too, taking my hand. "I'm glad to hear that. In that case, young ladies, please return to your classrooms, and perhaps you can spend your week beginning tomorrow composing a mission statement for 4H that will convince me of your intent to honor our agreement."

"No doubt, son." Marcy holds out a fist for him to pound; he looks quizzically at it for a moment, then chuckles softly and taps his knuckles to hers.

EPILOGUE

Live at Holyhill: The Sister Mischief EP

Tonight, I'm on a midnight jaunt out to Lake Calhoun, my TC oasis, the sandy beaches where I once tore naked across the shore, sand now indistinguishable from snowdrifts. As I come at it from the Excelsior side, I see a litter of fishing huts still settled out on the lake, and a few trapped buoys protruding from the ice like birthday candles. After I chain my bike to a tree, the only sounds are cars passing and my feet miffing the snow. If anyone needed evidence to be convinced of my hard-wrought Midwesternness, here it is: I can bike in virtually any weather. The long winter's only half-gone now, and everything is frozen solid despite the best efforts of climate change.

I got new headphones, a surprise from Pops. They cover my whole ears and make me feel like a magical cyborg, a girl robot wired into the root system of the music. I just feel like there's so much work to do, so much time and so little all the same. And then other times I make myself remember, *Yes, I do have time.* Time to be seventeen, to catch up to everything sixteen ran out on, time to create and re-create myself and everything I create. Some things you do in high school don't turn out as well as you'd planned—your first self-mixed drinks, believing that detagging yourself from incriminating Facebook pictures erases them, at-home hair color or any tattoo—but the truth is, some of the things you do at sixteen turn out better than you'd planned. Like growing older on the holy soil of Minnesota. Like girl rappers in Minneapolis.

We were at a family friend's cabin in Wisconsin, I forget whose, for Mom's last Thanksgiving, the winter she drove the Colt Vista out on the frozen lake.

"That ice is two feet deep!" she declared, persuading me out of my tryptophan coma after dinner. "We could drive a Mack truck out there and we'd be fine. Come on. Let's have an adventure."

I trotted after her even though I was scared, still protesting, *What if we fall in?* and *Would Pops be able to get to us in time?* I was an anxious kid, far topped by my mother in fearlessness. I remember her mouth stretching in delight, her white teeth glinting as we careened from the boat landing onto the lake and across the ice, her action-movie steering sending us in lunatic figure-eights that left the snow still scarified in the morning.

"Isn't this fun? Don't you feel *wild*?" she screamed, I think.

At first all I could do was clench the door handle and pray, but when she stopped the car and dragged me out in the middle of the frozen lake, I think I began to feel what she felt—a need to drive recklessly with no one around to see, to feel enormous or tiny in the face of something enormous, to be confronted with a carpet of stars and a raw night of possibility. They say that children who lose parents at an early age freeze developmentally at the age of that loss—that part of me will always be five years old and speeding in pigtails across the lake, hoping Mom and the ice car will come back to shore before spring. I spread out my blanket on the marbled frieze of Lake Calhoun, facing the Minneapolis skyline, and dig my boot heels into the snow, nestled in Pops's parka, not at all cold.

Mom's seventeenth-birthday letter came a few weeks late, predictably. I didn't open it right away, didn't see the point. *Dear Esme*, it would read. *Let me offer you another year of self-absorbed and badly organized line items that may or may not make any sense to you. Oranges, reflections on your life before age five, & etc. Love, Mom.*

Shaking my head, thinking *what the hell*, I draw the

envelope out of Pops's coat pocket and pull off my glove with my teeth to slit it open. Unfolding the paper, I notice with shock that the letter doesn't seem to be just a list. As I skim it, it still doesn't seem to make a lot of sense, at least not "sense" in the conventional understanding of the word, but hey, some of it actually has, like, syntax:

Dearest Esme Ruth (spawn of mine),

I can't believe you are seventeen already. I think of what you must look like now, probably more like the young woman I used to be instead of the child I used to know, and it makes me feel old. I read your letter and it meant so much to me to hear from you, even if it meant hearing how angry you are with me. You can't know how angry I am with myself. My visa expires next year and I may have to return to the United States whether I like it or not, which both scares me and fills me with hope, a hope that we might open that bottle of wine and close down a restaurant together talking someday soon, a hope that you turned out better without me, just as I thought you might. I was selfish. But please believe that I thought it might have been for your own good.

It occurs to me that maybe I never stopped to tell you it wasn't your fault. I'm sorry I couldn't stay to explain the hard things to you. I loved you — still

love you — so much, Esme, and I love Luke too, and
it was all my fault for getting married too young
and boxing myself into a life I wasn't ready for. A
Jungian psychoanalyst from Gstaad arrived on the
kibbutz a few months ago, and she and I have been
spending some time together — she told me I ought
to try to write you a letter without relying only on
lists, so here I am, trying. I know it isn't enough,
but maybe it's a start. We all move forward, Esme,
even those who have been given up on, even those
who have given up.

Knowing you are seventeen now made me
wonder whether you have fallen in love yet even
before I read your letter. Something told me, some
uterine sixth sense, that you had fallen in love,
and that it was unexpected and raw, and it made
me think yes, my darling girl, say yes, don't ask
questions, open your mouth and breathe out and say
yes. You are doing exactly what you should be doing.

1. *Just as hair always grows back, so do the sea-*
   sons change.
2. *Three baskets of oranges this morning, but the*
   orange groves are beginning to disappear.
3. *I ought to send you some oranges.*
4. *Remember how young you are.*

*5. I named you Ruth after the only woman author
in the Old Testament (or at least the only one
who didn't have an awful name like Esther).
Keep writing. Honor who you are at the center
of your name.*

*I love you, Esme. You'll hear from me before
eighteen. Your Mama*

For the first time since she left, I think Mom might be okay. Crazy, but a little—what would you call it?— self-aware, or something. I sprawl all the way out like the Vitruvian Man and tuck away the letter. Everything changes, I guess.

I still don't know where I want to go to college, but I know I want it to be in a city. I think I want to live in New York first and let it slug me around a little, then run away to the beach when I get too weary. My secret dream is to sort of get adopted by a hip-hop crew, or any good-hearted passing band of freaks, really, and whisked off to Brooklyn or San Francisco for a series of indoctrinations that'll transform me into the Real Thing, whatever that is. It's not like I want to get discovered, exactly, the way you hear about actresses getting picked off at diners. It's more about my own road to discovery, like pecking my way out of a shell. I just want to roll deep with a pack of talented bastards. Doesn't everybody?

I take out my iPod and scroll through to the feature presentation of tonight's listening. *Live at Holyhill: The Sister Mischief EP* is the newest little bundle of joy in the blended family that 4H has become, and I've been saving my first experience of it for just the right setting. It's been selling like hotcakes under the counter at school, and Yusuf has sort of become our unofficial manager-producer, whisking us around to check out other acts in the Cities and jam with his homies. He and Marcy are a match made in heaven—if heaven were the hip-hop section of the Electric Fetus—on the beatboxes and turntables, and it's sweet how they think we don't notice their furtive groping the minute we leave the room, the hands reaching for knees under the soundboard. Even though she doesn't admit explicitly that they're together, she gets this kind of proud tone in her voice when she talks about all the shit they work on together, all of which has a bunch of Radio Shack jargon that kind of sails above my head. It's funny. Now I know how Tess knew.

As per Principal Ross Nordling's proffer, the 4H cohort set to work on a mission statement during our suspension for the assembly that rocketed us into bona fide high-school notoriety.

"That shit is hot," Marcy proclaimed as we huddled around my laptop last week.

"It's basically the sickest mission statement anyone's ever written," Tess said, joining the self-congratulation.

"I'm going to make it my college essay," I said. "Don't worry—I'll credit you guys."

"I gotta admit, I was always super afraid of getting suspended," Rowie said. "But now, after getting suspended for the most bomb-ass show Holyhill's ever seen, I'm pretty effing proud." I looked at Rowie, glowing softly. In my mind, I reached out to ruffle her hair.

"*Hell*, yes." Marcy offered a fist-pound and we tapped a knuckle quartet. "Rhythm and poetry, motherfuckers."

"*Be* somebody, motherfuckers." Tessie grinned as we crowed at her dropping the F-bomb.

HIP-HOP FOR HETEROS AND HOMOS: OUR MISSION

Hip-Hop for Heteros and Homos, or 4H, is a sex-positive hip-hop collective devoted to thoughtful discussion of the intersections between girls, boys, beats, rhymes, and bombs. We are committed to nonviolence and the pursuit of lyrical happiness; all are welcome in our safe space. We celebrate the unexpected coupling, the sampled homage, the queer, subversive, multicolored, and mixed, and our task is to complicate, to investigate, to question everything.

4H holds central the First Amendment: that the public school, as an outreach of the government, may not make a law upholding any one religion over another, or prohibiting the free exercise of any religion; it may not abridge our freedom of speech, or freedom of the press, or the right of the people to assemble peacefully, or to petition the government for a redress of grievances. We believe that truth is found in words spoken out loud, and we accept love and brilliance in all forms in which they are found. We are Catholics, Hindus, Jews, Lutherans, Muslims, all faiths and all colors, and our common religion is the nation of hip-hop, of rhythm and poetry.

By combining our inquiries into hip-hop and sexuality, we aim to create a place for people and ideas that some might consider renegade. Queerness, as we understand it, represents a refusal to conform to roles prescribed to us by others and a belief that we are all equal as interconnected agents of love: each in our own way, whether we love women, men, or both, we are all queer, either because of our own orientation or because of the orientation of someone we love. We reclaim a word that once expressed hatred to express support for and solidarity with our GLBT brothers and sisters. By integrating feminist and sex-positive

language into hip-hop, our mission is also to make
hip-hop queer in our sense of the word, or to illumi-
nate the queerness that has always been inherent in
hip-hop. Hip-Hop for Heteros and Homos celebrates
sameness in collective otherness.

It's almost uncanny how much things between
Rowie and me have gone back to the way they used to
be, a playful camaraderie with subtly resolute boundaries, sisterhood with a perimeter. No more hair-ruffles or
biceps-punches, no hugs, only a parting fist-pound here
and there. It's an unspoken doctrine we both observe, as
though one stray of a hand could send the whole house
of cards crashing down. What sticks in my craw about
it is how electric the *un*touching is, a negative relief as
charged as its positive, an acknowledgment by denial
that something still courses in the space between us.
For now, we just don't talk about it.

I don't know if Rowie will ever be with another
girl the way she was with me—as much as I'd like to
claim sameness with her, I don't honestly think she's
whole-hog homo. I think the shape of a girl-body in her
bed was one that kind of snuck up on her. Maybe things
would've been different if we'd been in college, that
undetermined Other Place where things that haven't
happened yet happen, a place we understand only as a
space separated from here, like *abroad* or *the streets*. All

I want for her is that she finds a way to be who she is, the imp of an MC we've seen, alongside the images of model-minority MDs her parents have cast her in.

Maybe growing up is mostly just about learning how to play more parts at once, how to give them each their scenes.

"You can do everything you want," Pops tells me when I'm brooding. "Just not all at the same time."

I shift on the ice, starting to feel the cold a little. It's time to do what I came here in the middle of the night to do. I press PLAY.

The first few seconds are a fraught jumble of background noises: Yusuf fiddling with the controls, the four of us switching on our mikes and blowing into them, the crackle of Yusuf whispering to us that we're live over the walkie-talkie. He's left the recording all but uncut, I realize, and as I listen to it, I can hear every charged particle of anticipation, the crude rustles of a room packed with bodies, Nordling droning, *Ladies and gentlemen, please find your seats.* I hear our last words to one another before we brought the house down and blemished our permanent records all at the same time, and I hear myself barreling onstage.

In the first verse my voice is shaky and a hair too fast, tight-throated. I can hear myself begin to relax and roll with it, and I can hear myself pick up speed and realize I'm having the best time of my life, and I can hear the wallop in all our voices as we land hard on the *illest Sister Mischief*. I hear myself holding my breath as I wait for Rowie to plunge in, hear the release when she whips out her wicked and throws it down. By the second verse, I am fully my own irrepressible self, powerless to hold any of it in. And MC Ro and me are MC Ro and me like we always were, rhyming, soft and serrated aloft in a common rhythm, her sweet and my skanky all tangled up like skinny legs.

I hear Marcy scratching on her portable turntables and Tess's raging caterwaul, and it strikes me that I *do* roll with a cast of talented bastards, that I'm getting ahead of myself again, and that this is the way I'll always remember them: sixteen and throbbing with a heavy mixed-up beat, authors of their own chaotic destinies, caught in between one thing and all the becoming still left before the next, wild-eyed and wide-mouthed, jamming hard with our joy spilling out all over. Careening across a frozen lake on a prayer that none of us will fall in.

Yusuf's added a little coda to the EP that I haven't heard before, some B-roll of the four of us fucking around in the Njakas' garage-studio when we didn't know he was recording.

"Yo, do you all remember that time we made Ross Nordling crap his pants?" Marcy's voice drifts in over the laughter. "That was the sickest."

"Dude, I done saw it with my own eyes," a disembodied Rowie says. "Homeboy had to throw away that pair of boxer briefs."

"Cracka got served!" I crow. "Let's jam on this for a minute. Marce, count it off."

"One. Two. Three. Four," she gutters. She's live on the beat, hammering on an old drum kit Yusuf scrapped together for her birthday.

"Sister Mischief all up in here," Rowie starts. "MC Ferocious in the house."

"I got sick-ass sistership," I call.

"Lemme get a hit of it," she responds.

"I got the wickedest mischievists," I call.

"Yo, lemme get a hit of it."

"I got a Rooster J."

"Yeah, lemme get a hit of it."

"Yo Ro, you got deodorant in that purse?"

"I got it, Fero."

"Lemme get a hit of it."

The beat peters out as all four of us scatter in laughter, tossing good-natured insults at one another, loving in name-calling. *You dirtbags. SheStorm, where's my beat? You fools didn't even let me get to my hook. I got a beat for you right here, slick. Perv.* It's so un-self-conscious, freed from the body, just the casual intimacy of four girls amassed as something greater than any lone one of them. There's a slow fadeout, our jabs and postures and laughter slowly dying, as if I were a car pulling away from a party still in full swing. It leaves me bitten by something like awe, feeling overwhelmed by the magnitude of our becoming.

The cold has hooks now, and the whole span of my dorsal side feels like it might be frozen to Lake Calhoun. The little dipper in the southwestern sky points me home as I count the constellations I know, a fistful of pinpricks in an unbounded galaxy, so many still nameless in the mass of everything I haven't learned yet. *It's the naming,* I think. *The naming is the question.* I stand up and shake the snow out of my blanket. Cocking my head at the crescent moon, I say a silent prayer that life will always feel like this, all shot through with magic words and glittering samples hovering just out of reach, just the same as now, except — I pull my headphones back over my ears as I dust off the snow and cue up the *SM EP* again — except I'm listening, really listening this time, and older now.

MAD PROPS

To Rachel Gaubinger, Meera Menon, and Victoria Baranetsky, my wickedest mischievous sisters, most beloved friends of my mind, baddest bitches on the block, Brooklyn rollers, whiskey-pourers (or I poured), discourse without borders, who inspired me with genius e-mail chains, no-joke dance parties, etc. Without you, this book would not be a lady, would have no title, no samosas, and no staying up laughing until dawn. Thank you for showing me how to be somebody. Mad, mad, fiercest Thuggette love.

To my boo Patrick Cushing, partner in all journeys, for his love and support throughout the unenviable task of living with me as I was writing this book. My heart, my home.

To my parents, the indomitable Lar and Car, who have always believed in me, or at least suspended their disbelief at my most outlandish dreams. I love you. Thank you.

To the ferocious mind of my editor, Katie Cunningham, who got it from the beginning, and to my agent, Ted Malawer, dear genius, who first talked me into this adventure.

To Justin Hulog, my San Francisco sibling, and to our understanding of the search for sameness.

To my poet cadre — Ethan Hon, Emily Wolahan, Sara Femenella, Stephanie Adams-Santos. To words, and toward them.

To my teachers at Columbia — Timothy Donnelly, Sophie Cabot Black, Leslie Woodard, Eamon Grennan, Julie Crawford, Michael Golston — for their generosity and mentorship.

To Sandy Close and the NAMily for giving me the time, space, and brain food I needed, and for their truthtelling. Love especially to Rupa Dev and Neela Banerjee for being such clever desi babes and to Carolyn Ji Jong Goossen.

To Justin Lopez and the max unit B8 of the San Jose juvenile hall. Stay up.

To my Minnesota homies — Jess Dunne, Mike Fabio, Brother David Highhill, Alison Silvis, Laurel Somerville, and Maureen O'Connor, who is not adopted. To Paul Farris, departed brother, who pointed me home.

To Sara Blachman and her mama, Eve, whom I love no shit. To Lauren Lillie, the original Lizzie Borden.

To Vince Passaro (Virgil) in particular, and 1020 Amsterdam (Inferno) in general, who raised me from a pup.

To Jon Brilliant, for his beautiful portrait of an author as a young authors' portrait.

To Yvonne Woon, with whom I commiserated hard, and Kate Berthold, who shared her openhearted history with me.

And to all the smart girl word nerds. This one's for you.

Laura Goode was raised outside Minneapolis and now lives in San Francisco. She received her BA and MFA from Columbia University, and her poems have appeared in the *Denver Quarterly, Slope, Cannibal, JERRY,* and as a chapbook in *Narwhal. Sister Mischief* is her first novel.

YOU'RE ABOUT TO GET ROCKED

by the fiercest, baddest all-girl hip-hop crew in the Twin Cities, or at least in the wealthy, white, Bible-thumping suburb of Holyhill.

MC Ferocious is a Jewish lesbian lyricist and a smart, sassy die-hard word nerd. In her crew, she's got the butchest straight girl in town and the pretty, popular former super-Lutheran teen queen.

But she's got feelings for MC Rohini, a beautiful, brilliant, beguiling desi chick on the stick, and it's going to be more complicated than the rhyme schemes of their dreams.

AN AMELIA BLOOMER LIST SELECTION

AN AMERICAN LIBRARY ASSOCIATION
RAINBOW LIST TOP TEN SELECTION

★ "Full of big ideas, big heart, and big poetry."
—*Booklist* (starred review)

"Welcome to the queer hip-hop revolution."
—*Vanity Fair*

"*High School Musical* this ain't."
—*Publishers Weekly*

Front cover photograph copyright
© 2013 by Simon Tonge

Age 14 and up

0813

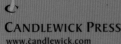

CANDLEWICK PRESS
www.candlewick.com

U.S. $8.99 / $10.00 CAN
ISBN 978-0-7636-6456-5

EAN

9 780763 664565   50899>

Also available as an e-book